GERALDINE MOORKENS BYRNE

The Body Count

To the best mother in the whole wide world, the redoubtable and amazing Maria Moorkens Byrne,our beloved Evil Old Woman.

Contents

Foreword — iii

Acknowledgement — iv

Glossary of Irish Terms and Slang — v

Chapter One — 1

Chapter Two — 9

Chapter Three — 14

Chapter Four — 26

Chapter Five — 32

Chapter six — 45

Chapter Seven — 50

Chapter Eight — 57

Chapter Nine — 62

Chapter Ten — 68

Chapter Eleven — 71

Chapter Twelve — 79

Chapter Thirteen — 91

Chapter Fourteen — 96

Chapter Fifteen — 103

Chapter Sixteen — 114

Chapter Seventeen — 120

Chapter Eighteen — 127

Chapter Nineteen — 134

Chapter Twenty — 141

Chapter Twenty-One — 146

Chapter Twenty-Two — 151

Chapter Twenty-Three — 158

Chapter Twenty-Four 163

Chapter Twenty-Five 168

Chapter Twenty-Six 174

Chapter Twenty-Seven 179

Chapter Twenty -Eight 184

Chapter Twenty-Nine 192

Chapter Thirty 200

Chapter Thirty-One 206

Chapter Thirty-Two 210

Chapter Thirty-Three 214

Chapter Thirty-Four 219

Chapter Thirty-Five 224

Chapter Thirty-Six 244

Chapter Thirty-Seven 252

Chapter Thirty-Eight 256

About the Author 261

Also by Geraldine Moorkens Byrne 263

Foreword

A brief word about the setting, for both Irish and international readers. The first book The Body Politic was set circa 2010; this book is set in 2012, as the Banking scandals erupted and recession deepened its grip. In Caroline's world, we have the leadership of Michael T O'Mahony, as the Prime Minister or Taoiseach, ready to reform and eager to winkle out corruption.

He is fictional. Derek Fields, his wise and progressive advisor, is likewise a figment of my imagination. They are the leadership we needed and deserved, but didn't get.

Otherwise, lots of things mentioned are real if sometimes chronologically incorrect. For example, the orphaned security deposit boxes exist, but plans to open them have only recently surfaced. If it helped the story, I took liberties with it. That's just how we murder writers roll.

A note on the police: The Irish force is called An Garda Siochána. An individual member of the force is a Garda, the plural is Gardaí. There is no Special Branch per se, that's a commonly used term inherited from years of British rule. The official name for that department is The **Special** Detective Unit (SDU) (Irish: Aonad Speisialta Bleachtaireachta) but especially in Dublin, it's almost universally still called Special Branch.

"Detective Sergeant" e.g. DS Doyle is not an official rank in Ireland, the correct rank would be Detective Garda Doyle. For the purposes of clarity and ease I fudged it into D.S.

A lot of places mentioned are real and accurately described, some are fictional but represent a range of real places and you would recognize them if you strolled around Dublin some day.

I hope you enjoy Caroline's Dublin, and of course, the murders.

Acknowledgement

Deepest thanks once again to everyone under the PPP Publishing umbrella for their help and encouragement. My husband Mark is my first and most helpful beta reader and he was ably assisted by the kindest team of volunteers, for whose feedback and critique I am endlessly grateful. Special mention goes to Joseph Lysaght for the four hundred and fifty four last minute revisions he presented to me at the eleventh hour.

As ever, I relied on encouragement from my "Wagons" Kristen, Edda and Marie. To friends like James O'Farrell, Deirdre Gaffney and Gina Bass to whom I owe a great deal of my sanity after a hectic year of changes, much gratitude. And thanks to everyone who took the time to provide feedback, constructive criticism, reviews, kind remarks and more about Book 1 (The Body Politic.)

The cover art is by Ceolnet Irish Design.

Glossary of Irish Terms and Slang

An Taoiseach - Irish Prime Minister and Leader of the ruling political party

Dail / Dail Eireann - The Irish Parliament

Leinster House - the common name for the building in which the Government sits.

Cumann na Laochra - Cum-mahn na Lay-chra (League of Warriors) Fictional Irish Political Party. Irish traditional political parties tend to have Irish names involving soldiers, warriors, destiny, etc.

Police

An Garda Siochána, Guardians of the Police (On Garr-dah Shee-ah-cawna)

Garda, usually for individual members e.g. Garda Murphy

Garda (garr-dee), usually the plural e.g. The Gardaí

Amadán -an Eejit

Eejit- a Gobdaw

Gobdaw - an absolute Amadán

All three mean a fool, a gormless twit

Wagon

Either a rude and unpleasant female or an affectionate term for your best mates, a Wagon makes a bad enemy but a great friend.

Similarly, **Weapon**.

Goat - lecherous eejit of a man

Poxy - Rotten

Irish Names:

Aoife - EE-fah

Declan - Deck-lan

Dermot - DER-maht

Donal - Dough-nall

Emer - EE-mer

Murrough - Murr-oh

O'Dwyer- Oh Dwy (rhymes with why) -err

O'Mahony - Oh-MAH-uney

 (*note: not under any circumstances is O'Mahony pronounced oh Mah-HONE-EE. Thóin pronounced Hone is the Irish for your backside. O, Mah HONE EE translates as O, she's my backside. Except it's not as polite as "backside."*)

Peadar -Padder

Una - OOOhnah

Chapter One

arie Flynn

M Marie sighed and looked around her glumly. Only half eleven in the morning and it was already an awful day. Her computer taunted her with the blue screen of death, the paperwork she should have been completing sat untouched on her desk and the slight ache behind her eyes had blossomed into a full-blown hormonal headache. Which meant backache and stomach cramps were sure to follow close behind.

She closed her eyes and tried to look on the bright side. While being a receptionist in the Bank of Leinster Headquarters was hardly the height of glamour, it was rarely quite this bad. She had been lucky to land this temping job, even with the outdated dress code and feudal attitude towards female staff in certain departments and while she worked hard for her money, it was at least a decent wage.

Marie ran a hand furtively over one of the (non-regulation) silver bangles on her wrist. She kept them hidden as much as possible, as her eagle-eyed supervisor (or *Empress Evil* as she liked to call her) would rip them from her, if she saw them. But she could not bear to be stripped of every ounce of identity, especially not these. In her real life, the one she was *supposed* to be living, Marie was still a jewellery designer; in that life, she still had her workshop and her tools and made her living crafting exquisite, silver jewellery in a Celtic inspired manner.

In this life, thanks to her faithless and feckless soon to be ex-husband, she was stuck in this horrible job. It would be another couple of years before she would be fully free but at least they were legally separated now.

Working in the company headquarters of a Bank had not been part of her life plan, especially not the notorious Bank of Leinster. Recent banking scandals and an unprecedented cock-up with their computer systems had made dealing with incoming calls an exercise in fear and trembling. But it was money, money to pay off the debts her husband, Declan, had landed her with and money to keep going. It was a job, in a country where jobs were increasingly scarce. And it was above all, temporary.

Her phone pinged. She sneaked it from her pocket and keeping a careful eye out (it was strictly against the rules to look at your phone while you stood idly in an empty foyer) she opened her text.

AMANDA: OMFG they're laying people off in Pharmacy Plus, 400 job losses!

Her sister Amanda, who refused to say Declan's name now, and instead referred to him as either "that man," or "the weasel," texted her every morning with titbits of news about the failing economy.

Marie knew Amanda was terrified she would rebel against this job, strip the hideous green Bank of Leinster uniform from her back and run screaming through the leafy streets of Ballsbridge, an exclusive area of Dublin filled with millionaires, Embassies and banks. Amanda thought these updates about job hell and financial misery would keep her focused on how lucky she was to be earning. It was her way of helping. Marie hardly needed the reminder though, considering she had a drawer full of bills and final demands.

The ominous click-click of heels (regulation 1 and a half inch, black leather) on the marbled floor brought her back to reality and the reception desk. She started to shuffle papers before glancing up to meet the steely blue eyes of Monica Delahunt. Technically her direct supervisor, AKA the "Evil Empress."

Monica cast an expert eye over Marie's ensemble and snapped, "Your hair is untidy. Ponytail, black bobbin. How many times have I to tell you this?"

Marie smiled and said politely "Sorry Miss Delahunt." And waited. She knew Monica wanted to see her squirm, so she took a perverse pleasure in never showing one ounce of the annoyance she felt.

True to form, Monica's eyes raked over her appearance trying to find some other point of contention. Marie wondered if her obsession with enforcing the outdated and frankly sexist uniform some kind of fetish for Monica, like those women who read Fifty Shades of Gray and had a delicious little tremble at the thought of being dominated.

Monica tut-tutted on general principles but said "Well, make sure you fix it on your break."

She stared around the foyer. "Where's Tomas?" Tomas was the security guard, six foot two inches of Polish muscle and he was supposed to be there, by the front door, to herd any stray customers off the premises.

Headquarters, as Monica liked to remind them, was not a "customer facing building" which meant hopefully no one the bank had shafted would arrive demanding justice. However, every so often someone was put on hold one time too many, hopped in their car, drove to Ballsbridge and demanded to talk to a human being. Then Tomas was supposed to gently persuade them to leave and discreetly note down their car registration.

Marie sighed. Tomas had gone on break twenty minutes before, something Monica should well know. She supposed making her state the obvious was part of the woman's plan to drive her completely insane.

"Break. He's gone on his break." She indicated the clock on the wall and sighed. "Half eleven to twelve, Ms. Delahunt."

Monica shook her head. "Nonsense!" It's almost ten past 12 now," she bleated, her helmet of spray-held curls quivering with indignation.

Marie stared at her. "It's ten *to* twelve" she pointed out. "The clock says ten to twelve."

The clock was an ancient timepiece that had been built into the wall of the lobby when the building first went up in the 1890s. It was renowned for its timekeeping, and the legend was that all the clocks in the company were set by it. Once upon a time, before digital clocks and computers this was true. It had been the job of some unfortunate clerk to check that every branch had the correct time according to the Great Clock. Now only the Headquarters went by the old clock, but according to the Board of Directors it was as precise as it had ever been, and questioning it was nearly heretical. The last President of the Bank before the current incumbent had insisted that the famous Great Clock was to be the final arbiter of any dispute about time.

Monica stared in confusion and then, with an effort, shrugged it off.

"Well, he's cutting it fine."

Marie rolled her eyes discreetly. A poxy half hour for lunch and they begrudged you taking it. Not even allowed sit behind the desk in an empty foyer, she thought bitterly.

"Was there anything else, Ms. Delahunt?" she asked sweetly.

"No. Yes. Yes, of course. I actually came down to check on room 4."

There were four conference rooms off the spacious entrance foyer, two doors on either side, used for the rare occasions when clients couldn't be fobbed off without a face to face, or the more frequent occasions when the team leaders needed to bawl out their teams for utter incompetence.

They were spacious, soundproofed and equipped with tea and coffee making facilities which meant you didn't have to pause in either placating or berating. Marie consulted her sheets.

"Room four? Room four is empty."

She looked expectantly at Monica.

"No, it's not," her boss snapped peevishly. "I was down here at half ten and the door was locked."

It was fairly common for management to lock the door if they were dealing with something very confidential or very embarrassing. It was probably against half a dozen EU workers' rights regulations, but the Bank didn't seem to care.

Managers also locked the conference rooms because Monica was known to be a snoop and a tattletale. She often "accidentally" walked into meetings.

Marie checked again. Because her computer had been dead all morning, all the information usually contained on a spreadsheet had been written out by hand. If there was one thing Marie could do, it was pay attention to detail. She was a perfectionist when she created something and brought the same eye for detail to admin. She rarely forgot a task, or a phone number and she absolutely never wrote down the wrong information, because she always double checked.

"No," she said firmly. "Officially, room four is free. If there's anyone using it, they didn't run it past me."

Monica squinted at the sheets and frowned.

"But the door is locked," she complained.

Marie shrugged. "I don't know about that. I can only tell you that no one booked it."

Click, click, went Ms. Delahunt's heels over the floor to the conference room. She shook the handle aggressively.

"Locked!" she said triumphantly.

"What is wrong?"

Tomas appeared behind the desk, trying to hide the cup of coffee he had sneaked in from the canteen. Eating and drinking on duty were strictly forbidden for both the security and reception staff, despite their lack of breaks. Marie took the cup from him with a smooth movement and placed it in her desk drawer. Tomas mouthed "thanks" as he passed and continued to Monica Delahunt's side.

"Is there a problem, Ms. Delahunt?" he asked politely. Marie caught Monica glancing surreptitiously at the foyer clock and smiled to herself. The auld cow really didn't give up easily, but Tomas was back with at least four minutes to spare.

"Why is this room locked?" Her querulous tones suggested that it was Tomas' direct fault. "It's supposed to be free, and I need to use it. I can't see why you people can't keep to a simple system and write these things down correctly."

Marie flushed angrily but managed to keep her voice level.

"I do write them down correctly, Ms. Delahunt. No one booked the room."

"Well, who's in there then?" Monica snapped.

"I don't *know*. I didn't see anyone go in there, all morning. Mr. Clarke has booked room one for an hour this morning and Mrs. Petroni had room three for the team leader briefing – and that's it."

She looked enquiringly at Tomas. "Did anyone come in while I was on break, Tomas?"

He shook his head emphatically.

"No. While you were gone, no one went in or came out. A few of the girls from customer service went out just after half past ten and were back inside by ten forty-five. Smoking," he mimicked the action disdainfully, "around the corner of the building. The smell of their clothes when they come in… why do they do that?"

Marie grinned. "Never mind that now, Tomas. There was no one else?"

She picked up the phone, curious now. That meant whoever is in there had been there since before half past eight that morning.

"Half the computers in the place are down," she told Monica, "That's why we've been double checking everything and writing it out. They were down when I came in this morning. I'll ring around and see if there's any way someone overlooked a booking."

She started with the customer service department.

"Hi. It's Marie here on reception. Who's that? Oh, hello Adele. Listen, Adele do me a favour? Ask up there and see if anyone is using Room four. Hi? Oh. No one? OK thanks." She shook her head at Monica and dialed another number.

"Hi…Lacey? How are ya? yeah…us too. Not a single computer in the building is working as far as I know. IT are going spare over it. Here, Lacey can you do me a favour please? Could you check and see if anyone in mortgages or corporate is using room four at the moment?"

There was a pause and then, "Oh, OK. No one is down here, that you know of? Thanks a million, Lacey. Talk to you later."

Marie shook her head at her colleagues. "There's only Clarke and Petroni booked in that anyone knows of. Mr. Clarke is meeting Jordan PR but they haven't arrived yet."

Jordan Public Relations was the up-and-coming public relations firm in the city, thanks to impeccable contacts and its owner's reputation for fearlessness. The owner, Caroline Jordan was one of the public relations advisers to the leader of the Irish Government. They were a prestige firm, and here for an important meeting with the Head of Marketing. There was no way Frank Clarke would be meeting them in either of the small rooms. Only the main conference room with the impressive mahogany table and the oil paintings of long dead Bank of Leinster officials would do for Ms. Jordan and her team.

Marie knew, without having to second guess herself, exactly who was using each room. Heavens above, but Monica was a pain.

She came out around the reception desk, searching through the bunch of emergency keys that lived in the back of her drawer.

"There must be some explanation," she sighed pointedly. "Someone must have locked the door by accident. Or something."

She located the right key and held it up triumphantly. "Now Ms. Delahunt, I'll open it up for you in just a jiffy!"

Tomas grinned at her behind Monica's back but made no move back towards his post. He was as curious now as Marie was, both as to why the room should be locked and why Monica was throwing such a hissy fit over it. Marie tried to catch his eye to give him the nudge not to push his luck and get back to his place, but he wasn't looking at her anymore. He was staring over her shoulder at someone approaching the front entrance.

As the HQ wasn't – in corporate speak – "customer facing" it could only mean that Frank Clarke's VIP guest was arriving.

Marie could head Monica muttering under her breath. Anxious now to placate her and greet the newcomers Marie jammed the key in the lock and turned it, pushing open the heavy door just as a tall, athletic looking blonde flanked by another woman, a brunette, and a tall thin man with dark hair, started across the marbled entrance towards them.

As they approached, Marie pushed the door open for Monica Delahunt and then turned towards the approaching guests. She fixed her bright receptionist smile on her face and stepped forward to greet them as Tomas tried to look security conscious. It was a good effort, but the effect was somewhat spoiled by Monica Delahunt screaming at the top of her lungs.

Marie saw the tall blonde, whom she recognized as Caroline Jordan from the gossip pages of the Evening Herald, stop dead, her face paling visibly. Jordan's hand was outstretched towards the other woman, preventing her from stepping forward. She was shielding her from a view of the room, Marie realized afterwards. The tall man looked sick, Monica was still screaming, and Tomas swore volubly as she turned and finally saw what was upsetting everyone else.

Frank Clarke drooped from the small chandelier in the centre of the room, a miniature version of the larger ones that shimmered over their heads in the marbled foyer. His neck was a slash of bright red, a bloom of red spread over his shirt front and across the cream carpet beneath him. His two wrists were bound together, and he hung from them, from the central stem of the light.

"But he booked the other room!" Marie blurted out, just before she realized she was about to faint.

Chapter Two

Caroline Jordan

It had been a funny old year or so since my previous employer Damian Fitzpatrick, Minister for Justice, had shuffled off this mortal coil. I had been targeted by a murderer, embroiled in a police investigation, and generally mistreated by fortune. It had taken an effort to shake it off and return to work, and for a long time I felt like I was faking it, but it paid off in the end. Life had returned to normal, as normal as life as a Public Relations advisor to socialites and politicians can be.

One good thing from that time was securing a contract with our beloved leader, An Taoiseach Michael T O'Mahony and through him, several of his political cronies. The cachet of being an adviser to the Irish Prime Minister also brought in a lot of society types. Next to politicians, we found socialites and minor celebrities were the most obsessed with their image and the most vulnerable to unflattering press coverage. Jordan PR had built up a nice portfolio of steady, if demanding, clients.

And working with O'Mahony meant working with Derek Fields, a legend in political and PR circles. Before I worked for him, I had admired him. In the eighteen months since becoming his protegee, admiration had turned to deep respect and liking. He was a remote but kindly, very business-like, slightly scary father figure. He was the power behind the throne; not that O'Mahony wasn't an impressive politician in his own right but he would be the first to admit Fields was a genius.

Professionally, things had gone well and were getting better, despite the recession and my insane overdraft. But I won't deny, when the chance arose to pitch for the Bank of Leinster contract, my calloused little heart had beaten faster, and my palms got a little sweaty.

The shameful truth was that Jordan Public Relations consisted of three people; my colleagues Paula and Steven, and me. Paula and Steve were loyal to a fault, and thanks to our combined hard work, Jordan PR had been able to pay them a respectable wage, but the Bank of Leinster contract would push us over the line into comfortably solvent. The Celtic Tiger boom may have ended in 2008 but the repercussions were only being felt in many sectors in 2012. We needed every solid contract we could get.

"We're OK, Caro," Pauline would insist, but with this contract I could give them raises and hire someone – *anyone* – to be office manager so that the three of us would no longer have to play various roles like receptionist, secretary, or general dogsbody. Plus, Paula and Stephen had long since stopped longing for each from afar and were getting married in seven months, so I wanted to be able to offer them something more than the hand to mouth existence we had endured so far.

We went into this meeting like soldiers planning a military coup. Despite their protestations, I knew they were as eager as I was. Both were preparing like demons. I found Stephen reading a huge tome entitled "Perils of the Irish Banking Sector," and muttering phrases like "differential share distribution." As Paula was a real, live, qualified accountant I expected that from her, but he rarely read anything heavier than a best seller.

The contract had long been held by Duggan and Fines Advertising and PR, coincidentally the very firm in which I had started my career. It was also the place I met Paula Hughes for the first time. She had been languishing in accounts, until I lured her away. Her sister Anne still worked there as a secretary to one of the higher up executives. It was not the most encouraging place to work, as a woman and after a few years of working all hours and getting little recognition, I persuaded Paula to move on with me. Shortly afterwards Stephen also jumped ship and came to work at Jordan PR.

When we left, shaking the dust of the place from our sandals, our ambitions ran solely to making a living. My bosses poured scorn on us, warning that we would never survive. The idea that four years later we might be in a position to nick a contract out from under their noses never crossed my mind. Yet here we were, and Duggan and Fines only had themselves to blame.

Paula had summed it up, as we shook our heads over the bank's antics, plastered all over the media.

"Duggan and Fines sat on their hands and watched the Bank lurch from one disaster to another! That system…that ridiculous new system." She shook her head in disbelief.

The Bank of Leinster prided itself on being cutting edge when it came to technology; it had weathered the worst Bank scandals of recent years with its reputation battered but basically intact. Then, in an attempt to push back against the recession, it had launched an all-singing, all-dancing, online banking product – smart phone friendly, filled with apps and widgets and all kinds of extras.

You could transfer money to New York while topping up your mobile phone credit and ordering flowers for Mother's Day – their advertising campaign promised a "unique and unforgettable" banking experience.

It had certainly proved to be both unique *and* unforgettable when their shiny new system froze. Just froze. Refused to process anything, became inaccessible, locked thousands of Irish consumers out of their accounts and left them temporarily penniless. To compound the horror, the tech team that had created the system proved unable to fix the damn thing and what should have been a minor glitch turned into a month-long war of attrition, with lawsuits and angry scenes outside banks and questions in and out of parliament.

"It's financial Armageddon," Ethan Sullivan, opposition spokesman on Finance tweeted, *"presided over by a corrupt government."*

Derek was outraged, he took that one as a personal insult. I wasn't naïve enough to imagine any politician was squeaky clean, but Derek Fields had kept O'Mahony away from anything overtly dodgy, and certainly fiscal corruption wasn't an issue.

He wasn't the only one furious. As Ireland was working hard to rehabilitate our image abroad as a responsible fiscal entity, Michael T was only barely restrained from taking out a hit on the head of the Bank of Leinster, Sean O'Dwyer. There was absolute war, and the dressing-down the unfortunate O'Dwyer received at the hands of An Taoiseach is set to go down in legend.

All the while as far as anyone could see, Duggan and Fines sat on their thumbs and watched.

They finally managed to release one asinine press statement so badly thought out that it was picked over for days by the media pundits.

"Listen!" Stephen had taken to reading the daily commentary over morning coffee in the office. "This is the best bit… *While it has obviously inconvenienced people on a personal level, it remains a triumph on a more important level!*" More important than thousands of people nearly losing their homes and savings! How did they think that would help things?"

It takes a genuine talent for cock-ups to manage to patronize your entire client base in one fell swoop.

The one public relations event of note the firm managed was to have Sean O'Dwyer and his horsey wife Veronica pictured at a *staggeringly* exclusive Hunt Ball. The subsequent media coverage, including pictures of them swanning around in designer gear sipping champagne, convinced the average customer of the Bank that their money had been embezzled to support the lifestyle of a bloodthirsty upper crust twit.

I don't know what they were thinking, frankly I would have him serving dinner at a local soup kitchen sooner than posing on the steps of a mansion, dressed like an extra from Pride and Prejudice. But then Paula solved the mystery.

"The person in charge of the BOL account," she announced solemnly "is one

Fintan Tormey, a gobdaw of unparalleled idiocy. All has become clear!"

She had the gossip straight from her sister Anne, who still worked in the secretarial corps in D & F. Anne was considered a sort of satellite agent of Jordan PR. She hated her bosses and loved a bit of intrigue. Tormey was a smug git who surfed through his working life bullying and cajoling more talented people into making himself look good. I had always sworn he would perish on the rock of his own arrogance. I was pure delighted when he managed it.

Other than those two ham-fisted attempts at salvaging public confidence, no real steps seemed to have been taken to mitigate any of the horrendous publicity the Bank received.

Meanwhile the press merrily painted them as evil greedy magnates stealing the pennies of the poor. I am no fan of journalists, but I have to admit, they had the nation entertained for weeks. Once the Bank had recovered its equilibrium from the debacle, the first head on the block was Duggan and Fines. However, besides enjoying the utter humiliation of that collection of witless worms, I didn't see it affecting me or Jordan PR in any way.

Not until I received a call from Derek Fields, a friendly little chat that ended with him asking me if we were interested in pitching for the Leinster account.

"Why not? You have little to lose, Caroline and much to gain."

Derek was planning to retire soon, slowly handing over the reins to me; he had also taken a kindly interest in our little enterprise and if he could do us a good turn, he did. He was possessed of the most astoundingly astute brain I had ever encountered and if he had told me to jump off a cliff, I would have given it serious consideration.

So here we were, about to make a play for financial security, massive kudos, a huge opportunity and a great big fat pay cheque. The only thing that could spoil it was the rather obvious dirty great big corpse of the man to whom we were supposed to pitch.

Chapter Three

C*aroline Jordan*

I'm not sure how long we stood there staring at the crime scene but the older woman had at least stopped screaming. I barely managed not to scream myself and my heart went out to the receptionist, who looked as if she was about to vomit.

I honestly thought that the pressure had finally got to me, and I was developing some kind of hideous monomania, seeing a gruesome corpse at moments of pressure. The fact that the woman with the helmet of hair and the rather funky, cool receptionist were also seeing it, was some comfort.

The security guard stood there, muttering a string of curses in English and Polish, staring at the bloody spectacle. He looked almost as green as the receptionist.

I had managed to protect Paula from the full horror of the scene. As it was she saw quite enough, her face blanching as she turned sharply away. Stephen was the only one of us with any presence of mind. He pulled open his phone and, hands shaking, dialed 999. I could register this with one part of my brain, but the rest of me was just underwater, barely hearing, barely breathing.

It's not something I like to tell people generally, but this wasn't my first dead body. The memory of another bloodstained corpse, my friend, at his desk… feelings of panic I thought I had managed to control were bubbling back up.

"You OK, Caro?" Paula whispered, giving my arm a gentle squeeze.

Finally, some sense trickled back into me, as I realized the older woman was about to walk into the room.

"Stop!" I must have sounded sharper than I intended as she jumped and looked at me resentfully. "Sorry, but you can't go in there."

She opened her mouth to argue, inching her way slightly further in but I pressed the point firmly. If my experience with dead bodies has taught me anything, it is don't interfere with a crime scene, it irritates the Gardaí no end.

"The police…" I reminded her. "The police will be here any minute. You can't go in there, it should be left exactly as it is."

The receptionist seemed to come back to herself at this, innate professionalism I suppose.

She touched the other woman on the shoulder, quite gently, and said "Monica…Ms. Delahunt…you have to step out of there." Delahunt turned slowly and stepped back over the threshold. She hadn't done more than put a foot into the room, so I didn't suppose any harm was done, but still ….

"Should we shut the door?" I wondered aloud.

The security guard looked at me blankly then shook his head. "We have already left the fingermarks, opening it and banging on the outside. We should not touch it again…I think the police would say to leave it."

He spoke excellent English with a touch of both Dublin and eastern Europe to his accent.

We all stood there trying not to look into the room but somehow unable to walk away. Walking away seemed…disrespectful, as if we were leaving the unfortunate man to his lonely fate. Gawping in was equally disrespectful.

"Etiquette of Crime Scenes," the little perverse voice in my head whispered, "How to avoid faux-pas at bloodied kill sites." My internal PR voice had a bad habit of kicking in at inappropriate moments.

The younger girl turned to me and said politely "Ms. Jordan, is it?"

I nodded.

"I'm Marie," she said, "Ms. Jordan, you were here to see Mr. Clarke, weren't you?"

Something in the tone made my heart sink. "That's him, isn't it?" I said wearily.

"I'm sorry," she said, looking it. "Yes, that is – was – Mr. Clarke."

Oh for feck's sake.

Stephen waved at me discreetly. He looked anxiously at Paula, but she was fully engaged in helping Monica Delahunt who looked as if she might reprise her fit of hysterics at any moment.

I excused myself from Marie and sidled up to him.

"They're on their way," he said quietly, "I explained as much as I could, they said not to touch the door again, leave it exactly as it is now."

Involuntarily we both glanced at the open doorway and as quickly as we could, looked away again. "But it seems obscene to leave it open, if anyone walked in it would be horrific."

I turned back to the security man, and the receptionist. The foyer was a wide rectangle with two wings leading off at either side of the reception desk. The desk was opposite the entrance; I could see two closed, frosted glass doors behind it and stairs just visible to its right, disappearing around the corner. The corridor leading to the left was unmarked but I guessed there must be lifts somewhere around.

"I'm sorry, I don't know your name" I peered at his name badge, "…Tomas? Tomas and Marie. We need to make sure no one except the police come through those doors, or down into the lobby. Marie, you need to take care of the stairs and Tomas you man the doors." I sighed. "The Gardaí will be here soon but until then we have to do our best to keep this area clear."

The pair of them bustled off, visibly relieved while I prayed the police would arrive soon – I didn't relish standing guard over the lobby area of the Bank of Leinster for any length of time. The seconds crawled by, the huge clock ticking away inexorably, so loudly that I fantasized about ripping it off its moorings and jumping on it.

To avoid looking at the doorway – it seemed to draw my eyes without giving me any say in the matter – I mused on the trio we had found standing around the door.

Marie the receptionist was a pretty, tall, slightly funky looking girl. Woman, I should say; I guessed early thirties but she could have been older. A woman who despite the idiotic uniform on which these places insisted, had managed to add some individuality. Her hair was tied back but not in quite the regulation style. Her entire outfit had some little touches here and there, very subtle. Her demeanour too – she was confident but not in the loud, snooty way that so many receptionists embraced.

Monica Delahunt was older, early forties at a guess, with just a bit more make-up than suited her face, her hair just a little too styled, her clothes expensive but inelegant. She wore a uniform of sorts though I doubt she realized it – her outfit was typical of many women her age who bought labels rather than had style. You'll find ten of them at a time in Harvey Nichols or Brown Thomas, any day.

She had on a very patterned blouse, in strangely clashing yellows and pinks, visible underneath a very tight cardigan and paired with a pencil skirt. It looked uncomfortable. And I say this as someone who believes in growing old disgracefully; I'd prefer to see her dressed cheerfully in punk gear than so dourly in a set of expensive, but soulless, labels. The security guard – Tomas, I reminded myself – shifted uncomfortably and cast another, miserable glance back towards the meeting room from his post at the door.

"This will be bad," he said sadly, half to himself rather than addressing anyone in particular.

"Don't worry," I tried to sound confident. "The police will be here soon, and they'll take charge. You've done everything you could. I'm sure it'll be fine."

He looked at me and shook his head. "Always the trouble, miss, if you're foreign. You'll see. They'll try to find a way to make this my fault."

I didn't ask if by "they," he meant the bank or the Gardaí. I suspected he was less afraid of the boys in uniform than the men in suits, upstairs. From the background Derek Fields had fed me, the atmosphere in Leinster Bank was far from pleasant at the moment. Staff morale was at an all-time low, and the general opinion was it was better to admit to being a traffic warden than an employee of the bank.

Callers to talk radio shows confided their stories of abuse, ranging from "Seriously, when I said I worked for a bank she looked at me like I was pond-life and walked away muttering," to "So, I said he couldn't withdraw money without a bank card and he tried to smash the bullet proof glass with a claw hammer." It was not a good time to be in banking.

"Hopefully, the cops will get here soon, Tomas. Don't worry, they'll have to tread carefully. This is a sensitive one, a senior bank official murdered in a Bank headquarters." Lots of important people, sensitive information, I thought, they will send – oh no. Oh no, no. They will send their Special Crime Squad, won't they?

No, I thought firmly. The local cops will arrive first. The chances of it being the SCS initially are very slim. "It'll be fine," I told him.

I was spared the burden of lying to comfort Tomas, when the doors to the foyer opened and a coterie of grim looking men and women entered, some in uniform and some in what passed for civilian clothes among the Irish police force. In other words, you could have picked them out at a hundred yards and identified them almost down to rank, despite their attempts to look normal. I scanned the faces and – yes. Yes. There he was. DS Doyle, the oddest and grumpiest policeman ever to wear out shoe leather in pursuit of justice. He was flanked by at least three faces that I recognized. The SCS were out in full force.

My previous experience with Special Crimes – lest you all think I'm some kind of hardened criminal – was when my old boss, the now disgraced politician Damian Fitzpatrick, was found murdered at his desk eighteen months ago.

DS Doyle became the bane of my existence for a short while, alternatively accusing me of having an affair with the loathsome Fitzpatrick or embroiling me in attempts to flush out his murderer. Okay so to be strictly fair, he did technically save my life in the end, but honestly, considering he put me through all that in the first place I think I was justified in feeling a bit resentful about him.

And it had been his colleague Claire MacPherson who really saved me anyway and I liked *her*. Jordan PR kept Claire and her girlfriend supplied with tickets to every event worth attending, and VIP passes to every festival. But I kept in touch with Doyle too, because apparently, it's also rude not to keep in touch with someone who technically helped someone else save your life. It was a challenging friendship though. Doyle often seemed faintly annoyed to hear from me but then out of the blue would fire off a friendly sounding text. God help anyone he dated; they would need counseling.

Of course, he had to turn up now. I felt a flash of irrational anger – I mean, how bad did this look? Once again, I was standing over a dead body, holding my hands up and saying, "Wasn't me, Guv', honest."

It was ridiculous.

DS Doyle scowled at me, recognition and irritation at war on his ugly mug. (Not exactly ugly, in fairness, but because he looks permanently annoyed, not exactly pleasant either.) I mustered a civil nod in his general direction, braced myself for impact and made a stern resolution. No matter what, I was not getting involved this time. I was nothing more than an unfortunate bystander. I knew no one and nothing. I would get this over with and then go back to trying to land a contract for my business. And nothing DS Doyle could do would change that.

For over an hour the lobby of Leinster Bank was a hive of activity with crime scene techs in tyvex suits, swarming around, taking photos and samples and huddling together in groups. I recognized Dr Lorraine O'Toole, the State Pathologist. She was an impressive figure, at the epicentre of the scene, directing every move with calm authority.

I only caught a glimpse of her though, before Jordan PR was ushered into a small room, with the three bank employees, and stashed there under the watchful eye of a young female garda. She was very pleasant, kind even. We were offered tea and coffee and she positioned herself at a discreet, and non-intimidating distance from us. She didn't even seem to mind Monica

Delahunt having mild hysterics every few moments and let me tell you, in a confined space her screeching was thoroughly irritating.

The minutes dragged. Paula and Stephen sat close together, obviously comforted just by knowing the other was there. I sighed. Much as I enjoyed living vicariously through their romance, it depressed me slightly that I had never had a decent relationship. In fact, since my last attempt at one had turned out to be with a raving psychopath, I had gone off the whole idea of dating. Not that work would have left much time for it anyway. Still, right now if someone half presentable had offered to hold my hand and sit beside me, I would have given it a go.

Finally, the door opened, and a middle-aged man appeared. His face looked familiar –Detective Inspector Graves. Yes! He was a *much* nicer proposition than his bad-tempered colleague. I smiled hopefully at him, and he rewarded me with a nod and a grin.

"Ms. Jordan" he said. "It's nice to see you again. Another workplace, another body, eh?" I opened my mouth to snap back but shut it firmly when I saw the grin on his face. Timely reminder, folks, never let your guard down around a Garda.

He passed on to the others, confirming each name one by one. When he got to Tomas the security guard, he indicated to him to follow him. Tomas stood up reluctantly, looked at me as if to say "See? I told you so," and slowly followed the Detective Inspector from the room. I sighed and exchanged looks with my colleagues. Paula rolled her eyes and glance pointedly at her watch. We'd be here all day at this rate.

After a comparatively short while however the door opened again and uniformed officer stood there, looking slightly lost. "Um…Ms. Jordan? Caroline Jordan?" Bless Graves! I thought.

I smiled at Paula and Stephen – at least he was moving through statements quickly. We might be out of this nightmare quicker than I feared. That little bubble of optimism lasted until the garda opened the door to the next little broom cupboard sized office and ushered me in. There behind the desk looking as cheerful as ever was DS Doyle himself.

Great.

He barely acknowledged me, instead continuing to sift through a pile of papers on the desk. I made myself comfortable on the only other chair and waited. He glanced at me a few times but said nothing. This was going very well, I thought, at this rate he'll take my statement sometime tomorrow afternoon.

"You found the body?" he shot at me suddenly.

"No." I smiled at him and added, "Nice to see you too, by the way. Hope things have been going well for you?

He stared at me like I had two heads.

"Never mind." I said wearily "No. The people who found the body were Tomas the security man, Marie the receptionist and Monica the - I'm not sure what Monica Delahunt does but she seems to be some kind of general manager. She bosses the receptionists and the like around. They were opening the door to the meeting room just as I arrived. Monica started screaming, I looked in – and well, there he was." I swallowed trying to block the memory of the slashed neck and blood. "All I - we – did then, was stand there and make sure no one went inside. And Stephen called 999."

"I see…" he studied one of the sheets of paper in front of him for a moment. "Did you know the victim well?"

"No." I said firmly. "In fact, not at all. I had a meeting here with him this morning, arranged through his secretary last week. I've had email correspondence with him but no personal contact. I've never actually seen him before today and," I added for emphasis, "I know absolutely nothing about him other than work related matters."

Doyle raised an eyebrow.

"You seem intent on distancing yourself from the victim, Ms. Jordan."

Oh good, I thought, you noticed.

"Do I?" I smiled sweetly. "No, I just wanted to be sure you understood, Detective. I am merely a peripheral observer to this tragic event. My interest in poor Frank Clarke was purely business."

"What kind of "business"," Doyle managed to imply I was habitually involved in drug smuggling or human trafficking at the very least. God above the man was an irritating sod.

"Public Relations," I replied not rising to the bait. "Surely you remember?"

"Ah yes…." he smiled faintly. "PR. Remind me…you're still Michael T O'Mahony's PR girl?"

It was my turn to raise an eyebrow. "I still work for the office of An Taoiseach, Yes."

Doyle grunted. "Right, what business brought you here then?"

I hesitated but decided there was no point in being obstructive. "I'm here to pitch for a contract. I'm sure you're aware of Leinster Bank's recent problems. It's been a PR disaster for them. They're looking for new blood -" I almost choked on my poor choice of words. "I mean, for a new firm, someone to help lift them out of this bad period."

He snorted this time. The man was a master of non-verbal communication.

"I see. And Clarke was the person in charge of awarding this contract then?"

"He was the first person to talk to. If he had approved of our general approach then we would have expected to pitch to the board in a week or so, a more in-depth detailed set of proposals. After that it would be a matter for the board to approve."

"Right. I suppose you've no motive to kill Mr. Clarke then." He sounded deeply regretful. I gave him my best "Die roaring, snot face" look.

"I would have no motive to kill anyone, DS Doyle. I'm not in the habit of murderous rages."

Without warning, I felt the fight seep out of me as I realized I was terribly tired and quite upset. I just wanted this to end. I wanted to go with Paula and Stephen and sit somewhere quiet and drink a hot drink and eat something and cry. A lot.

Stuff it, I thought. I didn't think we were bosom buddies, but I thought we were friendly acquaintances at least. He didn't have to be so rude.

"Look," I tried again. "You know fine well it wasn't me. Look at the CCTV footage, there's cameras everywhere. I walked in after the door to the room was opened. I've no motive and I didn't even know the man. And – and it's a bit much to have to go through all this again, frankly. I'm begging you - if you've any relevant questions, ask them and then please, just let me go home, okay?"

There was a pause while Doyle stared at me, looking even more annoyed than ever. He then shuffled the papers on his desk and cleared his throat.

"I just need to walk through exactly what happened this morning, what you saw and what happened. Then, yes, you're at liberty to leave."

I recounted everything I could think of, exactly where everyone was standing, the door swinging open as I approached, Monica Delahunt screaming…it was all pointless I thought but I recounted it as faithfully as possible.

"Again," I couldn't resist pointing out, "all this will be visible on the CCTV footage, there are at least three cameras on the way in."

He looked at me as if he was about to say something then clamped his lips shut.

"Indeed." He looked over his notes and asked a few random questions. I answered. He asked a few more. I answered, praying that I'd make it out of the room without being up for bashing a Garda in the face. At last, he seemed to reach the end of his pointless questions and stood up. It took me a moment to realize that the interview was over.

"Well, then Ms. Jordan. We'll be in touch, I'm sure. Make sure we have your current details."

I paused at the door and said "Well you have all my details, Detective, just check my last email or text. You know, the ones offering you tickets to the new Bond Film premier? Or the new Rockabilly Punks gig?"

I managed not to slam the door.

I found Paula and Stephen huddled outside, trying to shelter from the cold autumn wind. September in Ireland could be mellow and mild, or maliciously wet and wild. Sometimes both on the same day.

"What kept you!" Stephen exclaimed anxiously.

"Why? Was I long?"

"Jaysus, Caroline. Stephen and I were done and out here twenty minutes ago. I thought they'd arrested you or something." Paula hugged me. "Are you OK? You look so pale."

"I always look pale," I brushed off her concern. "But…What a horrible morning. What a rotten fecking morning." I blinked back unexpected tears. "Look. How do you two fancy getting something to eat? Or drink?"

A half hour saw us sitting in the nearest pub, sipping scalding coffee and eating horribly fattening but rather nice bangers and mash. Ballsbridge is one of Dublin's most expensive suburbs so even the basic pub grub is nice. Finnegan's Blue was an especially posh pub with a load of foodie awards, named for a famous horse. Ballsbridge was also home to Ireland's largest show jumping arena, and massive annual horse show. Most of the pubs around here had some kind of horsey theme, odd looking paintings of jockeys and lots of old horseshoes nailed around the walls.

I began to feel a bit more human once I stopped feeling so cold and weird. Just having the other pair for company helped. I think we were all fairly shocked.

"I should ring Derek," I pulled out my phone.

"I did it. I rang while you were still being interviewed." Paula looked sheepish. "Honestly, I was getting worried, he had you in there that long."

Oh lord, she probably had Derek Fields speed dialing every criminal barrister in the city.

"He asked me every stupid question you can think of," I said sourly. "But first he practically accused me of bumping off that poor man."

"It's Doyle," said Paula, smiling. "I honestly don't think he can help it. He probably thinks he was sickeningly nice to you."

"It's so unreal" Stephen shook his head. "I mean, the door was locked and according to that receptionist, someone was in the foyer since at least half past eight this morning. And they never leave the desk unmanned, either the security guard or the receptionist is there. So poor Mr. Clarke must have been there from extremely early this morning or last night."

"Yeah," I replied absentmindedly. "The blood…" A wave of pure nausea swept over me. "I mean…it wasn't recent looking." Oh god. For a moment, the entire snug seemed to shift and move like I was on the deck of a small boat in a large swell. I fought for control. "Anyway – it's their business not ours. The Gardaí, I mean. It's nothing to do with us. I'm not sure I even want this contract anymore."

Except, a treacherous ruthless little voice in my head chimed in, except now they need damage control more than ever. Even now, some board member would be on the phone, looking for someone to smooth all this over. The media would be all over the Bank of Leinster again. Nothing like a murder to bring out the ghouls…*You could ring to rearrange the meeting; they owe you one now…*

I'm only slightly ashamed to say that I made that call. At least I waited a few hours though.

Chapter Four

D*S Doyle*

Dr O'Toole waved to catch our attention and Graves moved swiftly to her side. From her animated gesturing, I gathered she had some preliminary thoughts to share; she was far too professional to commit to anything definite at this stage, but she had a soft spot for Graves. They were old friends and united against the old corps of self-satisfied and lazy cops who had wormed their way into positions of power in the force.

When I had joined the unit, it was still in its infancy. Offically named C Squad no one called it anything but SCS. On my first day Graves had taken me to the local pub, bought me lunch and given me a crash course in the politics involved in my new job.

"The very existence of SCS annoys a lot of higher-ups," he pointed out. "The good ones see it as protecting the status quo - giving special treatment to high profile figures. The lazy and corrupt among us are afraid we've the power to investigate them and their cronies should the opportunity arise." He sipped his coffee and laughed. "In short, everyone hates us."

It wasn't strictly true but true enough to make life difficult. O'Toole was a godsend; her goodwill went a long way to making us effective. If I am being honest we sometimes took advantage of her.

She disappeared back into Room 4, and Graves called me over.

"They're moving the body now,"

"What had the good doc to say? Anything interesting?"

"He's been dead at least since 6 am, probably an hour earlier. She'll give a better estimate when the autopsy is done. Also, he was tortured prior to death. Someone worked him over, very efficiently she says. Stab wounds, shallow cuts, bruising and contusions. Then they finished him off."

"Ah."

"Yeah. Nasty case, Alan. I don't like it."

"A variation on a tiger kidnapping?" So-called tiger kidnappings were now a thing in the city. Gangs would abduct or hold hostage the family of a bank official who would then go open the bank or withdraw cash under duress. Could Clarke have been targeted – except they thought he could be forced to open up the vaults by rough persuasion?

"I don't think so. It feels wrong. This whole thing feels hinky."

"Well, that's our specialty. Hinky, high profile, sensitive crimes."

Graves didn't laugh. "Finish up here. Let's convene back at the incident room. We need to get a handle on this and fast."

It took a while to clear the scene and even longer to deal with the bank officials including Sean O'Dwyer himself. He answered every question by referring us to someone else, not unusual in itself when dealing with senior officials, but the way he spoke about the dead man rubbed me up the wrong way.

"Frank was efficient. I found him most reliable." And "Frank was a dedicated employee. I had no reason to complain of his work." As if he existed only in relation to O'Dwyer.

None of the bank employees we interviewed seemed particularly cut up by the death of one of their executives; shocked, obviously and deeply disturbed at the idea of a murder on hallowed Bank property but not what you'd call personally affected. It was odd. Everything appropriate was said, but with a sort of polite detachment.

Dr O'Toole had the place secured by the time I left; it would be a few days before anyone would be allowed enter Room 4, and then it would a clean-up crew. Promising to have her final report for us as soon as humanly possible, the pathologist disappeared into the night, with her flock of white suited acolytes fluttering around her. At last Locke and I, the only two left standing, handed over to the unfortunate uniformed garda on duty overnight and headed back to the SCS.

For as long as I've been in Special Branch, both the main body and SCS, there's been talk of a new building, a state-of-the-art Headquarters with all mod cons. Like working lifts. Or any kind of lift. Windows that close fully in Winter or can be opened in Summer. And actual Wi-Fi – about a fifth of Garda stations have no internet access. People don't realize that. I tell people that all the time and they think I'm making it up. It's 2012 and we have stations dotted around the county as isolated as they were in the 60s and 70s. As it was the SCS was luckier than most, we at least got a share of the scant resources allocated to Serious Crimes, but I knew colleagues who used their own mobile phones because the radios in their cars wouldn't work. Some of the young fellows on the beat complain they use theirs because even the walkie-talkies are crap.

Talk of this new, amazing HQ was a time-honoured tradition in the force, and despite the Office of Public Works swearing they had bought a site in the city centre, no one was holding their breath waiting for it. In the meantime, we were housed in an ancient building in the south centre, where the outer wall encasing the car park was a listed monument and there were things growing in the damper areas of the building that were probably illegal.

You approached it be driving through an archway covered in lichen and through an alleyway with our building on the right and an equally decrepit, abandoned building on the left. This alleyway of an entrance was a regular stopping point on the Dublin Ghost Bus Tour, so you can imagine how cheery and welcoming it was. The General Public used a slightly less macabre entrance on the main road. Even so, their car park was badly lit, and inadequate for the volume of cars using it.

Inside was a warren of small offices, shoeboxes masquerading as situation rooms and on the ground floor, a suite of interview rooms and holding cells that we were afraid Amnesty International would get wind of someday. Being made sit in there was cruel and unusual punishment, for us as much as any suspect.

The point of our unit, Special Crimes Squad, was to investigate crimes involving high ranking figures, or sensitive institutions. A murder in a Bank headquarters certainly fell under our remit; O'Dwyer, the Bank's president was already chewing the ear off the top brass and in turn, we were being kicked around by Superintendent Looney. But we had a job to do and them rushing us wasn't going to make us do it better or faster.

The rest of the team certainly hadn't been sitting idle while the crime scene was being processed.

"I've tracked down every camera on the main road, including shops and traffic," Powers sighed. "There's nothing of much help, but we caught a few cars between 11 and 3 am, mostly clear reg numbers so I've passed it on to uniform to check up. It's possible one of them might lead back to an employee of the bank."

Graves echoed his sigh. "What's the story with Clarke's personal life?"

"Nonexistent," Locke rapped the table. "He was a bleedin' ghost, boss."

The first step in every murder case is to find out as much as possible about the victim; the solution so often lay with their nearest, dearest, most trusted friends and family. Graves claims that this is why murder cops are so suspicious and untrusting in relationships – so would you be, if nearly every case ended in the arrest of a spouse.

Locke handed me a sheet with details of next of kin, associates and so on. Usually, we had a range of people to interview, chase up and generally annoy until we either eliminated them or they confessed. Frank Clarke was an exception, I had never seen anything quite like it. He lived alone. He had two brothers, neither of whom lived in Ireland, and two elderly parents in Mayo who seemed to know next to nothing about his life in Dublin.

"I had to break the news to the brothers," Locke said. "The local uniforms visited the parents. They did their best but apparently, he rarely talked about his work, or his colleagues or anything of the slightest use to us.

"He visited them every few weeks. The general consensus seems to be that he was a good son. All I heard was, "Frank was great like that.""

To his siblings, he was even more of a mystery. One lived in Birmingham in the UK and the other in Jokkmokk in Sweden. When interviewed by Locke the brother in Birmingham, Damien Clarke, had explained succinctly.

"I emigrated more than 25 years ago, Detective, straight out of school. So did Jamie. We were gone before Frank finished secondary. He stayed, we left. It didn't make for a good relationship."

Reading between the lines, I imagined Frank resenting his elder brothers leaving at the first chance, staying away and putting all the responsibility for two elderly people on to their younger brother. Damien Clarke was brusque, Locke remarked, "and while it's hard to get a sense of a person properly on the phone, I'd say that he was genuinely shocked by his brother's murder. But I doubt he's deeply grieving him as a person, if you follow me."

"We'll be home for the funeral, whenever that will be." Damien Clarke had told Locke.

"I hadn't the heart to tell him how long it might be 'til the body is released." He sighed heavily, "Do you know what his parting words were? "God knows what we'll do about Mam and Dad now." I tell ya, I feel even sorrier for the unfortunate Frank."

There wasn't a lot more we could do that night, except catch a few hours' sleep and start first thing in the morning. When we arrived at the Leinster headquarters, a breakfast of coffee and pastries awaited us but no sign of senior management. The Board of Directors were huddled in a hastily convened meeting, and a helpful young man was assigned to show us around and line up people to be interviewed.

The murdered man's colleagues were equally unhelpful, despite their best efforts. Over and over that morning we heard that he was a nice man, quiet, efficient, popular in a low-key way. But he wasn't reall friends with any of them outside the office, he never mentioned hobbies or activities, he didn't seem to have a personality other than mild and inoffensive.

But people didn't get to be senior officials in an institution like the Leinster by being mild and inoffensive in my experience. There had to be more to the man than that.

"I tried," Locke insisted. "His brothers are a dead end. Maybe he told his parents something, or maybe he just didn't have a social life."

"Like Doyle, then," Claire grinned at me to take the sting away.

"Let me try again," he continued. "I'll see what a direct chat with his parents yield. And while I'm at it, I'll reach out to the local boys again. They must know something about our Mr. Clarke. And someone needs to check his finances, phone calls…"

"On it," MacPherson waved a sheaf of papers at us. "Just got the records now, it'll take a while."

"Get some uniformed to help," Graves instructed. "We need a break. We need something, anything, to happen." He looked like hell, his face grey and lined. Superintendent Looney had called twice an hour for updates since the words Bank of Leinster had reached his ears. He pointed at me and said, "We need background. O'Dwyer has a lot of political clout, far above our pay grade. We need to know whose toes we're stepping on. Which begs the question, who do we know who can give us that insight?"

Caroline Jordan. Again.

Chapter Five

C*aroline Jordan*

The Monday after the disastrous Bank of Leinster meeting saw Paula and me sipping beautifully made lattes in a tiny restaurant on one of my favourite areas of Dublin, South William Street. Not five minutes from its more famous counterpart Grafton Street, it's a long, narrow, winding haven of cool independent retail, hip coffee shops, hairdressers, and pubs. It also boasts the Powerscourt Townhouse, a shopping centre in an historic building filled with the kind of shops that ate my budget and spat it back out.

I was hoping that the nice surroundings and decent caffeine would help with our difficult client.

Best Budgets wasn't Ireland's biggest supermarket, but they were a good contract for us; lots of rural reach, with franchised stores all over the west and south and a smattering of city-based ones around Dublin, Cork and Galway. It was a nice one to have on the books and I knew it did us no harm with the rural politicians. It made us less of a Dublin firm. Some non-Dubliners, known as Culchies, viewed anything from the capital with suspicion. Obviously being from Dublin, I viewed them as strange, cow-rearing troglodytes in return. Best Budgets helped us bridge that gap.

Oh, but they were a trial and a tribulation, and we fought like cats in the office to pass them off on each other. Demanding and capricious, they constantly changed their minds and then blamed us; and now on top of their usual roster of promotions and events, they were launching an in-house magazine. This meeting was with the new head of department, the man responsible for editing and producing it. The idea was we were to launch it and try to make people in the Best Budgets family actually read it.

Yeah.

Paula had tried her best to push them towards an E-zine, something modern and easy to update. It didn't wash with the Best Budgets management; they were all, to a man (no women on this board of directors,) devoted to the idea of a glossy cover, featuring a z list celebrity and pages of self-congratulatory guff about the firm's achievements. To this end they hired a guy with a background in trade publishing and let him loose.

So far, we'd talked on the phone or by email - I was intrigued to see him in person.

"You need to come too," Paula pleaded, "He's a piece of work, it'll take two of us." She had done most of the work on the campaign and was more than capable of pitching it but she had found McDonnell as difficult to deal with as I had, and we were all still feeling a bit fragile after the tragic events in the Bank.

Also, not to put a tooth in it, John James McDonnell gave the impression of being a pompous misogynist and I hoped two women might confuse him sufficiently to get him to agree to our campaign proposal.

Every phone call had been a quagmire of innuendo, him talking over me, bizarre commentaries on his previous employers and current colleagues. At one point, I could hear him in the background on another line, shouting at some woman.

"I left it beside the bed!" he roared, "It's an expensive watch, I want it back, Yvonne…"

I was certainly expecting a suit with a bit of attitude but what arrived far exceeded anything we could have dreamed up.

McDonnell announced his arrival in advance, shouting into his mobile phone with gusto. You could hear him from the far side of the room, and

I could see heads turning as he passed. His sentences were peppered with language even I found excessive, and I swear like a navvy. "I told you to wrap it up, pronto!" He squeezed between two tables taking the opportunity to openly peer down at one buxom lady's top, "they either pick up the pace or they're out. Yes, yes, I know…" He sat down and held one imperious hand up to command our silence, "Sorry Jimmy I'm at a meeting. What? Oh yeah, two lovely looking young ones."

He favoured us with a gurn that was part wink, part lip smack. "Bye, bye, bye, bye, bye…"

Paula tried to catch my eye, but I couldn't. I just couldn't. If I looked at her even once, I'd start laughing. Instead, I tried to focus on our guest with my serious business face.

"John," I extended my hand, "Lovely to meet you in person. This is Paula, my colleague." His grip on my hand was uncomfortably firm and to my horror, his clammy fingers started stroking the inside of my palm. I once had a very brief relationship in college with a boy who thought that made women swoon; it didn't work then, and it wasn't working for lover boy here either.

I wrenched back my hand with an effort. Paula stuck her hands firmly under the table out of reach, smiling at him to cover the snub. "Lovely to meet you, John."

He frowned. "John James. Or JJ." He puffed out his chest and angled his chair so that he could man-spread his legs so far apart he took up the space between our table and next. "Most people call me JJ. Or Big John," He leered openly at us, and gave another grotesque wink. My internal voice started screaming before he could get the next, inevitable words out. "Yeah, Big John…or BJ, if the ladies are willing. Har."

All we could do was stare at him. I remembered old men from my teen years, friends of my mother, who thought it hilarious to talk to women like that. To find one under 50 still doing it was both depressing and fascinating.

"Well." Paula, bless her, was unflappable. "We have some fresh and exciting ideas for you, JJ. I've already compiled a selection of the most effective trade and in house magazine strategies from major firms in the last 5 years, with some very surprising trends I think we can make great use of." A hefty file appeared from beside her. Even I was impressed.

"Shall we start?" she had barely opened it when the redoubtable JJ intervened.

"Hold your horses there, Missy," a smug grin and another greasy wink. "I don't recall agreeing to anything yet. Best Budgets might use Jordan PR for the odd wee opening or to handhold our regional stores, but this is a bit… well, it might be a bit beyond two girleens like yourselves. I don't want to boast but at my level, you need to vet these things carefully." He reached across the table and grabbed my hand again. "We need to see what you're offering first."

Paula looked at me, her eyes wide. I'm fairly sure she thought she was going to have to pull me off JJ's neck in a minute. Much as I would have liked to launch myself at him, my professional instincts were too well honed. Instead, I picked up the nearest fork and stuck it, playfully, in his hand. He yelped and pulled away the offending article.

"JJ," I said sweetly. "I think there's some kind of misunderstanding here. You don't have a choice. No choice, at all. The decision to award us the contract - a legally binding, very *hard and fast* contract - was made so far above your pay grade, you'd get a nosebleed climbing up there to complain. I have a long standing and excellent relationship with your bosses, especially Mr. Collins himself." Collins was the CEO of Best Budgets , and I had met him several times. He hadn't hated me. "So. Much as we enjoy your little joke, ha ha, we do need to get down to work here."

Paula offered him a sheaf of papers her face carefully blank. McDonnell hesitated for a moment, before snatching them ungraciously.

"Sure, you can't even make a joke these days," he muttered, unable to make eye contact with either of us. "Let's see these earth-shattering suggestions then."

A very difficult half hour passed between ordering and food arriving, JJ giving a begrudging and reluctant pass to only 3 out of all of Paula's carefully curated content suggestions. From her anxious glances at me I could tell she was feeling deflated, but experience had taught me to ignore sulking men. In a few days we'd come back to him with the same suggestions, phrased slightly differently and he would pass them, because he knew they were good. Let him have his petulant tantrum now, at least we all knew where we stood.

Whatever his annoyance at Jordan PR, JJ didn't let it affect his appetite. He interrupted Paula twice to wave at the waiter, a lovely man whose name tag identified as "Javier," barking orders at him. "What's this? Onion Jam? What's that when it's at home? Falafels! Jaysus, you can't ate anywhere without coming across them yokes. No. I don't want a falafel. Don't you do any normal food? Burger. Chips. Toasted sandwich."

The bewildered waiter seized on the one thing he recognized from McDonnell's diatribe and offered a Croque Monsieur. I could see trouble looming when a luscious confection of sourdough and gruyère arrived at the table rather than the pub favourite of thin sliced bread and ham with a processed slice of easy single melted in. Sure enough, McDonnell looked up and wrinkled his nose. "Ah here, what in the name of god is that?"

Paula and I cringed in sympathy with the unfortunate Javier.

"Oh, that looks so nice," Paula beamed at McDonnell and added, "How clever of you, I wish I'd ordered that instead of this salad!"

Torn between his hatred of anything he deemed "foreign" and his need for the soothing balm of admiration, he contented himself with snorting derisively. Then he stuffed his face noisily. Honestly, I was already plotting how to get him fired.

"I suppose we'll have to leave it at that for now." Almost two hours of torture had passed by the time he unbent enough to sign off on phase one of the campaign. Paula had managed to soothe him into some kind of good humour although even then he was far from pleasant.

We walked him to the door of the restaurant then doubled back in to apologize to the staff.

"Mother divine," Paula said as we trudged back to the office, a fair stretch away past Christ Church Cathedral but with Dublin traffic, still faster to walk. "What a specimen."

"Isn't he a joy? Bet you're glad you didn't have to meet him on your own" I laughed. "Don't worry about JJ. Or BJ to the *lay-deez*. He tried it on, he got slapped down, now we just manage him until this blessed magazine is up and running."

Paula looked doubtful. "Mark my words, JJ McDonnell is going to drive us all mad. If he gets too bad, maybe we should palm him off on Stephen?"

I hated that idea. "Honestly, we should be able to manage him, Paula. But yeah, I suppose as a last resort."

We had enough to worry about, without getting too sensitive over a sleaze like him.

For example, we still had the bank contract to worry about and a few hours later I found myself back in the Leinster Bank. A rather imperious email had arrived in my inbox, from one David Howard, asking me to come in for a "chat." It wasn't clear exactly what the chat was to be about but at least we were still in the game. The thought of returning to that building didn't appeal, if I'm honest but I found my backbone and presented myself at the appointed time. The same receptionist was behind the desk, and I was glad to see Tomas on duty at the door. He greeted me like a long-lost friend; obviously finding a dead body together was one of life's bonding experiences to Tomas.

"Everything OK?" I asked him quietly. He nodded.

"Yes, they are all very angry about poor Mr. Clarke but at least not blaming me."

"Thank feck for that." I was relieved for him. It was no fun being the foreigner when people started pointing fingers.

I nodded at Marie Flynn, standing primly behind the reception desk and she smiled wanly. "Ms. Jordan," she scanned the list of names on her clipboard. All the computers in the world and they still made her carry a damn clipboard. "Mr. Howard, is that right? 3.30?"

She had on a very pretty silver brooch, discreetly holding her Bank of Leinster uniform neckerchief in place.

"That's me." A horrible thought struck me "Where...where's the meeting being held?"

She looked at me sympathetically. "Upstairs in Mr. Howard's office." She lowered her voice and said, "They haven't used any of the rooms down here since – well, since Mr. Clarke."

And thank feck for that too.

"Great. Should I go up?"

She shook her head. A rather rebellious expression on her face belied her professional, deadpan delivery. "I'll have to call someone up there to come down and escort you up, Ms. Jordan, it'll just be a few moments."

I rolled my eyes. Leinster Bank's reputation for being more than a little hidebound was proving accurate.

"Grand. I'll just sit here then and try not to touch anything."

She suppressed a grin and pressed a button on her desk. Sure enough, after ten minutes a polite young man in the ubiquitous grey suit so favoured by bankers escorted me up two flights of stairs.

Puffing by the time we hit the top landing, it was hard to appreciate the architectural splendour of the place. I know it's an old, listed, landmark building but come on, people, lifts! The Nice Young Man ushered me into a very spacious, bright office. Another man, in his early forties, sandy haired, good looking enough with a very warm, pleasant manner seized my hand and shook it.

"Ms. Jordan!" He had a very noticeable English accent, a proper rugger bugger accent. If Paula was here, she'd try to make him say "crumpet" and "mummy." "I'm so pleased you could come in again. I just want to say, and I speak for the board here too, we are so terribly sorry about your awful experience the other day. I'm David Howard, please call me David..."

I nodded, trying to convey both bravery in the face of a dreadful event and the fact that it was nothing to a good PR woman like me to shake off a mere murder and plough on in the interests of my client.

"Poor Frank," he continued, shaking his head. "It's unimaginable. He was a very popular colleague, you know. It's absolutely shocked us all, shocked. And I can't imagine how awful it must have been for you!"

"It was – yes. And of course, for Marie and Tomas too. And Monica of course," some inner demon prompted me to reply.

He looked completely confused. "Ah…your um, your staff?"

"No, David. *Your* staff." I smiled at him. "Marie the receptionist, and Tomas your security guard. And Ms. Delahunt of course. They were terribly upset. It was a horrible shock for them."

He only faltered for a moment. It was an interesting moment though, as confusion gave way to comprehension, then annoyance, then the smooth mask slipped back down. Hah! Two years dealing with Irish politicians had given me insights into men like David Howard that clinical psychologists would kill for.

"Oh of course, yes. I believe Ms. Delahunt is still on leave, poor woman. I'm sure they are all being well looked after though."

I wondered. Sure, Monica Delahunt was off having the vapours but the receptionist and security guard were back at work and I would have bet my last toffee pop biscuit that was because they wouldn't get paid otherwise. I knew all about Leinster Bank's approach to worker's rights if you were a lowly paid, temporary contract only, type of employee.

"Did he – did Frank have any family?" I'd been wondering about this all weekend, whether there was a widow or kids somewhere.

David shook his head. "No, he was unattached. Elderly parents, and I think, two brothers. Very sad for them, especially in such circumstances."

He shrugged slightly as if casting off the entire distasteful subject of murder and minions. "Of course," he said diplomatically "We at Leinster Bank are now in a doubly embarrassing position…"

I could recognize an opening when it was bulldozed in front of me. With as much confidence and aplomb as I could muster, I launched into my sympathetic, optimistic, happy to be a part of the glorious future of Leinster Bank pitch. As this was an "informal" meeting, I steered clear of committing to too detailed a campaign but managed to hit the main points. Including my personal thoughts on the best way to limit damage from the murder investigation.

I'd done a bit of digging, aided by Derek Fields' encyclopaedic knowledge of everyone who is anyone in Ireland, and Michael T's endless fund of scurrilous gossip and rumours. As a result, I knew several very sensitive issues that the individuals that made up the board of the Leinster Bank would prefer – would *really* prefer – to keep quiet. The trick was to touch lightly on them, show that I knew about them, but also reassure that I would not expose them. Nay, that I would move heaven and earth to protect them.

In short, I lied through my teeth, obliquely threatened, and basically begged. A normal kind of high-level pitch, in fact. By the end David Howard and I had reached a cozy mutual admiration that seemed to bode well.

I shrugged as I left – I'd done my best. Either all three of us would be in pitching for our lives in a week or so, or I'd never hear from The Leinster again. At least we had moved forward a little and considering the importance of this contract to our little firm, I was expecting a welcoming committee when I arrived back in our tiny but glamourous office. Instead, a frantic looking Stephen intercepted me at the door, mugging and gurning like a mad yoke. There was no sign of Paula, but I could see through the frosted glass door someone was sitting in my office.

"He's in there," Stephen hissed. "Doyle. He's in there!" He disappeared behind his desk, only to emerge clutching the chocolate biscuit and sweet treats box. Doyle was one of the honoured few who received the best biscuits, a sort of a thank you from Stephen for not letting me be murdered by a maniac last year.

My heart sank. For a glorious moment I thought about sneaking back out, but I couldn't abandon Stephen. Instead, I just walked in, my head held high, as if finding rude, annoying detectives in my office was an everyday occurrence. He looked up as I entered but otherwise made no move either to greet me or explain himself. I smiled at him, suspecting that it made him deeply uncomfortable.

"DS Doyle," I said, settling myself behind my lovely Cillian O'Suilleabhain desk (it cost me an arm and a leg, was definitely too big for the room but it was worth every penny right now.)

He nodded. "I have to ask you to confirm some of the times given in your statement," he said without preamble.

Wearily I nodded back. In fairness to the man, I couldn't blame him double checking. My track record on accurate times was a trifle spotty where he was concerned.

"Go on,"

"You say you arrived at twenty past twelve."

"Yes."

"According to Marie -Ms. Flynn - the receptionist, and Mr. Warskowski the security guard, you arrived at 12 on the dot."

I blinked. I opened my mouth to say "yeah, maybe," but then I remembered…pulling up into the car park, and obsessively checking the clock in my beloved Jaguar XK series black coupé so that we wouldn't walk in too early or too late for our half twelve meeting. I know in my bones we walked into that building at twenty past the hour.

"No," I said firmly. "I checked the time. I wanted us to walk in no later or earlier than ten minutes before the meeting. My car clock is always right."

He gave me a disbelieving look. "Always?"

"Yes. Always." I added smugly "It's one of the things a Jaguar XK is famous for."

"I see. Well, the problem is, that while both the aforementioned witnesses put you arriving at twenty minutes earlier, Ms. Delahunt agrees with you. And insists that she had the correct time all along, with her watch putting the time she came downstairs at ten past twelve and you arriving at twenty past twelve."

"Okay." I hesitated to point out the obvious but, "So what? I mean, that man was there for hours surely. It wasn't done between twelve and twenty-past. What difference does it make?"

He didn't reply but instead showed me a glossy photo of the famous Leinster House clock. "You know this?"

"Yes. It's the clock, the one in the main foyer they all say is so accurate and the whole company takes its time from it, yada-yada-yada."

"It's out. By twenty minutes."

I looked at him. Obviously, this was meant to mean something but instead all I could think was "So what?" and something told me Doyle wouldn't appreciate that reply.

"OK."

"It was correct the day before - everyone seems to agree on that. It was out by twenty minutes on the morning of the murder. The receptionist and the security guard continued about their day using the clock as their guide. Tomas Warskowski says he adjusted his watch to match the clock when he came on duty. He was surprised to find that instead of being his usual five minutes early he was twenty-five minutes ahead of schedule according to the clock. Ms. Flynn apparently doesn't wear a watch." He stared into space for a moment. "She said it makes her feel too tied down, outside work."

I smiled. I did quite like Marie Flynn, what I'd seen of her. She seemed wasted on Leinster Bank.

"Okay. Right then. If the accuracy of my Jaguar is any help to you then I can confirm that I was there at twenty-past. Which would imply that somehow the blasted clock was wrong."

He looked at me expectantly and I finished in exasperation, "You do realize, the thing is probably not accurate at all? I mean it's ancient, and this legend about it being so accurate is more than likely just an ancient marketing myth."

He shook his head.

"It's regularly serviced by the firm of James and Patterson." James and Patterson was like, 150 years old and renowned for their precision and accuracy. They sold watches that cost my yearly mortgage payment and people swore they were worth it because they would last a lifetime.

Doyle continued "That clock is apparently, and I quote, "more accurate than any digital clock."

I doubted it. But I took the point – presumably, someone had deliberately altered the clock. It seemed fairly pointless though, a total red herring.

"It'll all be on the CCTV cameras anyway," I returned to my favourite, and obvious, point. "Surely you can see who went in between 8.30 and 12.30 and it won't matter if the clock is wrong?"

Doyle gave a sour look at the floor and muttered "Yes. Well, it appears the CCTV cameras were also interfered with."

I stared at him. "Interfered with? *Oh.*"

"Yeah. No trace of anyone going into the lobby since 11 pm last night. And they were disabled remotely through an untraceable IPS address." He shrugged "Or something. I don't get a lot of this techie stuff. At any rate no one can figure out who disabled them, at least not yet."

It made me uneasy that he was sharing information with me; the last time he did that it turned out he wanted me to be an unpaid undercover spy for him.

Doyle was as odd as two left feet, in my opinion and I would not put it past him to try to embroil me in this again. He was a great believer in inside information.

"Well," I said encouragingly. "I've every faith in the Gardaí. I'm sure you'll work it out." I even half stood up, trying to convey a not too subtle hint. Doyle completely ignored me.

"I am not sure we will." He actually looked weary. A lesser woman might have felt sorry for him. "The problem seems to be that no one knows where Frank Clarke was since 5pm yesterday, when he's clearly visible on the system, leaving the building for the day. Between then and 11 pm he must have been somewhere; we just haven't found where. At 11pm the CCTV is disabled, and then he must have returned, and died, between 4 am and 6 am, as near as medical science can determine."

Dr Lorraine O'Toole was our state pathologist and if she said he died between 4 am and 6 am, you could bet on it she was right.

He was mainly talking to himself at this point.

"What makes no sense is why the clock had to be altered."

I sighed. "When exactly was the clock altered?"

He shrugged, Doyle language for I don't know.

"Okay. Say it was altered before five pm yesterday, was it done to ensure Frank left early?"

"No. It was definitely all right at five, according to the staff."

"Then it was altered later, to make him or someone else think that it was twenty minutes earlier than it was."

He looked skeptical.

"I know it's only twenty minutes and it's hard to see how that could be important to anyone. But if you think the clock was changed for a reason then it can only be because twenty minutes *were* important to someone. Someone needed either to make something happen twenty minutes earlier or make someone think it was twenty minutes earlier."

Despite myself, I got interested. "Here! Maybe the clock itself makes things happen? From what I can see everyone in the place is obsessed with the clock being perfect. Maybe they time something by it, and it had to be altered because of that?"

"Hmm. There are time-locked vaults. Maybe." He stood up abruptly. "So. Anyway, thanks."

And without another word he stalked out of the room. My teeth clenched involuntarily. He truly was the most annoying man, and now it irritated me that he had dismissed my little theory so offhandedly. And then I was irritated at myself, for being irritated. I did not want to be involved, so why on earth care what he thought.

Awful man.

Chapter six

Marie Flynn

Marie hesitated.

It seemed paranoid to be worried. Tomas was rarely late, but everyone had a bad morning now and then. He was a hard- working man; she knew he often went straight from a day's work at Leinster Bank to a barman's job in his local pub. He was engaged to a girl back home and saved every penny for their future. It wouldn't be surprising if he overslept now and then.

She stared at the phone and tapped her pen absentmindedly against the desk. People often got the wrong impression about Tomas, thinking he was surly or reserved but in fact he was a dote. He covered for the girls on the reception desk and when your break was only a measly half hour, often taken away at Ms. Delahunt's whim, it was a huge deal that someone would help you when you were a few minutes late.

He also minded the girls when they left on dark winter evenings, more than once walking them out through the dark grounds to the well-lit road beyond the gates.

She glanced at the clock again. Ms. Delahunt had had a fit over that stupid thing yesterday. She had moaned and bitched and whined somehow seeing it as a personal affront that anyone could have tampered with it; Marie could have smacked her. Who cared if an ancient creaky old clock was a few minutes slow or fast? It wasn't as if it made any difference – She and Tomas could tell them that the room hadn't been entered before 8 am on the day they found poor Mr. Clarke. So, who cared? Especially when someone was dead.

It was now almost 9 am. Tomas would never be this late and while there was no concrete reason to worry, the fact that one colleague had already been murdered made Marie a bit nervous. Rather than waste more time thinking about it, she dialed the number on file for Tomas' flat and waited. It rang out. She rang his mobile again and it went straight to voicemail.

Bugger.

On impulse she dialed Linda in personnel. Linda lived under the heel of Monica Delahunt and if possible, hated her even more than Marie did. She often slipped things past her, requests for days off or sick notes. Maybe Tomas had actually called in already and Linda had not had a chance to tell her.

"No," Linda hissed quietly into the phone. Obviously, the Evil Empress wasn't far away. "I haven't heard from him at all. He's never this late. She'll freaking kill him."

"I know." Marie chewed her bottom lip worriedly. "I've rung his flat and his mobile."

"Maybe he's chucked it in," Linda whispered. "Maybe he's free of this place."

"No. No, I really don't think so. He was only saying the other day how much he needed to hang on to this job. You know what he's like, it's all about Milena and their wedding. I can't see him just upping and going."

Linda sighed. "If he's not in soon you know what'll happen."

"I know."

Marie had a feeling Monica would only jump at the chance to fire Tomas, she seemed to have taken a sharp dislike to him. "Oh well, there's nothing much I can do."

There was a long pause then "There might be something I can do...." Linda whispered. "I could put a note in saying he called in sick. It would be the first time, so there's not much she could say about it. I know the temp agency should be told too but most of the time that never happens anyway, or at least not until the end of the week."

Tomas, like Marie and a lot of the Leinster staff were technically "temps" employed through an agency, thus denying them the luxury of things like sick leave, worker's rights and benefits.

"Oh, you're a pet! That would be fabulous, Linda. At least give him a chance."

"Grand. Leave it to me." Linda hung up.

Not for the first time Marie offered a little prayer to the God of Employment that she wasn't stuck up there with Monica all day. How Linda managed was beyond her.

The morning wore on with no sign of Tomas. Eventually Carl, the alternate security man arrived in.

"Howya love," Carl was a cheerful Dubliner with a perpetually optimistic outlook on life. "Linda called me in. I hear the Iron Man is out sick? Jaysus, it must be bad – that fella would drag himself in here with two broken legs."

Carl hailed from the inner city, from the heart of Dublin Liberties and was a font of information and anecdotes that passed the time. His cheerful prattling made the day easier, but by five o'clock Marie was ready to go home and sit down. Not even allowed to sit behind the desk, she thought bitterly. Rotten place. What difference would it make to allow her to sit, seeing as the general public wasn't allowed in? Not for the first time, she cursed the random meanness that drove attitudes in places like Banks, the endless pointless rules that served no real purpose.

She shivered a little as she walked down the dark, tree lined avenue, not just because the Autumn chill had crept in. It was typical that the Bank poured thousands into decor and fancy lighting inside but wouldn't bother with a few poxy lights to make the driveway safer. Of course, most of the staff had cars, and didn't need to walk through the creepy gloom to the bus stop.

Her car had gone months before when the credit union had called about the five-thousand-euro loan Declan the Weasel had persuaded her to take out in *her* name, to help his business over a hump, and of which he apparently hadn't bothered repaying one red cent. Her bus stop was just outside the gate, thankfully.

She looked at her watch and did a quick calculation. If she got the bus halfway to the suburb where she shared a house with two others, she'd be just outside Tomas' flat. She could ring the bell and see if he was there. Maybe he was sick after all. At any rate she could check on him and be back on the bus half an hour later.

At Larrington road, one of the many streets around Rathmines, she hopped off the bus and walked the five minutes to Tomas' address. Rathmines was another of Dublin's historical villages submerged by the sprawling growth of the city, in this case transformed into an sea of flats and apartments. Long, wide streets were flanked by Georgian and Victorian houses that had been divided and sub-divided over generations, first bedsits for students and now studio flats for young professionals.

At its heart was a high street of restaurants and pubs, a commercial college housed in a red brick Victorian building and a small, but ambitious shopping centre. It was in the process of being gentrified but it was still a little scruffy, slightly rough but cool. Walking through it now made Marie feel older than normal, conscious of her very middle-class working uniform that screamed establishment. Feeling more than slightly foolish by the time she reached Tomas' place, she stared up at the building. An old Georgian converted to bedsits in the 1970s it was dingy and not at all welcoming; Tomas had often described it but told her it was cheap, and there was worse in Poland. He had seemed to quite like the place. She remained unconvinced.

As she stood dithering on the doorstep, looking at the bell for "T.Warskowski Flat No. 6," the door opened and a rough looking young man sidled out. He held the door ajar and looked at her inquiringly.

"Goin' in, love?" he rasped. Despite looking about 16 he already had the cigarette addled voice of a 60-year-old heavy smoker. On impulse, and half to get away from him, Marie nodded, slipped past him and shut the heavy front door behind her.

She glanced around the dingy hall. There were three doors, each marked with the kind of gold numbers her sister put on her wheelie bin. She counted the doors; the ground floor was comprised of numbers one to three. She climbed up the stairs, and at the top of the landing saw numbers four to six. She approached number six, her heart beginning to pound uncomfortably.

When asked afterwards, she realized that she had unconsciously recognized the fact that the door was very slightly ajar. Without thinking about it, she pushed it fully open and gasped at the scene beyond. Tomas had not wasted too much money or time on decorating; just a couch, an armchair, a bookcase and a coffee table. The couch was overturned, and the bookcase half prone across the back of it, the books and magazines scattered across the floor.

She swallowed and forced herself to take a step inside, calling out "Tomas?" There was no reply. The room was in darkness, only the streetlights outside and the landing light behind her illuminating the gloom. She felt around for a light switch, feeling more and more uneasy by the moment. "Tomas!?" she shouted this time. "Are you here?" Her fingers failed to locate a switch. "Blast it!"

She picked her way across the room. The place felt empty, but she could still feel a cold sweat on the back of her neck. She saw a door at the far end and pushed it open. A kitchenette. She felt around again and this time her fingers hit a switch. The kitchen light was at least bright, and she could see a lot better.

Almost immediately she regretted this, when she saw what lying at her feet.

Chapter Seven

D *S Doyle*

When a murder like the Clarke case stalls after a few days, with few leads to follow, you hope something, anything, will happen to kick-start the momentum again. But not like this. I hated to look at the poor man, lying in a narrow hospital bed, his face a horrible mess. That he was alive at all was a miracle. He was at death's door when Ms. Flynn happened to call in on him and had crashed twice in the ambulance. Now, twelve hours later, he was at least stable, but they weren't expecting him to wake up any time soon. The grim-faced Doctor wasn't making any promises either.

Graves appeared by my elbow, looking even more sombre than usual.

"Poor fella." He remarked. "He put up some fight, the crime scene's a mess. But whoever did this was both strong and armed. Some kind of steel bar or possibly even an aluminium baseball bat. We'll know in the morning."

"It is the morning," I pointed out wearily. It was 3.30 am to be precise. "What about the girl?"

I felt almost as sorry for Marie Flynn as for the poor man in the hospital bed. She struck me as a very capable, nice woman. It seemed unfair she had been subjected to two violent situations in less than a week, but if she hadn't gone to check on Warskowski, he would be dead.

"I sent her home hours ago, with a nice lad from Larrington Road Station as escort. She went to her sister's home in Dundrum. I thought she was going to puke on me more than once." Graves winced in recollection.

"Hmm." People tell me I have a suspicious nature. They're probably right. I couldn't see Ms. Flynn as a viable suspect, and something in me hated asking but I had to consider the possibility. "I suppose finding two bodies in a week will shake anyone up. Did it strike you as genuine?"

I caught a sharp glance from Graves. "You think she's involved?"

"Do you?" I countered.

He considered a minute then shook his head. "No. His phone records show that she's been trying to contact him since he didn't show up for work this – sorry, yesterday morning. She called the ambulance for him. If she wanted him dead all she had to do was leave him there until morning. And she seems genuinely upset. She keeps talking about his fiancée…Milena something or other…back home in Poland."

Great. "Someone needs to contact the fiancée."

Graves nodded. "Yeah, I've already asked MacPherson to get on it."

Claire MacPherson was the only woman on our team, but that was not why Graves had asked her. She was the type of person who could wrinkle a confession out of a complete stranger on a bus. People queued up to tell her their darkest secrets. If there was anyone who could establish a rapport with the fiancée and find out what, if anything, Tomas Warskowski was up to that got him attacked, MacPherson was the one.

Failing that we could send in Dave Locke, he could charm his way in anywhere. MacPherson's intel would be more objective though.

"Good." I said, "Locke and Powers need to start chasing up the tenants in that building. I want to know how that man's door stayed half open all day and none of those skangers noticed or tried to rob the place."

Graves chuckled. For some reason he maintains that I have a jaundiced outlook on my fellow man. I call it reality.

"What about the lovely Miss Jordan."

I rolled my eyes. That woman. "What about her?"

"Nothing." He looked around innocently. "Just wondering how she was doing. Must be a bit of a shock to her to suddenly find herself in the middle of another murder investigation."

I hesitated. People think I don't try with social interaction, but I do. I am never quite sure I'm doing it right, but I try. "Actually, I thought of that." I was rather proud of myself. "Indeed, I called into her work and had a chat."

Graves almost choked. "You didn't? Good feck man. I hope she appreciated it!"

"I think she did. We'd a nice chat about the murder case and she seemed fine. I think she's quite interested in it, if you ask me."

"Is she." Graves seemed a little at a loss and he sounded a bit strangled. "Wow."

I wouldn't say we were mates, but I had definitely managed to maintain a civil relationship with Caroline Jordan since our last encounter. It wasn't easy, she was a very irritating woman at times, but she has a good brain and I had to admit, she was generous with the tickets and invitations to events. Not the I would have time to attend but it showed she wasn't as hard-nosed and callous as you might think. And considering how often I'm told I have no people skills it was nice to be able to show that I could be diplomatic if needed.

MacPherson had some news for us later that morning. Despite only having a few hours' sleep, Claire looked far more human than any of the rest of the team. Locke and Powers both looked as if they had been up all night and I knew I looked as if I had slept under a hedge. As usual our incident room looked nothing like you would see on TV. It was dingy, badly lit and filled with crap. The desks were untidy and the only thing that looked remotely like the conventional idea of a cop's investigation was the board. Already covered with photos and notes from the Clarke case, someone -probably Powers, as his was the only legible hand-writing – had placed a photo of Tom Warskowski and written in the details of his case as well.

"What have you got for us, Claire?" Graves smiled benignly at her. Claire was thirty-odd, with shoulder length dark hair, sallow skin and a very pleasant face. She looked kindly and approachable; something that had been a source of regret to many a gangster over the years. It would be easy to dismiss her, at first glance, unless you noticed the gleam in her eye as she sized you up.

"We-ell. Poor Milena – that's Tomas' fiancée – is absolutely distraught. I had an interpreter ready to talk to her on the phone, but it turns out she speaks excellent English, and worked in Dublin until two years ago. That's how she met Tomas, they were both immigrants and both trying to get work around the bars and stuff. Fell madly in love, decided to stay in Ireland full time, and were all set to move in together. Then her mother got sick – badly sick. She's dying from what I can make out. Milena goes home to mind her, and three weeks later Tomas flies out after her, proposes and tells her he will earn the money to support them both while she nurses her mother."

"Ah Jaysus, that's rough." Dave Locke shook his head sadly.

"And ever since that's what he's done." MacPherson continued. "He works at least two jobs, sometimes more. He pays his taxes, no cash in hand stuff, all above board. Milena says he hates anything "not straight." He sent money to her regularly and she has access to their joint online account where he also stashes money for their wedding. According to her, he does nothing but work and occasionally plays a bit of football with some lads in his building. Every penny is saved. She said he hasn't been home even for Christmas or a holiday, every penny goes towards supporting her mother and her."

Everyone remained silent. This sounded like a rotten kind of victim – innocent, decent, hardworking. It was easier when they were greedy or venial or crooked. All those courses on criminology, where they tell you the victim usually has something in their life that makes them vulnerable - they avoid talking about the ones where pure dumb luck or rotten twists of fate are the only explanations.

Claire consulted her notes. "So. Last week he rang her to say that he'd been offered a bit of extra work; he was asked to help one of the senior personnel of the Bank with some after-hours work in the building, and it meant working overtime. He told her that it was cash in hand, which he initially wanted to refuse but was afraid of offending this guy, for fear he would fire him. Then, the man told him that while it was cash in hand, it would go down as a bonus and would all be above board and legal."

Graves snorted.

"I know," she said, impatiently. "The point is Tomas believed him because he was and I quote, "A big guy here, one of the top guys, he knows all about tax and laws.""

Everyone stirred and looked at each other.

"He told her he wouldn't be able to ring her at his usual time, because he would still be at work. And that was…." She looked around triumphantly, "That was last Wednesday."

"The day before Frank Clarke was found murdered."

Locke whistled softly. "Tomas was asked to stay back and do some "work" on the night Clarke was murdered."

"But by whom?" MacPherson peered at the board and made a move towards the marker to add in her new information. Powers intercepted her smoothly and began to fill it in. She scowled at him but sat down again – like most of us she had handwriting that was barely legible and she knew it. If anyone was going to have a hope of reading the damn thing, we needed Powers.

"It could be any one of the senior management. Or the Board. Anyone in there specialize in tax?" Locke asked.

"It could actually have been Frank Clarke," I said slowly. "We don't know where the hell he was between 5pm and whatever time he arrived back in the building. He could have been with Warskowski or setting up whatever he had planned for that night."

Powers made a note on the board.

"Any chance that Warskowski will recover?" Graves asked.

They all looked at me hopefully.

"It's touch and go," I parroted what the doctor had told me. "It's too early to say. He's had massive trauma to the head and is currently in a medically induced coma."

David Locke swore loudly. Graves shook his head, not unkindly. "There's no point in that, Dave. No point at all. We all feel for the poor bugger so let's get out there and get whoever did this."

He pointed at the white board. "Tomas Warskowski was bullied into helping some stuffed shirt banker do some dirty work. Sure as I'm sitting here it has something to do with his attack. I'm going to talk to Looney, see what we can get in extra man-power to help, and we're going to go over every inch of that stinking bank 'til we find the answer."

Locke nodded. Usually he was the office joker, an irrepressible force. But he had a soft spot for poor eejits like Tomas, decent sorts who were pulled into other people's messes. Today there was a grim set to him, no humour at all.

"I have mates in the Fraud squad and the Financial Regulators office, Sir. I'll find out exactly what we're looking at in the Leinster."

Powers, the youngest and least experienced of our team was practically bouncing in place and only short of raising his hand like a school kid. Graves acknowledged him with a wave of his hand.

"I actually know a fair bit about the tech stuff," Powers tried for modesty, like a good lad. "I could go over the set up in there, see what exactly that clock controls."

"Controls?" MacPherson sat upright and asked sharply, "I thought it just told the time."

"Noooo," Powers flapped his hands expressively, "it does a lot more than that. In the late nineties they had a huge refit done, that clock controls the time locks on the vaults." He looked at our faces and laughed, "Not that they store, like, cash there. But securities, bonds, paperwork and stuff."

Something about that sounded familiar; it was more or less what Caroline Jordan had suggested. I relayed her comments to the team. "Well, it's a theory," Locke said. "It's better than no theory at all."

"OK," Graves clapped his hands together and rubbed them gleefully, "Maybe there's something in that. Let's see. Anything you can find out about that side of things, Powers, see if that stupid clock is a red herring or what."

He turned to the board again. Two names, one dead and one hanging on by a thread. "I don't like this one. I don't like it at all. Let's go get them."

Chapter Eight

C*aroline Jordan*

Life goes on. It's brutal but it's true. We were shocked to hear about the poor security guard, he was a nice chap. And the sight of poor Frank – well, it would be a long while before that would fade. Paula was subdued, Stephen was worried and anxious, and I was snapping at everyone. But we had to prepare a pitch for the Bank of Leinster contract, arrange events, fulfil my duties to Michael T and the political landscape of Ireland and somehow, life just started moving again.

Within a week newspaper and media articles on the murder gave way to other, new, murders and scandals. And a very horrible thing, when you stopped to think about it, was that Clarke's death was tangled up in the rest of the Bank of Leinster scandals. People posted about their disastrous App experiences or rumours of shady back-room mortgage deals in the same breath as the murder.

Stephen stalked Facebook and Twitter for any mentions of either the murder or Jordan PR. He set us up an account on the new one, Instagram. Which I wasn't at all sure about, because it looked to me like Flicker for mobiles, but he was adamant it's the next big thing.

"Caroline, leave it to me, please." He waved his iPhone at me and pointed proudly at its array of icons. "You know you have trouble using modern tech."

Which was accurate, but cheeky.

Leinster House, where the Irish government sits, was taking up a lot of time as usual. Fresh off their 6 weeks summer holidays, Irish politicians liked to get their names in the papers as soon as they could to show the constituents that they were working hard. "No," they assured local voters "Far from sunning myself in Portugal like that other shower, I was formulating important initiatives." I had heard variations of this speech so often "Formulating Initiatives" was now our office code for dossing.

Michael T O'Mahony had galloped to victory in the general election in January, which reflected well on Jordan PR, but now we had a raft of legislation coming up. He might be smooth and crafty, but he did actually want to change things for the better. Anti-pollution laws, reforming zero hours and exploitative contracts for workers and of course, Banking regulation reforms were all in the works. Sleepless nights were spent trying to predict where the problems would rear their ugly heads and what we would do when they did.

I suspected Derek Fields had an ulterior motive for getting in on a Bank contract -he liked to have inside intel and was a master of the "keeping your enemies closer," strategy.

And we had our society contracts to worry about too. Some firms do brands and products, and those contracts tide you over the lean months. Jordan PR does Beautiful People, and their Glittering Events. Sometimes Sparkling Events or Fabulous Occasions but you get the idea. Dinner parties, balls, charity events, pet projects and birth/death/marriages.

Our golden contract was with the Foxrocks. For no apparent reason, Lady Foxrock had picked Jordan PR out of a list and handed us the work. Elderly, dotty, but shrewd in unexpected ways, she ran an eccentric and surprisingly effective cat charity, Cat's Paws. Every year she hosted a fundraising ball, generally considered to be the most important social event of the year. Old money, Anglo Irish landowners, establishment types and a certain type of celebrity were the main guests, sprinkled with politicians and lawyers and Beautiful People. It was just exclusive enough, thanks to Paula's ruthless approach to a guest list but with enough up to date figures to make sure every newspaper wanted a photo.

Successfully handling the ball led to a lot of other work from one-off events to some interesting long-term enterprises. As it happened, an email from one of them was haunting my inbox, waiting for a response.

Leslie Howard had been about my age, with an overdraft that made mine look healthy when she inherited a castle from her uncle. A real castle, of the type some of my ancestors would have tried to burn down at regular intervals, with land and a lake and a big dinner gong in a wood panelled entrance hall. She was initially delighted to receive it and then not so delighted as the extent of the debt on the estate became clear.

At this point I'd have sold the place, but Howard was made of sterner stuff. "Also," she admitted "I can't afford to sell it, I think it's in such a bad state, I would probably end up owing money to the buyer!"

Instead, she took a look at her options and started to plan. With the kind of reckless optimism I admire, she plunged further into debt and created a hipster paradise of "wild gardens, Eco-friendly camping, vegan friendly café and water sports."

"Water sports is a bit of an exaggeration," she confided, "At the moment it's my friend Peter with some second-hand paddle boats and his mate's scuba gear but we're getting there." But there was a real lake in the middle of the grounds, with pike fishing and tiny islands to explore.

Leslie came to us, with an introduction from Lady Foxrock, a vision for her estate and an infectious optimism. It was shortly after the events surrounding my late employer's death and my judgement was probably impaired, but we decided we would give Howard's Castle Hideaway a bit of pro bono work. Stephen got his journalist mate to spend a weekend there, with his partner and kid, warning Howard to show them a good time. The wife was a good-natured hippy-type whose Facebook feed was soon full of pictures of an adorable toddler, dirty and happy with the caption "Heaven! Magical place, back to nature, best weekend ever."

The Hideaway took off like a rocket after that. Leslie proved to be the unicorn of clients (loyal) and we certainly lost nothing for having helped out when she was broke. I liked her, despite my inherent distrust of rich, Anglo-Irish types. My mother was a rich Anglo-Irish type and she had soured me on the breed.

"Read the email again," Paula shouted from the outer office. She knew I was procrastinating.

"Dear Caroline,

Hope all is well with you and the firm. Please say hi to Paula and Stephen for me. Thanks for the great work you all did on that last promotion, it was a great success. Can't believe we never thought of it before!

I know you are terribly busy but I could really use your help. We are in with a chance of hosting an art exhibition in November, works from the Loxburg collection. My father and Charlie Loxburg are great friends, so we have a fighting chance. Obviously if we get it, the PR contract will be yours but in the meantime Loxburg and his family are coming to visit this weekend with some friends in tow, see if Howard Castle would suit.

I wondered if you and the team would like to come visit too? You would be so much better able to handle them than I. Dad will come over and butter old Charlie up, but the son terrifies me, and the entourage of arty types are beyond me!"

"The rest of it is basically bribes of food and drink and some begging." I finished.

"Please, Mammy, can we go?" Stephen appeared in the doorway; hands clasped like that orphan in Dickens. "I could do with a weekend in the country!"

"Oh yes!" Paula sighed. "It'll be horrible weather and dark mornings before we know it. Let's get one nice weekend in, and it's freeeee."

I sighed. "It's also work, or did ye ignore that bit? A two-day hell of art lovers spouting pretentious crap at us."

Paula laughed. "Ah you know we're going, Caro. I'm going for the change of scenery, Steve's going for the walks and nature and you're going precisely because it is work and you can't pass it up!"

That stung a bit.

"Fine so, we go then," I muttered sourly. I shot off a reply to her and tried to forget about it. Half an hour later I was googling Loxburg Collection and looking up art terms.

One blessing was I hadn't heard from Doyle at all, although Locke had emailed me a few follow up questions. A tabloid had run a story on possible gangland involvement, with hints about a tiger robbery gone wrong. It began to feel as if it was tragic but commonplace violence, and we were just unlucky to be on the sidelines.

Chapter Nine

D *S Doyle*

Being part of SCS had its perks, and it had its drawbacks. Perks included interesting cases, involving high profile individuals and a chance to overreach the normal boundaries of case work – vice, corruption, theft, murder, all could potentially fall under our jurisdiction in the right circumstances. We could liaise with any other department without the mountain of paperwork and politicking that usually followed. Our boss, Superintendent Looney, was a boot-licking, social climbing Yes-man but he was well in with the top brass, and knew how to smooth things over.

The downside of SCS was that high profile cases involving important people could end your career with spectacular speed. One wrong step, and at the very least you'll end up sliding down the ladder. Each case needed a different approach, each brought its own troubles.

This Bank case – well, it was a mess. And in the background, always, the shadow of Cumann na Laochra and Shane Donoghue squaring up against Michael T O'Mahony, and the Government. We needed movement on this, and fast.

Leaving aside the problem of the seemingly innocuous Clarke, and his lack of social life, we had few other avenues to explore. We huddled in the incident room to bring each other up to speed, and see where best to apply ourselves.

First came the pathologist report. Dr Lorraine O'Toole was both thorough and professional. She was a godsend to SCS but her relationship with

Superintendent Looney was not great at the best of times, mainly because his misogyny was legendary even in a traditionally male dominated force. We also had to tread carefully and bend rules gently when dealing with the influential and rich, something Lorraine found reprehensible. But she was too savvy not to understand that it had to be done and she never shirked her duty. Her reports were detailed and prompt, and impervious to even the most devious of barristers.

The most important things from our point of view were time of death (no real surprises there, 4 am to 6 am had been narrowed down to "likely to be" between 5 and 5.30 am) and method of killing. O'Toole was adamant that Clarke was killed in situ – standing on the desk, his weight tipping forward so the blood ran down onto the polished wood, and to the carpeted floor beneath, his arms tied above him, and his throat slit.

It was nearly impossible to pin down who was there when it had happened, without the CCTV cameras or Warskowski's testimony. We knew Frank Clarke had returned to the building at some point. We knew at the time he returned the building should have been otherwise empty – no one was there past 8 pm. We had checked the alibis of everyone who was in the building at any point during the day (Locke and Powers were sick of ringing people and calling to doorsteps asking "Excuse me, can you confirm the following…") What we had was extremely slim.

From across the room, Locke threw a scrunched-up ball of paper at me and shouted "Well, your favourite receptionist was where she claimed to be!" He seemed to think I would be particularly relieved to hear it. Sometimes I wonder about that chap.

"Quit clowning,"

"Aw sorry, just thought you'd like the good news. Ms. Flynn was at home, as vouched for by both her flat mates. A couple of mature students, Donal and," he consulted his notes, " …Fiona. They say she got in around 7 pm, made herself some dinner, was in her room for a bit, watched TV with them 'til around 11. Went to bed. Donal was up 'til around 3.30 am – he says he was working on a paper, but I say dossing and watching late night TV. At any rate he swears she couldn't have left the house without him knowing.

I think it is reasonable to assume she wasn't back at HQ murdering Frank Clarke, not without a car. No buses on that route after 12.30 am and no sign of her on any CCTV flagging down taxis."

Claire looked up from her computer. "At least that's one ruled out. Not that I would have pegged her for it anyway. What about Tomas?"

"No way of confirming what he told us. He definitely arrived home, one of his neighbours saw him, but after that we can't be sure. His fiancée said he was due to go back in, but we can't get anyone in there to admit to asking him to work overtime." Locke sighed heavily. "Then we have Ms. Delahunt, she lives alone and no one can confirm or deny her times. Upstairs, as it were, we have confirmed alibis for most of the secretarial staff, the clerks, the mortgage team…most of the staff, in fact. What we are left with are the higher-ups."

It made sense. Every organization has a layer of people at the top who could be dancing the tango naked at 4 am in the foyer and no one else in the building could ask them what the giddy feck they were playing at. In this case, three Board members were viable suspects– Sean O'Dwyer the chairman, Emily Cleethe, a prominent figure in finance and banking, and a bloke lumbered with the frankly unlikely name of Loxburg.

"Like, I hate to say it, but these are the most likely. Warskowski's fiancée said he was afraid to say no, the person who wanted him to work overtime was a senior figure in the bank."

"Man," Claire objected. "She said it was a man."

"Yeah, well, when I double checked because I thought I could rule out Cleethe, she said she thinks he never specifically said male or female. He said "person" and she assumed it was a bloke. She's still mostly sure it was a guy, but just can't be sure that he definitely said so."

"Bugger. Well then, what do we know about the four of them – Delahunt, Cleethe, O 'Dwyer, Loxburg?"

Graves rumbled a reply from his desk at the window. "Sean O'Dwyer is a big shot, politically. He's in with Shane Donoghue, and that whole gang."

Donoghue was the long-time leader of the main Opposition party, "Cumann na Laochra" or "Society of Warriors." Revolutionary zeal in the early 19th century had led to all our main parties boasting various versions of warrior, hero, or soldiers in their names. A less likely band of heroes you couldn't imagine in reality; the party faithful of Cumann na Laochra were mainly middle aged, middle class, professionals or comfortable farmers and developers. Shane Donoghue used to be a teacher, before he entered the Dáil thirty years previously and legend had it he still drew his teacher's salary.

"O'Dwyer is getting on though. He must be 70 now? I can't see him clambering up on a desk and stringing Clarke up by the wrists."

A moments silence while we all visualized the portly form of the Bank of Leinster chairman trying to hoist his senior manager up on the desk of conference room four then Powers said, "It doesn't seem likely."

"Understatement, laddie, it's your superpower," Graves sighed. "Next we come to Monica Delahunt – physically unlikely, but we can't rule out her involvement in some other capacity. Same with O'Dwyer. Which leaves us Cleethe, she's in her forties and fit but again, can't imagine how she would get him up there."

"I can," Locke said. "I'm not trying to be funny but, say they were having a kinky session?"

The room went quiet, and he reddened. "I am being serious! Say he thought this was foreplay, "let me tie you up" stuff and then once she had him in place, she produces the knife."

Graves laughed. "It's a theory, Locke, but come on– you're stone cold sober, you're in your workplace and there are a dozen more comfortable places with easier set ups to use. Would you seriously go to a ground floor conference room, climb up on an awkwardly placed, highly polished table, your partner trying to tie your arms to a chandelier …"

Locke shrugged. "You might lack a sense of adventure, but some of us are up for the challenge."

Graves snorted but conceded, "Well, we won't rule it out completely. But I think it's more likely he was coerced and manhandled into place. Bruises on his arms," he read from the pathologist's report, "Bruising on the neck, consistent with being held in place, possibly by an arm around neck in choke-hold."

Held in place, while being tied up.

"More than one person," Claire said decisively. "No way one person could both control him and tie him up." She stood up and gestured to Powers. "Up. You're about Clarke's height. Get up there now on the desk."

Powers obeyed, leaping nimbly onto the table without a word. His hero worship of MacPherson was well known. "OK, Doyle – you're about the strongest. Get up there and try it out." My ascent was far from nimble, and less than dignified but I managed. It was immediately apparent that Claire was right.

"See, if he was incapacitated, you'd have to hold a dead weight, and get him tied up. If he wasn't, and could struggle, it would be nigh impossible and on that polished surface, there would be traces of scuff marks."

Graves disappeared back into the report. "Nope. Very few marks on the table. They're still analyzing what was there,but let's assume two for the moment; two sets of reasonably stable footprints, certainly little sign of a struggle."

MacPherson stood back and made a "finger gun" with her right hand. "Seeing as we're assuming, let's pretend we have two suspects. One covers Clarke with a gun. He climbs up, the other suspect ties him to the chandelier. He may not suspect yet what is truly happening. Suspect two ties him up, they work him over and one of them slices his throat."

Powers interjected, "There's another scenario. Maybe he thinks this is part of the plan. Say he's in on whatever the hell they were doing. He's supposed to be tied up, to make it look like he was coerced. He hops up, his accomplice ties him up, he isn't fighting hard because this is what is supposed to happen. Just enough to rough him up, look authentic."

"And then they go over him very heavily, for some reason." Claire considered for a moment. "Nice, Powers. That works too, if we can figure out why they attacked him once he was tied up." Powers went pink and jumped down, trying to look cool.

"Write it up," Graves directed. "We have two working scenarios there. Three, if you count Locke's Femme Fatale. What else have we got?"

"I'm in the Bank tomorrow," Powers offered. "I've had a good look at the tech set up in there and I've a mate with a real insight. I have an idea about the clock, but I want to see if it's viable."

"G'won. Anything good turns up, let us all know."

Locke pointed at his screen. "I'll have something later today. My contact in Finance has a lot to say about the Bank of Leinster. I'll owe her big-time for this. She's sending me over her thoughts on the Board and senior management but it's to be kept confidential."

We all exchanged significant looks at this. Rumours abounded that Locke had a secret girlfriend, some mysterious woman he dated but never brought to anything public. Up to now he had been the office Romeo so any hint of a serious love affair at all was fodder for the gossip. I got the impression he was well aware of the effect.

"Is this your lady friend?" Graves asked, with the air of a pompous uncle. Locke shook his head. "Try again, Detective. Adrienne is a friend."

"But there is a girl somewhere?" Claire asked. "Some poor, blind, deluded young one that you've brainwashed into dating you?" Locke made a rude gesture in reply.

The meeting broke up, everyone eager to follow their own trails at this stage. Graves and I drifted into a corner, and he handed me the pathologist report. "Chase up the trace evidence and the other physical evidence, won't you?" He rubbed his eyes and sighed. "This is a nasty one, Alan. Too many sensitive issues. Looney is having a conniption over it all."

Our beloved leader should never have been put in charge of anything as politically charged as SCS. Panic and insecurity brought out the petty bully in him.

"No problem. Also, we need to get a handle on these people, O'Dwyer and Loxburg. And the rest."

Graves eyed me and I knew he was leading up to something. "We know someone who knows a lot about this level of individual."

Didn't even bother arguing with him. Caroline Damn Jordan again.

Chapter Ten

C*aroline Jordan*

"Onwards and upwards," Derek Fields boomed genially down the phone. "I hear you will be helping with the Loxburg Collection?"

The man had a crystal ball, or he had our offices bugged. Neither would surprise me.

"Yes, or at least we're trying to secure it for Howard Castle."

"You'll get it," he said, "Charlie Loxburg is going to oblige Philip Howard, once the place isn't actually falling down around his ears. He just wants to see that young one jumping through a few hoops first."

Derek knows everyone. Even better, he knows the important bits of their personalities. All those little failings and vanities that makes them easier to manage.

"I'm glad you're going for the weekend, Caroline. There are some interesting people surrounding Charlie Loxburg. His son, for example. Strange man in many ways, quite a character. Academically brilliant but some very extreme politics. I'd be very eager to hear what you make of him. You should also meet Emily Cleethe. Do you know who she is?"

The word "smug" wouldn't do justice to me. Working with Fields had honed my skills, and hours of studying the whole Loxburg menagerie were about to come in handy.

"She's his partner – business and personal. English, originally but has lived here for yonks. She was an artist but soon gave it up and became a sort of broker – putting artists and buyers together. Very influential and has a desperate reputation for rudeness. How am I doing?"

Fields laughed. "I expect nothing less from you, Caroline. Good research, and accurate. Rude – yes, to people she doesn't think important. I can tell you she can be very charming when she wants to be, but she is always shrewd and greedy. If she feels slighted, she'll go out of her way to make trouble."

I made a mental note to warn Leslie Howard.

"She loves a bit of flattery," he continued. "As does Simon Prendergast."

I leapt in. "Simon Prendergast, art critic, writer, gallery owner."

He chuckled. "Yes, simmer down. I see you have done your homework. Prendergast is like Charlie Loxburg's shadow but likes to think he's a trend setter in art circles." He paused before dropping one of his little information bombs, "A good few years ago, as a young man, Prendergast was suspected of dealing in fake art. Some major names but mainly minor, collectible artists, nothing too flashy. Fairly sure he was guilty, just between us."

"Good to know," I scribbled "Simon, flashy, crooked" on my notepad and asked "So you think this exhibition thing is worth our while then? To be honest I thought of it as more or less a favour for Leslie Howard."

There was a slight pause, and I knew Derek was weighing his words. "It would be a nice contact for Jordan PR. And, your evaluation of this particular group would be very interesting for Michael T. The Loxburgs are involved in a lot of things besides art. The son, , sits on the board of the Bank of Leinster. And Emily Cleethe is involved in quite a lot of financial deals. With Bank reform coming up, it would be worth our while knowing more about all of them. Even just personal insight."

I grinned. Derek was always two steps ahead, that was the kind of long-term planning that made O'Mahony our most effective Taoiseach in decades.

"Well, I'll do my best. If there's gossip to be had, we will have it."

Paula and Stephen didn't bother to hide their delight. Paula texted me three times to ask about appropriate outfits and I caught Stephen googling "fishing rods" when he was supposed to be drawing up a schedule of potential social media advertising for the BOL contract. Saving for the wedding sucked up every spare penny in their household so it was a rare treat to get out of the house and away from the city, even for work.

"You'll come down early on Friday," Leslie had rung several times to talk about the weekend. Her breezy email was belied by her nervousness. "I could do with a bit of moral support! I do appreciate it, Caro."

Friday morning saw us all crowded into the offices, our weekend luggage pretty much filling the tiny reception area. When I returned from a last-minute meeting with Derek in the Government Offices, Paula was taking her turn on the phones, while also trying to work. She held up a note as I came through the door. It read "Get a Receptionist."

Then she held up another one.

"DOYLE. YOUR OFFICE."

Chapter Eleven

Caroline Jordan

At some level I felt I knew it was too good to be true. Of course, Doyle would turn up again. Why couldn't it have been MacPherson, or even Graves? Locke or the young one, the one with the reddish hair and rabbit-in-headlights look?

"PR guru is ungrateful weapon," my inner voice hissed, and I tried to plaster a smile on my face. Rather disconcertingly, he seemed to be doing the same with a kind of rigid rictus grin. We grimaced at each other for a moment then gave it up.

"Caroline." He nodded.

"Detective," I responded.

Pleasantries out of the way, I sat behind my desk and waited. Doyle looked around him, as if he'd never seen the place before. "You changed something in here?" he pointed at the trendy mini shelf unit behind me, home to an eclectic mix of cactus (cacti?) and ornaments. "That thing."

"Yes, it was a present."

He looked mildly surprised. "Oh. Well, it's nice to have something new." With a wave of his hand, he indicated the general décor of the room. "This is all very bare."

It was minimalist, cutting edge and cost me far too much money, the cheeky git. I breathed in and out a few times, trying to remember one of those positivity mantras. All I could come up with was "don't smack a cop."

"Is there anything I can help you with, Detective? Need to check timings again?"

"No, no. Thanks. Well, yeah. There is something." He tried the rictus grin again, and I tried not to visibly wince. "I need to ask a favour."

He settled himself in the chair and with the air of a man delivering an over-rehearsed speech. "So. As you know, this unfortunate case has many troubling aspects." Pause. "It has brought us into contact with people in a position of influence, involving sensitive information and of course, people with ties to political parties and prominent, um, people." He paused again and nodded at me. "Like, the kind of people that *you* know. Which is great, isn't it. You can be of great help, which is…great." He looked at me hopefully and I resisted the urge to throw my ornamental paperweight at his head.

"I know some…people." Trying to be cautious. "Which of them exactly are you trying to find out about?"

The polite, careful demeanour vanished. "Great. Look at these and tell me anything you know about them."

A sheaf of pages slid across my desk, in batches of two or three pages stapled together. I could see photos attached to each batch. One of them was…Sean O'Dwyer President and Chair of the BOL Board. And Emily Cleethe. Ah here. O'Dwyer was the banker of choice for the country's second largest parliamentary party which also happened to be my main client's political rival. My brain did a little spin trying to weigh up the inappropriateness of this situation against the desire to find out exactly what crime Doyle suspected him of committing.

"You recognize them." Doyle was smug. "Go on then. Tell me, what should we know about them?"

"Doyle, I'm not…this is not on. This is my work, and while I am always happy to help, this doesn't…"

Hang about, Loxburg? I stared at the picture, Derek's words in my head. The difficult man. "Um. If I help, it has to be strictly confidential and no funny business, OK?"

Doyle looked outraged. "Funny business?"

"Yeah, funny business. Last time, you tried to embroil me in the whole mess. I'm not doing that again. Info is one thing, I owe ye that much. But that's it."

He frowned. "Of course we only want information from you." Outraged innocence, the very picture of.

"Alright then." I pointed at O'Dwyer's picture. "As you know, we are pitching for the BOL account. This is the chairman of the board, also a close personal friend of the Leader of the Opposition. O'Dwyer is hidebound, conservative, hates what he sees as the "descent into a liberal society," - his actual words - and he is rumoured to be extending financial supports towards the likes of the Colmcille Association."

Doyle grimaced and shook his head. It was a mark in his favour that he obviously didn't support that bunch of right-wing, un-elected meddlers in Irish Society, a collection of disaffected far right types who wrote complaining letters every time a gay person or a woman was mentioned positively in the media. One of them had called our lovely president, Her Excellency Ms. Mac Aonghusa, "a harridan bent on dragging the men of Ireland into chains." She had responded with a mild, "Not a harridan. And not chains. Kicking and screaming into adulthood, yes."

All she had done was mildly suggest men should be doing as much in the home as women.

"He is also into a lot of property development, and by a lot I mean, everything. His name crops up every time a large apartment complex or the redevelopment of a landmark building or sensitive site applies for planning. I know for a fact that he's considered dirty by a lot of senior figures, despite the façade he puts up. Say that outside of this room and I'll pluck your eyeballs from your head, by the way." He grinned but also, sat up a shade more warily. "From my perspective O'Dwyer is a nuisance, the biggest stumbling block to getting the BOL contract. He loathes Michael T."

The fact I was on our prime minister's team meant Jordan PR was anathema to O'Dwyer. "But because of the dog's mess they've made of things over the last few months, people in the know say that the Board are in full rebellion. He won't be able to stop them if they decide we can help them save face."

I pointed at Emily Cleethe. "Cleethe came to them in a twisty way. She started about as far from Finance as you could imagine and I doubt she'd have a place on the board of any other financial institution but the Bank of Leinster is a law unto itself. On the surface she's clean, well connected and very successful at capital investment but there's a shadow attached to her. In her favour, she has been on fundraisers for a variety of causes, none of which would endear her to O'Dwyer. She's on track to be the first female BOL chairperson, she is a Cumann na Laochra party member and is well liked among the more centrist party members. Not that that makes her exactly warm and fuzzy."

I pointed to the one of David Howard. "Him, I've met. Slick, charming, English accent and very well connected socially. No political ambitions, but hot on the pursuit of money and into a load of property deals. Nothing dodgy whispered about him, bit of bitterness that he got where he is because of posh Anglo-Irish connections rather than ability but he seemed competent enough to me."

A thought bubbled up even as I continued talking; I wonder if Leslie Howard is related. Maybe she's his posh Anglo-Irish connection?

The next one to hand was Murrough Loxburg, and I sighed. "I don't know him personally, and I know very little about him. Derek Fields says he's difficult and that could mean anything from "eccentric" to "harbours secret desire to be world dictator." I wish I'd more on him, but other than the basics you'd get from any google search, I don't. He doesn't do much on the Board other than vote, so he hasn't been on my radar. He wields a lot of influence behind the scenes though."

And that, right there, is where I should have stopped. But I had to open my big gob and let it out. "I might be able to tell you a bit more on Monday. And about David Howard too. We're all going to Howard Castle this weekend to help them pitch for an art exhibition. Charles Loxburg and a collection of his works. That's Murrough's father and both Loxburgs are going to be there."

My brain tried to shut my mouth up but lost the battle. Before I'd finished, Doyle bold upright in his chair and an eager light in his eyes.

"No." I said coldly before he could speak. "Whatever it is, no. I don't mind letting you know on Monday if there's anything about Murrough that would be of interest to you. But that's where I draw the line."

"I didn't ask you to do anything," Doyle protested.

"Okay."

"We understand you not wanting to be involved."

"Good."

He looked at a point somewhere above my head, and said "If you were to get chatting to him…"

"I am happy to give you my impressions of the man, of course."

"Of course. But if you were, say, talking about this contract you're after with the Bank of Leinster and he was to be drawn on the subject, he might say more to you than he would to an official inquiry."

"No. Look, Detective. I am not about to go to a client's home and put her chances of scoring a big event at risk by asking a man I've never met before what was he up to the night his colleague was murdered." I stared at Doyle but his face was impassive. "I'm not going to place my firm's chances of a contract at risk either. I am not going to mention the murder, nor am I going to pump people for information."

He nodded but went on as if I had not spoken. "You'd want to be subtle, all right. Lead up to it. Don't go leaping in asking leading questions. And you think David Howard might be there too?"

"What? Yes. I'm not sure." I picked up the sheets with Howard's information on them. Under "school" was listed a Church of Ireland fee paying boarding school, one that I knew Leslie's family attended. And under assets there it was, "Shareholder in Howard's Hideaway Castle.'" I knew Leslie had roped in everyone in her family to help out.

"OK. I think he's Leslie Howard's cousin. Which is only of interest to me, Detective, because he might support our bid for the contract if Jordan PR helps Leslie secure the Art Exhibition and make a success of it. Again, not going to jeopardize that by asking him questions about the murder, so don't even think about it."

Doyle ignored me. He seemed lost in thought and altogether too smug.

"I like it," he announced. "You get any information you can out of them.

Crucial thing is any hint of an alibi. Neither can account for their movements that night, Loxburg barely tried."

He pointed at Murrough's head shot.

"Do you know about the Kinsella robbery?"

I stared at him, and choked down the response "I'm not a garda, why would I know about some robbery?" with some difficulty. Doyle often acted as if he lived in a parallel universe to mine.

"It was in eighty-three, maybe eighty-four. There was a robbery from one of the big Houses, down in Carlow. Bellingham Hall. A professional five-man gang, slipped in and out very neatly. Cut the alarm system, knocked out an elderly caretaker, took as many paintings and valuable trinkets as they could carry. Very nice work. Only problem was, everything was as hot as hell. They couldn't fence most of it because every piece was so famous."

He leaned his long body back in the chair, almost tipping it over. "They off loaded a fraction of it, but most of the good stuff never surfaced. Then we picked up one of the gang, on something different, and he ratted out the whole lot of them to save himself a few years in Portlaoise."

Doyle chuckled, as if amused by the wee rascal of a thieving scumbag.

"None of the rest of them would talk. We got two of them, possession of stolen goods but the other two had more sense. No trace of them ever having had hands on the stuff and a jury declined to convict on the word of an informant."

"Fascinating, but if you'll forgive me pointing it out, it has nothing all to do with the issue at hand?" Maybe it was Doyle's only art related anecdote.

He grinned. "Not directly but, here's the thing. It was DI Graves' first big case. He worked it to the bone, every avenue and every sideline. He's the one who got the first guy to rat on his mates. He figured out that someone involved had real inside knowledge, both of Bellingham Hall and the arty stuff. Along with the four members of his own gang the informant gave up another name."

He looked positively wolfish at this point. "A young art student, very well connected, invited to all the posh Anglo houses, but short of the few bob himself. Allergic to work, no bar jobs or summers on construction sites for this chap."

"Charlie Loxburg," the name fell out of my mouth without my consent.

"Couldn't make it stick, but it was him. Crooked as a corkscrew, that's the great artist."

"Jaysus wept."

"Yup. Wonder if Murrough is a chip off the old block?"

I recalled Derek's circumspect but pointed words. "He might well be."

"Well, I've work to do. Enjoy your weekend, keep your ears open for us and check in on Monday. Sure, just let your Paula loose on them, she'll know everything by Friday night."

With a sense of horror, I realized he'd unbent to the point of chumminess. That man was never happier than when he was dragging us into some convoluted mess of a case. Attempting to regain control, I started out to object but he waved a hand and stalked out. I heard him call a cheery goodbye to Paula, who immediately scooted into my office and plumped herself down on a chair.

"You won't believe this," I complained.

Ten minutes later she was engrossed in the character reports he'd left on my desk. "Oh, I bet he's right, I bet Murrough's a chip off the old thieving block."

"Paula, it's Doyle. He's as odd as two left feet. He once thought I was having an affair with a Minister of State, on no evidence."

"Be fair, that wasn't his fault. He explained it was bad information given to them." Paula looked at me and said firmly, "You are very hard on him, Caroline. He's different, yes. He doesn't conform to all the niceties we expect, and he isn't what you'd call subtle. But that's him. You have to make some allowances, meet him halfway."

Jaw-dropping. "Are you kidding me? Paula, he's the most aggravating person I've ever met. He doesn't even pretend to fit in, he's like a -a blunt object."

"Betcha good money he thinks the same about you." She stood up, the reports in her hand and added, "I am going to read these through before we head off to Howard Castle. As far as I'm concerned, Doyle is a good guy. If we can help, we help. And you should think about this – why should Doyle have to pretend to fit in? He's straight-forward, he says what he thinks, and he says it to your face. Why don't we try to fit in with that and not expect him to be subtle and coy?"

She was back at her desk before I could tell her to feck off with herself.

Chapter Twelve

aula Hughes

P Castle Howard is – well, it's a fairy-tale castle.

First, as you turn off the main road from Carlow to Killeshen, you travel five kilometres down a twisty country boreen, under a canopy of trees holding hands from one side to the other. When you emerge from the leafy green tunnel, there's a sharp turn left, along a similar sized road but this time flanked by grey stone walls. Keep going until you see a pair of wrought iron, ornate gates. Turn in there, past the gate lodge, with its colourful cottage garden and roses growing around the door. Next, there's this huge sweeping gravel drive, that winds through pastures and meadows and a small forest, before opening out into a circular space, in front of a heavy, panelled oak door.

It's a proper castle, not just a posh house. The centre of the building is definitely old, started in Norman times and added to bit by bit over the years.

It has actual turrets, and crenelations - and yes, I know what they are because I used to date a guy who was mad into swords and dragons and fantasy books. He tried to put a row of them along the roof of his parents' garage and they went bananas. Especially when they fell off into next door's driveway.

Anyway, the ones at Castle Howard are the real thing.

It had been a fortified stronghold until after Cromwell; then, as the British got a better grip on Ireland they relaxed and started turning their forts into

"

houses. Howard Castle got two big wings added on each side. The windows in the middle are slits just big enough to shoot arrows out of while the rest of them are gracious, floor to ceiling, sash windows filled with glass and flanked by ornate, brocade and velvet curtains.

The grounds in late September were a mix of wildflower meadows, green paddocks and overgrown clumps of gnarled trees, already boasting early Autumn colours. I was afraid the inside would be modernized and generic "hotel" décor but instead there were original flagstones, dark oak panels on the wall, actual shields and armour and two large shaggy dogs stretched out on ancient sofas.

All of it was extraordinary, I could totally understand why Leslie loved it so much. Part of me was a bit guilty because if we're honest, all this was at the cost of my ancestors and I'm fairly sure the popular *"Dire Dungeons, Come the Way for Ghostly Fun,"* attraction masked a few centuries of atrocities against the general Irish populace. But it was also beautiful and full disclosure here, a perfect place for a wedding.

Stephen and I were now engaged.

As I hung up my best outfit, then my second best outfit and finally what I hoped would pass for smart-casual day clothes – not having much experience in being a country house party guest - I stifled down a little sigh. Being engaged was lovely but planning a wedding was not as much fun as I had hoped. Neither, if I'm being totally honest, was wedding dress shopping.

Every single bride I knew, girls from schools and cousins and neighbours' daughters and friends, were all thin on the day. Most went on diets before they even got the ring, and one of my sisters had a friend who went on a rigorous diet 6 months into any serious relationship just in case. I wasn't awfully fat, but the kindest eye in the world couldn't be fooled into calling me thin.

I had thought I was a fairly normal size before I started shopping in the realm of puff skirts and lace sleeves.

"Sorry," one rake thin sales assistant puffed as she shoehorned me into an ivory-coloured puffball. "The dresses are in very small sizes, and sure, you'll be so wound up over the wedding you'll lose half your weight without trying, ha ha."

It's not that I wasn't trying to diet, but no word of a lie, it was impossible. We worked late, we ate out, we snatched food at our desks. Then on weekends, Stephen loved to cook and let's be honest I loved to eat. We did walk, and I even tried to do the "Learn to run 5 k in as many weeks" routine, but that just meant I didn't get any fatter. It didn't help me get thin, like wedding thin.

A weekend away in a stunning castle, even if it was more a working weekend, was a guilt free break from everything else.

Caroline laughed at me for packing DS Doyle's lists but why not have a look? She may have forgotten how much we owed him and his colleagues, but I hadn't and if I could find out anything at all to help, I would be delighted. She was exasperated by him, but if she would only stop and think – the things that irritated her, like his bluntness and laser focus, were the very traits they shared. The difference was Caroline's mind worked like a serpent, and she could hide behind any number of facades at a moment's notice whereas his was more like a war machine, relentless and hell bent on removing any obstacles in his path.

They would both be a tad frightening if they weren't fundamentally decent people.

"Paula!" Stephen was ready to go, and I was still staring at my clothes wondering if they'd be good enough. He gave me a hug and correctly guessed my thought process. "Everything you brought is lovely, not too flashy, not too casual. Now, come on down with me." I hoped he was right.

Caroline was waiting for us in the hall. "They're all in there," She pointed towards a room that opened directly onto the hall. The door was ajar, and I could see pale blue walls, oak wood floors and an assortment of chairs, armchairs and sofas upholstered in palest blue silk and gold thread. It was quite a gloomy room, despite the light and airy colour scheme, definitely a part of the old castle with narrow grey stone windows only allowing a limited amount of the late afternoon sunshine.

As we entered, I realized there were two distinct groups of people already gathered. Near the fireplace, Leslie Howard was standing beside Peter, her friend, with a man I recognized as David Howard, and a girl who bore a clear resemblance to the Howards (another cousin, I guessed.) At a remove, near the window, a distinguished looking man in his late fifties or early sixties held court flanked by an entourage, listening deferentially.

A girl who looked about 20 was nodding enthusiastically, as was a tall man I recognized from my days of researching as Simon Prendergast. He was in his thirties, I knew, but looked younger. He had a serious look, heavily rimmed glasses and a goatee beard. You'd peg him for an art critic or gallery owner in a heartbeat.

The older man had to be the famous artist himself, Charlie Loxburg. He looked the way I imagined a famous artist would look – sort of sexy in a rumpled way and world weary. Looking absolutely enthralled by his every word were two tall, slim men in a sort of uniform of loose white shirt, leather trousers and wristlets in coloured beads. Even their hair was styled similarly, only one was blonde and the other dark.

The only one not looking directly at Loxburg, was a slim, attractive woman in leather trousers, a very expensive multi coloured loose blouse and a lot of gold jewellery. She had sleek black hair cut into a sort of voluminous bob and she had sharp face, all angles and cheekbones, her age hard to guess. She was watching the group, especially the young girl. That was Emily Cleethe.

Seated and looking bored was Philip Howard, Leslie's father. He had the look of a man dragged out of his comfortable home against his will, I knew that look well from my own dad.

Leslie's mother, a tall, attractive woman with strong features, and an air of glamour and expense was posed by the fireside. There's no better word for it than posed. It looked staged, from the way she angled herself to the way she held her head.

I had the weirdest feeling, as if all the others were carefully acting around her, trying to pretend they weren't affected by her at all.

You could have cut the tension in the air with a knife.

"Oh, you're here!"

Leslie greeted us with obvious relief, leaping to her feet and dragging Peter with her by the arm. Peter was her "friend" and we had never managed to work out if that meant romantic partner, best mate or business partner. Not even sure what his surname was if I'm being honest. He was almost entirely silent, and in public, he was never more than a few feet away from Leslie.

Caroline seemed as confident and relaxed as ever as she hugged Leslie.

"Hi! Thank you so much for having us here. I'm so excited about this project, I can't wait to get stuck in." If I hadn't known for a fact that she would sooner have stuck needles in her eyes than be there, I would have believed her.

"All business, I see," Mrs. Howard drawled, her voice almost a parody of an English accent with traces of Irish clinging to it. "Leslie, you might like to feed your… "guests" before they start working."

Leslie rolled her eyes, but I noticed she was careful to keep her back turned to her mother. Stephen stiffened at the gratuitously insolent tone, and I can tell you, I wanted to shrink into myself, but Caroline just laughed and tossed her hair. "Why thank you, Diane. You're so good to think of us. Leslie, I'm famished, I'd eat a horse."

I had to remind myself that as much as Caroline rejected the connection, her mother came from this world. Not that I would have known if Lady Foxrock hadn't let slip that she knew (and despised) the woman.

"Lunch will be just a few minutes," Leslie slipped her arm through Caro's and smiled brightly. "And I'm sure Charlie appreciates your enthusiasm for his art."

Diane Howard stared at Caroline and shook her head with an air of disdain. Caroline responded by grinning at her and waving a friendly greeting. "You're looking well, Diane. I like the hair." I heard a few quiet snorts of laughter from both sides of the room. Apparently, we could unite the various factions in dislike of Mrs. Howard.

Charlie Loxburg smiled at Caro and said approvingly "Ah the energy of Youth. I admire it. I like people who are not afraid to be enthusiastic. So many young people pride themselves on being bored and jaded."

"Oh, I'm a ray of sunshine, Mr. Loxburg and this pair are worse. Leslie will tell you we love nothing better than a new project and this one is something special. When I think the Loxburg collection against the backdrop of this magical place – I wish I'd thought of it, frankly."

"Call me Charles, please. Well, I am delighted to hear you say that." His entourage looked a bit put out by his sudden approval of the PR team, but they gamely fixed a smile on their faces and gravitated towards us. Stephen took the opportunity to drift towards David Howard and his companion, still seated by the fireplace. He was smiling and chatting with them immediately while Caroline chatted easily with the arty group. I noticed her making a special effort to include Emily, who unbent a little under the force of Caroline's sunny goodwill.

And I stood in the middle, feeling a bit lost.

I can organize any event, and deal with any number of people professionally, as long as I'm in the background. The bigger the party the better. Strangers, in such a small setting, are not things I find easy to deal with. Everyone else seems to know who to talk to and how to start a conversation. I feel like I am in a play, that I haven't rehearsed and there's no script for my character. My outgoing and glamorous sisters used to attribute it to my being an accountant, as if studying figures had robbed me of any social graces. But here I was, a competent PR executive and I still didn't have the knack of easy socializing.

I had the knack of listening though. Hearing two or more conversations at the same time is my super-power.

David Howard was introducing his cousin (told you so) Miriam Howard to Stephen. The girl had introduced herself to us as Danielle and was telling Caroline earnestly that her PhD was being written on the Loxburg Collection, hence her presence there. "Charles is so kind, letting me tag along everywhere. I'm gaining so much insight, just oodles, the kind of stuff you can't learn from books." Caroline shot me a look that screamed "I bet you are," because body language alone suggested young Danielle was learning more than art history from Charles Loxburg. His hands constantly touched her back, shoulder or arms as she spoke. Dirty auld man. I glanced at Emily and saw her eyes narrow and smile fade.

Leslie seemed anxious, and from the way she glanced at her mother, still standing aloof by the fireplace, I could guess why. She stood close to Peter and made small talk with the others. Her father stretched and stood up, ambling over to Stephen and the Howard cousins – I could hear him asking Stephen if he played golf and when the answer an enthusiastic yes, he launched into a detailed cross examination of courses played and handicaps. David Howard joined in and Miriam Howard seemed equally enthralled. I knew Stephen would be in his element, as a keen golfer, and with an eye to the BOL contract, it was no harm to find common ground with David Howard.

A middle-aged woman, with a short blunt grey bob and a pleasant face appeared in the doorway and shouted cheerfully "Lunch!" Leslie brightened up and replied "Great, thanks!," while her mother winced visibly.

"Leslie, must you shout like a fishwife? It's bad enough you can't teach your staff to announce meals properly." She hissed the words at Leslie as she passed us, and I saw tears spring into her daughter's eye. What a weapon.

Lunch was laid out in a charming room, rose patterned walls with dusky pink floor length curtains and polished wood floors. The table was set with a perfectly matched bone china service, rose patterned with silver rims, and a giant silver teapot, cake stands filled with mini sandwiches and cakes, and pots of jams and preserves scattered the length of it. There were also platters of cold meat and salads and baskets of bread rolls. If I wasn't on a strict diet, I would have been in heaven.

Maybe just eat the meat and salad, and one bread roll. Yes.

As I sat down, frankly preoccupied by the food, I realized David Howard was on my left and Peter the Silent on my right. True to form Peter responded shyly to my "hello" and "how are you" and then put his head down to avoid further interaction. I turned to David and smiled. "Hi, I'm Paula."

"Well, hello," Good God the accent, full on plummy English like a BBC drama. He smiled, bending his head closer towards mine. "Paula? You're Caroline's colleague, yes? Oh, of course! You were there when poor Frank Clarke – well, when they found him. What a terrible experience, I can't imagine."

"It was – yes. It was terrible. And Tomas Warskowski too – poor man."

David nodded, "Yes, we're all very worried for him, it's just appalling.

And so far from home, his poor family must be distraught." Caroline had described him as cold, and rather indifferent to the feelings of his lowly staff members, but he seemed genuine enough to me. Maybe he was one of those people who are very compartmentalized, different at work than in real life.

"Leslie has done wonders with this place, hasn't she?" Best move the conversation on a bit. "I can see why she loves it so much."

"Oh, she's a genius. Frankly I thought she was mad, but she was so persuasive and had such conviction she persuaded me to invest against my better judgement. And now I'm glad she did. It's already running at a profit and with careful expansion, there's no reason why Howards Castle Hideaway won't be one of Ireland's top attractions." He added in a quitter voice, "And she's had no help or encouragement from her parents, quite the opposite."

"Really?" My gossip sensors were tingling.

"Well, you know Diane and Philip expected to inherit? But Jeremy, my grandfather, he passed them over. He knew they'd sell it off as quickly as possible to some developer. Leslie adored the place, even as a child. We all did. The old man used to let us run wild here."

I had visions of an Enid Blyton Famous Five childhood, with wellies and tree-houses and bunting and ginger ale.

"And her parents resent her success a little?"

His eyes crinkled and his smile widened. "Oh, my sweet! A little? Philip was absolutely seething for months, although he's come around a bit now the place is doing well. If he can show off and use it for his friends like Loxburg, he'll mellow. Diane however..." We both glanced quickly at Mrs. Howard, sitting at the end of the table in splendid disapproval. "Diane will never forgive Leslie. Bad enough she inherited but to not have the common courtesy to fail horribly and have to concede defeat..."

I had to laugh. David was very droll and not at all stuffy.

"What about Miriam? Are you both investors?"

"Yes, along with Murrough. That's Charlie's son. Have you met him yet?"

"No. He's not here today?"

"He will be. It was his idea to have the Loxburg Exhibition here. "

"Oh, right. I thought it was Leslie's. But if he's in favour, and he's an investor here, surely his dad would agree?"

"Ah. Charlie has every intention of having it here. He just wants us to jump through hoops. The deference due to the famous artist, you understand."

I did understand. We dealt with egos on a daily basis.

"Well, that's our job, we'll butter him up. I know nothing about art, but I've googled, and I know how to pronounce Peredvizhniki and I know he studied in Russia as well as Germany and that his art was called "Supremacist" by some art critic. I couldn't find out what exactly Supremacist means in art, but I'm hoping to get away with that."

He gave a loud bark of laughter and without warning, covered my hand in his. Giving it a squeeze, he said "Oh, I can see we are going to get on famously."

I looked up to see Stephen staring at us. Extracting my hand, I waved at Stephen and smiled. His face relaxed and he went back to chatting. I turned back to David and explained, "That's Stephen, my fiancé. And colleague."

"Lucky man." David shook his head in exaggerated sorrow. "Why are all the good ones taken? I finally meet a pretty girl who laughs at my jokes and can pronounce Peredvizhniki, and she's engaged!"

"You'll survive." He was some flirt but harmless. Although I wasn't impressed by him grabbing my hand, he was a saint compared to some of the grabby clients I'd encountered. Like JJ McDonnell. "Now we've broken the ice, can I ask you a professional question?"

"You can. If it's about the Bank of Leinster contract, I can only say that it's being considered." He winked and added "But it's going well."

The rest of the meal passed pleasantly; he was great company. And it was nice to have the attention of a good-looking man. Like Anne always said, I was engaged not dead. Stephen had nothing to worry about and he knew it; there was no one like him in my eyes. But David Howard was that rare thing, a client who was also fun and easy to deal with. I caught Stephen's eye as we all trooped back into the drawing room after lunch and gave him a thumbs up. "Well done," he mouthed back.

"Right," Caroline perched herself on the edge of the sofa, "Shall we have a look at this exhibition idea, and get it out of the way? Or are we all too stuffed from that amazing lunch?"

The Howards looked towards Charlie Loxburg, waiting his lead.

"Well, my dear. I know what Leslie will say. I know what Philip there thinks. Why don't you tell me, why should I host this exhibition here?"

"Because it's your defining moment." Caroline stated this as if it was a fact, incontrovertible and immutable. Charles looked taken aback. He stared at her in silence waiting for her to explain.

"This is the moment you present a lifetime's body of work to the world and say, "Here is Charles Loxburg." You will paint more pictures, but they'll be known as "Post the Exhibition.""

Caroline smiled at him. "This event is going to frame everything that you stand for as an artist and nowhere can do that justice like Howard Castle. The Loxburgs are from a particular segment of Irish history. Howard Castle is too, but it's becoming part of mainstream Ireland, the Ireland of ordinary people, the Ireland of people who barely know who Charles Loxburg is. Without them, your legacy is left in the hands of a narrow demographic, which is nice and elitist and all that, but is that all you want?"

She gestured around her, at the wood panelled walls, the portraits of long dead Howards, the almost careless array of china and silver, ornaments and candelabra.

"People are coming here now, to see this. To enjoy the grounds. To wine and dine or camp with their kids. They'll come to see your art too, your story. They'll leave feeling that you're part of *their* Ireland, part of their experience here and that you belong to them. Charles Loxburg will be their artist, maybe the only one some of them ever get up close and personal with. Art critics and aficionados, you already own them. They love you. This… this is where the public falls in love with you."

She paused, stared into his eyes and added solemnly, "Plus, it's half the cost of a posh Dublin venue and you get Jordan PR thrown in. I'll have Michael T and half the government here at the opening, and the word "castle" alone will tempt every journalist from Belfast to Cork, watch and see."

There was silence for a long minute, the entourage again watching Charlie for their cue. The artist himself was silent, staring hard at Caroline. He sighed, a strange hard sigh, like the wind being knocked out of him.

"Yes." He answered her simply. "Yes. That's the legacy I want. Let's bridge that gap."

Leslie grinned at me from across the table. I knew everyone had assured her it was a done deal but despite Loxburg's friendship with her family, I doubted he would have gone against his own best interests. With a subtle shift in the balance of power, Charles was now aware of what Howard Castle brought to the table.

I just hoped Michael T and his party faithful could be relied on to show up, but if anyone could make it happen, it was Caroline.

"Don't worry," Stephen said, when we held post-mortem in our own room later that evening, "She'll get them there if she has to steal his diary and write it in herself."

The rest of the meeting had passed well, and once we got into the actual details of the exhibition, the pair I had mentally dubbed "the twins" turned out to be rather nice and very competent. Brendan Healy wrote critical pieces for newspapers and posh magazines and George Lyons sold, or rather "brokered" Art with a capital A. Under the mannerisms and nervous energy, both were experienced and capable. They also had a vicious sense of humour, that peeked out whenever Diane Howard interjected one of her barbed comments. Now that Charles had fallen in love with the idea of Howard Castle, as presented by Caro, they took any criticism of it as a reflection on Loxburg. Diane was outgunned.

Her final shot was to point out that the Great Hall, a huge function room cum ballroom space on the first floor, was in need of a lick of paint. We hadn't seen it yet but from Leslie's dismayed reaction I was confident Diane was right.

Stephen started to say reassuringly "Yes, we'll look at that -" but George cut across him, with a withering "Dear Diane. Always so comfortingly bourgeois. I don't think we need concern ourselves with painting and decorating just yet." He turned to Caroline and inquired with exaggerated politeness, "No doubt you can find some nice local handyman to slap Magnolia on the walls for Diane, no?"

Diane flounced out, banging the door behind her. Philip Howard sighed but made no move to follow his wife and the rest of us got back to work.

"Bless George," was Caroline's opinion. "With any luck she'll be so offended she won't interfere for a while at least."

I wasn't so optimistic, but we could only hope.

Chapter Thirteen

C*aroline Jordan*

"I can't thank you enough," Leslie beamed at me. "It was a nightmare when they got here. I don't know if you noticed but everyone was just sitting around staring at each other. David and Miriam gave up even trying to talk to Charlie's friends, and to be honest I was sure it was going to go pear shaped." She signed happily. "Then you three arrived and you fixed everything."

"Steady on, Leslie. We're good but we can't take all the credit. That massive lunch went a long way to smoothing ruffled egos."

She frowned and shook her head.

"Well, I'm most grateful and I think I am a complete genius for asking you down this weekend."

We were standing in a smaller drawing room, sipping cocktails before dinner. Like the rest of the Castle, the furniture managed to be at once ancient and opulent. The curtains that flanked the huge windows were thick and richly coloured, the rugs before the fireplace and artlessly arranged on the original wood floors were slightly worn but intricately designed with deep, vibrant colours. Another batch of ancestral portraits stared at us from the walls.

"You are a genius," I agreed. "We are all geniuses, and this cocktail is amazing."

"It's my own recipe." I jumped at the sound of Peter's voice. He was so quiet I often forgot he was there.

"It's a triumph. You should be serving bespoke cocktails to guests. I'd drive eighty miles for this any day."

His face went pink, and he retreated behind Leslie again. She smiled up at him. "See, I told you so! Peter is amazing, he cooks like a professional and his cocktails are to die for."

They were a sweet couple. I wondered how Diane Howard felt about them. Somehow, I wouldn't imagine her appreciating Peter as a potential son-in-law.

"We have a lot of work to do tomorrow," Stephen warned me, eyeing the cocktail consumption with alarm. "We only have these two days to nail down a lot of details. We won't be back on site until the week of the exhibition."

"Shut up, you walking work-diary. Have a drink. When was the last time we got a chance to relax for the evening? Take two paracetamols before bed and drink a glass of water, you'll survive."

Paula agreed, helping herself to a cocktail. "Cheat day," she grinned. Cheat day indeed. It had come to something when a woman with a figure like hers was worried about dieting. Paula had curves I would have killed for; she had no idea how attractive she was. Her sisters were great, and I loved them, but I hated the inferiority complex they had unwittingly embedded in Paula.

"It's all good," Brendan, or Twin One as Paula had privately named him, joined us, "Oh. My. God. That is absolutely lush, Peter" He dispatched one and grabbed another. "Don't judge me, darlings, I need this."

"No judgement here," I took a second glass. "Let's enjoy ourselves, Stephen will have us up at dawn measuring spaces!"

With the exception of Diane, everyone was in high good spirits at dinner. We were still missing Murrough Loxburg and as I doubt Charlie would have been as easy to handle with his son present, this was a bit of a relief. Derek Fields' description of him kept running through my mind – let's be honest, if a handler of Irish politicians calls someone difficult, odd and untrustworthy, they have to be a special kind of goblin. I was half fascinated, half dreading his arrival.

As it turned out, we didn't have long to wait. Halfway through dinner, this time served in the official dining room, there was a clatter of noise from the hall downstairs. "," Leslie murmured to me, and sure enough, the man himself appeared minutes later, accompanied by a young and attractive girl.

The photo Doyle had included in his suspect pack, as we had taken to calling it, had shown a good-looking, blonde man, with a rather hard stare and grim expression. In real life, he was better looking, and as he was smiling, didn't look half as sour. He also looked far more like Charles than I had thought from the photo and was taller than I expected. He was dressed in expensive, designer "casual" clothes, the kind that cost more than a lot of people's best clothes. He glanced around the table, giving a nod to those he recognized.

"Sorry to be so late." There wasn't a hint of apology in the tone, I noticed. He seemed highly amused at something. "I do hope you haven't been waiting for me."

"Of course not," Diane snapped, "I think you'll find everything has been moving on splendidly without you."

Murrough raised an eyebrow but responded politely "How nice. I would hate to think I inconvenienced you, Diane. Have I missed anything interesting?"

Charles looked up from his soup. "Nothing that concerns you, at any rate. Although it would be nice if you would cast your eye over Leslie's function rooms tomorrow and give us the benefit of your expertise. Caroline here can bring you up to speed. She has quite a vision for this exhibition."

Because I was watching him closely, I caught the flicker of anger. Otherwise, you would have though he was delighted. "Ah so it's all settled. And there was I worrying that I'd be holding you all up. And if I may ask, have you decided on a date as well?"

"The opening will be the 28th of November," Peter surprised us all by jumping in. He stared at Murrough, a challenge in his eyes. "That suits us and your father best."

Murrough nodded. "I see. Well, what a lot you got done in a one evening." For someone who had supposedly championed the idea of holding the exhibition here, he seemed oddly put out.

"My fault, I'm afraid." I thought it was time to enter the conversation. "Hi,

I'm Caroline Jordan, this is Paula Hughes and Stephen Walsh. You must be Murrough? It's nice to put a face to the name."

Well, apart from your mug shot attached to your police file, that is.

"We pushed ahead with the basic details, for absolutely selfish reasons. We don't get out of the office that often and certainly not trips to idyllic castles to meet famous artists. I wanted to enjoy the weekend without it hanging over our heads."

He stared at me and gave a tight-lipped smile. "Well, no harm done. Although I would like to look over anything that has been agreed. Dad is a genius with a brush, but when it comes to business, he does rather let people take advantage."

Charlie gave a snort of mixed anger and derision, Leslie exclaimed "Murrough!" and Peter sat up straight in his chair, like a guard dog ready for the signal to attack. Paula intervened smoothly before anyone could reply.

"Of course, Murrough, I'll be happy to email you a copy of everything we went over today. It's all preliminaries, of course and any insight would be great. We plan on choosing a space tomorrow, Charles says you and Simon are the only ones he'll listen to on that one! Oh, and we will need a list of the paintings, Charles said you have already got permission from owners and commitments to lend for the duration? That's frankly amazing, it must have been like herding cats?"

Murrough looked startled but couldn't resist Paula's disarming mix of sincerity and flattery. "Yes. Well, to be accurate, more like lion taming than cat herding."

David Howard laughed and said, "No better man, Murrough. It's made all the difference. There's no way we could pull this off in under two months without that work."

I'm not sure he was totally mollified but he defrosted enough to introduce his date, "Everyone, Phoebe. Phoebe, everyone." Poor Phoebe looked lost, he didn't even budge up enough at the table to let her sit down. Before I could offer to move, Stephen stood up and gave her his chair, moving himself a place further down. She sank into it gratefully, giving Murrough a resentful if furtive glance as she did so. "Thanks."

"Not at all," Stephen smiled reassuringly. She leaned towards Murrough, trying to get his attention but he ignored her and started an animated conversation with the young PhD student, Danielle.

Stephen noticed the snub and rolled his eyes at me. He launched into friendly chit chat with the kid.

"Are you into art too, Phoebe?"

She shook her head. "No, I'm studying Communications. My friend Aoife is studying Art History though."

How old was this child? She had the strangled vowels and exaggerated accent of the Dublin 4 wealthy, private school set. Friend mutated into "Frond" and every sentence ended like a question. But underneath the makeup she looked even younger than I had thought. Her initial air of self-possession had deserted her, although in fairness many a 30-year-old would have been at a loss if their date blatantly ignored them in a roomful of his family and friends.

So far Murrough was proving to be a rude, petulant ass. But unfortunately, he was an ass with a seat on the board of that benighted Bank and I didn't think Derek Fields would be impressed with the intel that he was a lecher and a dickhead. He was after something more concrete than that. We couldn't afford to alienate him. I was uncomfortably aware that I had half promised Doyle some insight into him too. Much as I would have liked to, antagonizing Murrough was not on the agenda.

Still, I promised myself, I would be keeping an eye on Phoebe.

Chapter Fourteen

aula Hughes

PSaturday in Howard Castle was a productive day, and despite the bad initial impression I had of Murrough, he proved to have a good eye and a real understanding of what was needed for this Exhibition to be a success. Leslie's "function rooms" – a long balconied gallery and the old ball room – he rejected out of hand. "Clichéd. And the light is horrible." Simon Prendergast tried to argue the point with Murrough but was over-ruled firmly. I felt a flash of sympathy for Prendergast, it wasn't pleasant to be on the receiving end of Murrough's snide comments.

As we explored, Murrough seized on a series of four interlocking rooms formed a kind of semi-circle around the central entrance hall.

"The public can enter here, go through in this direction and we can divide the collection to reflect different stages in his work," He explained. The "twins" looked at each other, some kind of silent communication flashing between them.

"He's right," Brendan pronounced firmly, and George nodded.

"Think about it," Brendan said. "I'm Joe Public. I'm a total pleb, never heard of Charles Loxburg. Last artist I heard of was Van Gough and that's only because of the Dr Who episode. I'm on my holliers, driving around with the missus and two screaming kids, bored out of my head and I see posters… no, *banners*…advertising Castle Howard. It looks good: activities, fun for the kids, café, and art exhibition. I dump the kids at the archery, sign a waiver not to sue if they get an arrow through the eye and off up to the Castle we go. At the main entrance we see the signs for the Loxburg Collection. "Ooh" sez the missus, a bit of culture!""

He mimed Mrs. Public, ecstatic, followed by a less than enthused Mr. Public. "We enter, to find a gorgeous usher ready to take our money…" George leapt into the role, obviously well used to the dramatics. "Suitably laden with brochures, we enter stage left to a room with everything I've ever thought a castle would have. High stone windows, ancient oak floors, tapestries…oh my god, that is a tapestry?…it'll have to be moved…I follow the exhibition around from here to here to here…and I we emerge back into the mundane oppression of daily life, what do I see in front of me? A sign for the café bar and gift shop. Perfect!"

He turned to Murrough and bowed. "Genius. Once you pointed it out, it's so obvious. Nowhere else could possibly do."

Even Caroline was impressed. "Perfect. Simple, keeps people moving, What about lighting? There's less natural light here than in the Ball Room."

"Natural light isn't what these paintings need." Murrough replied shortly. "They need atmosphere."

For the first time, Charlie and Emily looked impressed. "Atmosphere," She looked at Murrough and nodded. "Yes. No glaring lights and white spaces. Dark shadows, warm highlights. Make people work to see them." Her accent was such a strange mix of Irish and English, it made everything she said sound harsh, she didn't so much converse as bark at us.

Caroline was scribbling notes furiously. "I know a guy who is a genius at stage lighting. Full on drama. And we should ask people not to talk. Make this an Experience, not just an exhibition."

"The Loxburg Experience," Charles nodded. "Yes. That's it."

Murrough was in high good humour after this, though Simon Prendergast openly sulked. I made sure to ask Murrough's opinion on everything, and cc him on every email. To my surprise he was efficient, and he had a great eye for detail. As long as we were dealing with the nuts and bolts of the exhibition, I could enjoy working with him.

It was the rest of the time spent in his company that made me loathe him.

The way he treated the unfortunate Phoebe was atrocious; she was far too young to be hanging round a man like him and you could tell she was infatuated. Some age gaps make no difference, but Murrough Loxburg was toxic and fully grown adults found him hard to deal with. It was impossible to know where you stood with him. In the middle of a conversation, where you thought you were getting on well, he would be suddenly and inexplicably rude. He encouraged you to chat and then made you feel like a fool. He seemed to resent almost everyone present, from Emily to Peter. He was polite enough to Leslie but with an edge. In fact, there was an undercurrent in everything he said to the point where no one wanted to be around him for long.

It was worse when he talked politics. Between us, every shade of political opinion was represented and while personally I found the Howards en masse too conservative, even Leslie and Peter, they were far from fanatical. Murrough was different; he was forceful by nature and became quite vicious if the subject turned to immigrants, minorities or feminism. And he continuously turned the subject there.

Politeness, and professionalism, prevented us responding as we might normally have done, but he couldn't have been under any illusion about our reaction to his rants.

In fairness, he seemed to dislike everyone equally, except for his extra hostility towards Diane Howard. That was only too openly displayed, and most certainly reciprocated. They each went out of their way to annoy the other and make everyone else around them deeply uncomfortable. There is only so much sniping you can listen too, especially after a long, hard day. The surroundings were so beautiful, the weather had held up and I was dying to start enjoying the place but listening to Murrough and Diane sneer at each other made everyone sour and unsettled.

Saturday night dinner started well, but the talk turned from Art to politics too quickly. Emily Cleethe asked Caroline a few questions about her work which led to a discussion of some of Michael T O'Mahony's more liberal plans for the country. It was soon apparent that apart from David, the "twins" and our group, there was a decided lack of enthusiasm for his progressive agenda.

"What your boss doesn't seem to understand," Charlie prodded Caroline with one of his long, bony fingers, "is that no good comes from pandering to the rabble."

Caroline smiled, remaining heroically silent. Emily Cleethe chipped in, "I'm all for equality, but when do we consider the majority? Why do we always have to stoop to the lowest common denominator?"

Brendan and George exchanged laden glances. Cleethe ploughed on regardless. "I mean, don't we already have gay marriage? Isn't that what civil partnership is for?"

"No," said Stephen.

He smiled brightly at Emily. "Civil Partnership was brought in as a compromise, to placate the minority who oppose full equality. It'll have to be replaced."

She pursed her lips. "Don't bet on it, there's still a lot of people in this country who respect the institution of marriage, mark my words. They don't shout about it, unlike some, but they won't want to see marriage turned into a circus."

A silence followed this, some people smiling and nodding, the rest of us rolling our eyes. Considering the fact Emily and Charles had never bothered to get married, it was breathtakingly hypocritical. I could tell by the twitch beside Caroline's eye that she was weighing up her professionalism against a desire to throw the soup bowl at Cleethe's head.

Brendan turned to George and started an animated conversation about a music festival close to them in Dun Laoghaire. "It's pure mad," He exclaimed, "It's all ukes, just ukuleles everywhere. But it's massive craic."

We joined in, but there was some devil in Murrough that night. He dragged the talk relentlessly back to politics, this time bewailing the proposals to allow a few thousand extra refugees in under a new scheme.

I won't repeat his comments on that topic. But if he was any further to the right, he'd be wearing a black shirt and goose stepping around the table.

Even Diane Howard was moved to remonstrate at one point, which led to a fresh round of bickering between them. Charlie and Emily kept up a chatter of pointed comments, the gist of which was that our most important client, O'Mahony, was driving the country to perdition and wouldn't survive another election.

Caroline refused to be drawn, but I knew it was sitting badly with her. Especially as Murrough could be heard telling some screamingly unfunny joke about women and sex trafficking at the other end of the table. I glared down at them, and David Howard caught my eye. In fairness to him, he looked mortified and uncomfortable.

After dinner, Leslie drew me aside. "I'm sorry," she said helplessly, "It's a nightmare. Murrough is not usually so bad, but he can't seem to help himself around Mum. I wish they'd both shut up. Anyway, I just wanted to say, I've asked the lads to light the lanterns and set up tables by the lake. We've a lovely area of reclaimed meadows just by the boat sheds. You and Stephen go down, before the rest of them. Have a nice stroll around, look at the sunset and Peter will send down cocktails."

I thanked her and grabbed Stephen as quickly as possible. We escaped with unseemly haste; cocktails by a lake being a luxury so far outside our budget recently, it was a mere fantasy. I felt a pang of guilt at abandoning Caroline, but she would be the first to tell us to go, while we could.

True to her word Leslie had set up a little café style area beside the boat shed, with fairy lights and tables with brightly coloured cloths, flowers in jam jars and those candles that keep midges away. The lake shore was a few feet away, with a tiny pebble beach either side of the slipway for boats. And a huge pitcher of whatever the hell Peter put in his cocktails sat on one table, flanked by multi-coloured glass tumblers.

Stephen beamed at me over the edge of a salt rimmed glass and for a while all was well with the world. There was an otherworldly peace about the place, in the long Irish twilight. Crows flew overhead and circled low across the tops of the trees, while the water lapped on gravel and the tiny fairy lights twinkled.

The charm of the Hideaway was its mixture of laid back, bohemian chic with the opulence of a bygone era. There were manicured lawns and formal gardens, but they were offset by wildflower meadows, over-grown thickets of trees and undergrowth. It felt rich, but in such an easy-going way. You could daydream about owning this wonderful place if you ignored the fact that up until quite recently the average Irish peasant would have been shot for trespassing.

We looked at each other and laughed, I knew Stephen had been thinking much the same thing. Neither of us were Castles and Titles people; we were chips on the way home from the pub folk, and we liked it. But this was undeniably a lovely change of pace, just for a weekend.

"Down here!" Prendergast's harsh voice broke our happy bubble, "Come on, down the steps!"

Stephen grabbed my arm. "Come on!" he grabbed the pitcher of cocktails that Peter had sent down, the delicious Howard Specials, and shoved our glasses into my hands. "Leg it!" he hissed. And leg it we did. By the time the others had reached the tables we were out of sight and halfway down a grassy avenue flanked by rhododendron bushes. The flowers had long faded but even in early Autumn the leaves made perfect cover.

Giggling like children, and gasping for breath, we ended up nearer the house. "There's a kind of summer house around here," Stephen said, "We'll hide there and drink and go back to pretending we're rich and this is our country house!"

"Oh, imagine owning this?" I sighed. "Though it's also kind of weird to think of one family owning so much land, all those empty unused rooms. There's no getting away from it, it's not fair."

"Don't worry, my beautiful Comrade. We'll be benign rich people, we'll live here but we'll let everyone come and enjoy the place too. Up here, look – there's the summer house thingie."

I could see a small stone structure, circular in shape with a pointy roof, held up by pillars and open at the sides from waist height upwards.

It was only when we were nearly at the entrance that we noticed a faint light. It looked like the glow of a phone screen. We could also hear strange noises, scuffling noises and a kind of moan. Moaning. And a sort of sucky… .Oh. My. God.

Clutching Stephen's arm and frantically waving I managed to stop him from barging in. Realization dawned on him in time, and he stepped back;

we looked at each other and tried to stifle a fresh round of giggles as we melted back into the shadows.

"Someone's having a good time!" Stephen wheezed with laughter.

"Who's there?" With a shock I recognized Murrough Loxburg's voice. I could see him silhouetted against the fading light, but no sign of Phoebe. Once his head disappeared back down, we took the opportunity and hightailed it back to the grassy avenue.

"Oh my god!" Stephen exclaimed. "Well, that would have done for us with the Bank. Hi, Murrough, sorry about bursting in on you and young Pheebs, but can we have the PR contract, ta!"

"We should have taken photos and blackmailed him," I snorted. "Here, we'd better walk back down to the others. I don't want to bump into the lovebirds, they'll know it was us."

The second shock of the evening came as we approached the rest of the group around the table. Everyone applauded the sight of the pitcher of booze; Caroline favoured us with a wink and a knowing smile; and Phoebe asked us anxiously if we had seen Murrough?

"He went to get his jacket," she told me plaintively. "He's been gone ages." There was nothing I could say to that, only look at Stephen and shake my head. Then I did a quick headcount.

Everyone was there except Diane Howard.

Chapter Fifteen

aroline Jordan

"I swear," Paula said. "It had to be her."

I was woken at an ungodly hour by the pair of them, full of news. "That poor kid, Phoebe."

"Yeah."

"We should tell her. We should, shouldn't we? I mean…" Stephen trailed off, looking at Paula and me. "Well, should we?"

"No!" It came out more emphatically than I'd intended. "Sorry but, no. It's none of our business and let's remember, this is business. These people are not our friends. I like Leslie but she's a client. She can decide to go with another firm, and let me tell you, no matter how much she owes us if it was in her best interests to switch, she would. Do you think she'd stay with the firm that exposed her mother's affair? David Howard and Murrough Loxburg are on the board of the Bank of Leinster. We need them. Can you imagine walking in there to pitch, with the pair of them glowering at us? It's not our place."

Paula nodded, albeit reluctantly. "I agree. I hate it, I would love to tell that girl to run a mile from him but, we need to be professional."

"I don't like it,"

"None of us do, Stephen. But this is the reality. We're here to sort this exhibition out, make a commission, and make nice with Loxburg before the vote."

"And suss out any suspects for Alan, or any intel for Derek." Paula didn't give up easily. "We have a whole day left here, so let's make the most of it. I'm going to tackle David, Stephen needs to start chatting to Emily Cleethe, and you need to get Murrough on side, Caroline. And don't forget Simon."

Leslie had persuaded us to postpone our departure until after dinner. I had the impression she still needed us as a buffer, although the mood had improved greatly since Friday afternoon. Brendan and George, it turned out, were kindred spirits and excellent contacts to have made. We were already earmarking collaborations that might interest them and a night out was planned for the near future. Peter the Silent had overcome his shyness sufficiently to inform Stephen that he liked the direction we were taking Howards' Hideaway Castle. And we now knew his surname was Dwyer and he was Leslie's partner of 6 years, both business and romantic.

Simon Prendergast was a different story, he seemed friendly but there was an edge to everything he did or said. "He's insecure," Paula remarked. "Remember what Derek said? Flattery will get you everywhere with him." It did help but it was hard going. I tried talking politics to see if he was on Murrough's wavelength but to his credit he was obviously distressed by the attitude Loxburg had expressed.

"I don't like talking politics, Caroline. If you don't mind, I'd rather not bash people who are just trying to survive like the rest of us." He flushed and added, "I suppose you'll report that back to Charlie. Or Murrough."

"Ah don't be daft, Simon. Murrough isn't my client and he's certainly not a friend. Why would I drop you in it with him?"

He shrugged. "I don't know, I'm sure. But everything I say seems to get picked up and picked apart by him. I expect he's slagged me off behind my back already to you."

I was torn between exasperation at his sulking and sympathy for the way he was treated by both Loxburgs. And the older Howards too for that matter.

Changing tack, I mentioned the murder.

"Oh. Yes, I read about it. Very distressing." He seemed genuinely uninterested, beyond finding it all distasteful. As a last resort I pointed to the pictures and he lit up.

"These are his best work, by a long shot. Painted when he was mature enough to bring some experience to bear but before he became famous and bloated on praise. Not that I can put that on the brochure, ha. I'll find a way to praise them without pointing out how much his painting dipped since then. I think these should be next, they're the best of his later work – the contrast won't be as stark. Oh, and that one, yes." There was a childlike quality to his enthusiasm, despite his obvious disillusionment with Charlie as he was now.

I wondered why he stuck with him. In fact, if pressed I'd have to say I thought he was afraid of him.

Emily was another difficult person, although once she realized none of us were interested in Charles beyond a professional relationship, she relaxed. I made sure she was included in every discussion which seemed to help professionally. Socially however, she was distant and presented such a smooth exterior, I couldn't get a foothold. Not to be boastful, but there are very few people I can't get around when I apply my devious brain to it; Emily was one of the few. Maybe she was just one of those people whom you can meet many times, chat pleasantly and part not knowing her one whit better.

The only opportunity to talk to her privately fell to Stephen but she confined herself to golf; courses she liked to play, Europe's Ryder Cup team and whether an up-and-coming Irish golfer was likely to win on the international stage. Fascinating fare for Stephen but not much use to either Doyle or Derek Fields. I did however eavesdrop shamelessly on her conversations with the Howards Senior and as both Philip and Diane had loud voices, I could at least tell Derek that Emily was making noises about running for local government on a Cumann na Laochra ticket.

Murrough was next and I wondered a lot about him. Knowing he was having his wicked way with Diane Howard threw me. Much as I thought Phoebe was too young for him, she suited his persona better. It was more typical – *"overbearing, arrogant man dates young impressionable young woman."* Hardly the stuff of news. At least Diane Howard was his senior. Far better to date an experienced older woman than manipulate an inexperienced girl. Even the fact that she was married, I considered to be none of my business.

Who knew what arrangement the Howards had privately in their marriage?

What bothered me was their personalities. Diane was a narcissistic weapon, with a vicious streak. The way she treated Leslie was appalling, naked jealousy and resentment of her own daughter apparent at every turn. Murrough had a disturbing undercurrent to him, hard to quantify. Together I could imagine the pair being utterly toxic.

And again, it was none of my business, I reminded myself sternly. I was doing my bit for law and order. Murrough was a potential client, and even if he was a murder suspect it wasn't my business. In that spirit, I sought him out after breakfast. He was in the games room, equipped with a billiard table, darts board, and a pile of battered board games. He had a pack of cards at a small table, engaged in a hand of patience.

"Caroline," He nodded as I approached.

"I haven't seen that in a long time," I said truthfully, "Most people play on their computers now. I used to love playing it with real cards."

"I prefer real cards," He kept playing without pausing, "Real cards and real books."

"Now you're talking. Real books are the greatest luxury, did you ever think you'd see the day?"

He raised his eyebrow in that slightly supercilious way he had. "You surprise me. I thought you'd be all for kindles and e-readers."

"I am, in a way," I sat opposite him and watched him allocate cards. "I mean, I would hardly ever get to read if it wasn't for my tablet. But it's not the same as a proper book, the feel of one in your hands and the smell of a new book. Oh, and second-hand bookshops!"

This earned me my first genuine smile from him. Who knew sincerity could be useful?

"My favourite pursuit," he offered, "Exploring old book shops. There's one on the quays, the Secret Bookshop. Love that place."

"I go there all the time. Well, when I have the chance. Have you been to the one in Rathmines?" We played one-up-man-ship over obscure bookshops until he finished his game. He won by mentioning De Búrca rare books, a treasure trove in the city centre which sold the kind of books I could only dream of owning. It's not done in PR circles to show too much hidden depth but just between us, if I didn't spend all my money on vodka, takeaways and the dreaded clothes shopping, I would treat myself to a first edition of a George Russell or the famous storyteller Patricia Lynch.

Not wanting to push my luck, because he was as changeable as the Irish weather, I started to stand, saying "Well I'll leave you to it. Better go measure a wall or something."

"Sit down a minute longer. The exhibition is well in hand. I want a word about something else."

Surprised but interested, I resumed my seat. "Shoot."

Murrough tapped the table with the edge of the deck of cards and stared at me. "Jordan PR is pitching for the Bank of Leinster contract next week."

Okay. Well, that was news to me. We had been waiting on some kind of call back from the board but assumed we would have plenty of notice. My face must have reflected this, because he grinned and said, "Not expecting that? It's a favourite tactic of Sean. The old man likes to test people. Unannounced inspections, unscheduled meetings, and calling in firms at the last moment to see how they operate under pressure."

"I see. The "Baptism of Fire" school of management."

"From what I've seen, Jordan PR can handle it, but I thought, you might appreciate the heads up." He paused, and added casually, "You've done great work for Dad here. And after what happened with poor Frank Clarke most of us on the board feel it would be churlish not to award you the contract. But Sean can't give anything without feeling that the person earned it – jumped through some kind of hoop, I should say."

"I get it. We'll get a call midweek with about 24 hours' notice, so we have a panic stricken, sweaty palmed nightmare and he can feel good about us getting the contract." Murrough nodded. "Okay then. Well, the jokes on him, because we are prepared, we've been prepared for weeks. But if it makes him feel better, we'll fall in the door looking like we haven't slept and are functioning on caffeine and diet pills."

"Hah! Well, that might be overdoing it, but a little, what did you call it?

"sweaty palmed fear," might go a long way with him."

"Done. I appreciate it, Murrough, I really do. We are well prepared but that might just have thrown us. Especially," and I paused delicately, "Well, it's a bit strange walking back in there. That was an experience we won't forget."

"Ah. Yes. I have to say, the Board appreciated your firm's discretion at the time. To be honest, we expected a lot of lurid reportage. Not that there wasn't quite enough of that but at least, there were no eye-witness accounts and gruesome details."

"We would never do that." I said flatly. "I know what it is to be on the receiving end of public interest in a tragedy."

He nodded. "Ah yes. Sorry, I was forgetting."

You were in your bum, I thought rudely. I doubted he ever said *anything* without thinking it through ten ways from Christmas.

"Well, it was appreciated."

"Have you heard anything about the investigation?" I asked innocently. "Surely they must have some idea who did it. You'd think there would be some progress."

Murrough frowned. "It's apparently all very much a mystery. Poor Frank was either in the wrong place at the wrong time, or he was involved in something none of us knew about."

Shaking my head, I tried for a little more. "A bank robbery I could understand, it's awful but people do get shot or hurt during armed robberies. This was – well, it's hard to imagine who would do such a thing. Maybe it was personal?"

He shrugged. "Frank was a quiet man, as I recall. I can't see him being involved in any kind of personal crisis that would lead to this."

"Oh. Well, no doubt the police will get there in the end. They usually do. From a PR point of view, it's an added reason to get control over the narrative. It would be best to have it resolved quickly, better still if it's something the public can easily understand and not blame the "Bank" for."

"Indeed. And it's impressive that you're already thinking ahead."

"The Leinster contract is a huge deal for us," Experience had taught me that a well-placed nugget of honesty worked wonders at times. "We want it, and to be honest, I think Jordan PR can do a lot for you."

He looked pleased. "I look forward to the pitch. As I said, there's a lot of goodwill towards you from the board members. Of course, it's a little unfortunate that you're so closely linked with our glorious leader." The way he said it, that was no compliment to O'Mahony. "You must know that politically a lot of the Board would be on a different wavelength to our Government. Sean in particular is wary of that connection."

I smiled, hoping my annoyance was well enough hidden. I might privately castigate my political clients, but they were saints compared to the opposition shower waiting in the wings. Give me an bog-standard venal but liberal leaning professional politician over a right wing, conservative, Holy Ireland obsessed zealot any day.

"Ah, we keep these things separate," I said lightly. "Between us I'm sure we represent a variety of political opinions and points of view. Have to see the merits in each." Which is top class Public Relations waffle, right there.

Murrough swept the cards aside irritably and started dealing another hand of patience. "That is reassuring to hear. I know the two shouldn't overlap but politics do tend to creep in."

"Not with us. I keep my politics private, and I don't ask anyone else who they voted for."

"Now, I wonder is that cynical or merely professional?"

"Hah! I'm the first to admit to being cynical but in this case it's definitely professional."

"And if I were to ask you where you stand personally?"

"I think I'm like a lot of people. I have some liberal views and some conservative views."

"Ah yes. Without wishing to insult you, don't you think that's very... .weak?" He shook his head. "So many people, wavering all over the place. Seduced by some promise of leftism, but still wanting the protection of a stronger, conservative State. I bet your "liberal" views include so-called women's rights, yes? Equal rights for the gays too? Let in all the immigrants, no matter what they bring with them? And let's reward young women for being promiscuous, stick them in houses at the expense of married couples and families. But on the other hand, you want a strong police force to protect you, and you want antisocial thugs off the streets. The same thugs that are being reared by single mothers."

The absolute cheek, especially seeing as my Dad died when I was a kid and I was reared by a single mother. She was a disaster as a parent, but it was because she was always a narcissistic wagon not because she had no man to rely on. I was on the verge of a hot-tempered reply but since childhood, I've had a superpower. When dealing with outrageous and provocative people, time slows down, my mind works quickly, and a lot of thoughts run through the empty caverns of my mind. It had saved my neck since my schooldays; being educated by nuns gave one the instincts of a CIA operative. It kicked in now, as I smiled politely and thought furiously.

"Murrough holds the kind of views that make people say things like "Heil Hitler." He wants a fight, or at least to goad me into a hot-headed response. He thinks he knows my politics" – okay, in fairness he's right, I am everything he thinks I am but that's beside the point.

"This is some kind of test. If I respond defending my politics, I'm the enemy. If I equivocate, he thinks I'm weak and will despise me.

"He despises you anyway," said my inner voice, *"better he thinks you're no threat than you hand him any insight into your private opinions.""*

It was the voice of reason, I decided.

"You're very passionate there, Murrough. I'm not saying you're wrong, but I must admit I don't spend a lot of time agonizing over these things. I've enough to do to keep our political clients on the straight and narrow without debating policies. Mine is not to reason why, just to stop them appearing on Politics Tonight drunk." I looked at his spread. "You're missing that Queen, black ten will move there."

"Ah. So it will," He gave me another of his bland, disconcerting stares. "Good to chat, Caroline. I look forward to seeing you soon."

"Definitely." I was about to leave when a thought occurred to me, and some spark of mischief had it out of my mouth before I could stop it. "Oh – can I ask you one thing? Pure curiosity, to be honest! That Garda, Doyle?

Did he ever figure out what was wrong with the clock?"

His hand paused, mid placement of a card. He cocked his head to one side and favoured me with a hard, unsmiling stare. "Clock?" he repeated coldly.

"Yeah. Did he not ask you? Apparently, the clock was slow. Or fast. Out by a few minutes anyway. I thought it was a bit odd of him, harping on about it. Something and nothing, I suppose."

A tight smile. "It must be. I think he may have mentioned it, but I've no idea why."

"Ah well. As I said, idle curiosity. He seems to think it has something to do with the vaults. Or the records office. Probably barking up the wrong tree." He dropped the ten of clubs and bent to retrieve it with an annoyed Tsk. I dismissed myself with a cheery wave, content to have rattled him a little. It was time to find the others. A brief search located Paula in one of the west-facing small sitting rooms, on the first floor, still chatting to David Howard, with Miriam, Danielle and the "Twins" pouring over floor plans and sketches.

"Honestly, it's a bit too Gothic if you know what I mean?" Brendan was examining one of George's impromptu artist's impressions of a Loxburg hanging in situ, in gloomy light. I looked at it curiously. It was a very good little sketch and the picture was instantly recognizable as Lady Waiting in Sunshine, a vibrant but slightly sinister painting of a figure against a harsh sunlit beach, with the hint of storms and angry seas and a sense of mist closing in.

"I think it needs to be more softly lit," I suggested. "It has so much going on, if it's too brightly spotlighted it ruins it. Also, we need to leave enough light for people to walk around safely, not grope around the place."

"Grope your way around Charlie Loxburg," Miriam giggled. "It has a certain ring to it!"

David grinned. "I'll say. He's some goat for his age, isn't he?"

Danielle stiffened but stayed silent. No harm for her to hear this, I decided.

"He's a bit… handsy?" I asked.

"Oh my god, Caroline," Miriam rolled her eyes. "He's a terrible old lech. I'm fond of him, but he thinks every woman wants him. He was very good-looking, when he was younger, and I suppose a lot of women did throw themselves at him. That's what broke up his marriage, to Murrough's Mum Georgina. She stuck with him for years but, well the girls stayed the same age and he got older. I don't know how Emily deals with him. I couldn't."

The PhD student had too red spots on her cheeks and kept her eyes on the ground.

"It's hard on her, I'm sure. It's such a cliché too, the old man and the young girl."

Brendan chuckled. "It runs in the family. My dears, that poor wee thing Phoebe! She's had a miserable weekend. I hope she dumps Murrough."

"Anyone should dump a person who treats them badly and just uses them." Paula, bless her, was indignant on behalf of any underdog, but especially a fellow female. "It's just rotten behaviour. And being an artist is no defence, either." She glanced at Danielle and added, "Totally understandable to fall for a smoothie like him, but if they don't treat you well, walk away."

Feeling we had done enough by way of public service announcements for one day, I asked after Stephen – out playing golf with Emily Cleethe and Philip Howard – and extracted a solemn promise from Paula that they would be packed before dinner so we could head off as soon as it was over.

"I'd better go pack now," she sighed, "Stephen takes forever so I'll do it while he's not there to rearrange it all."

I sank into an armchair and chatted lightly with the others. Part of me wished we were already on the road. It had been a productive weekend overall, but we had been working for most of it and a quiet Sunday night in front of the TV sounded good to me. One by one people drifted away to change before dinner or pack. I was as dressed up as I intended to be and packed since morning so I stayed and watched the shadows lengthen through the French doors and the room grew slightly dimmer with every passing moment, until my eyes may have shut briefly.

I started awake to terrified screams, coming from the floor above. From the bedrooms, I thought groggily and then with sharpening clarity, "Paula! That's Paula!"

Stumbling out into the corridor I could hear Stephen's voice from the

Hallway below, as he threw his golf clubs into a corner shouting "Paula!"

"Upstairs!" I roared, taking the stairs to the bedrooms two at time. Stephen overtook me before I could reach the top landing, just as the screams stopped abruptly.

Chapter Sixteen

Paula Hughes

My form of packing a car is to throw everything into a suitcase and stuff both it and the overflow into the boot. My beloved finds this my only real flaw and vice, and if it was left to him everything would be packed with military precision and neatness. I usually let him pack when we're going and I pack when we're leaving, so we've reached a compromise of sorts. Still, I was conscious of needing to get everything done before he finished his round of golf; I didn't want to discuss whether his shirts should be rolled or folded. My plan was to have the cases ready to go, so we could enjoy dinner and leave in good form.

It had been a good weekend, in my opinion. Well, Stephen and I had enjoyed it, it was the nearest to a holiday we'd be getting before the wedding at this rate. My diet had taken a battering which made me feel a bit guilty but next week would be like boot-camp, I promised myself. No sugars or carbs and I would make it to the gym once a day no matter how tired I was.

Pushing down memories of cream teas and cocktails, I forced the zip closed on the last bag and did another sweep of the room. The last hotel I had stayed in I left a pair of sandals under the bed and never managed to replace them. Lesson learned, I swore, as I peered under the bed on my hands and knees.

Without the slightest warning, not even a floorboard creak, I became aware of a shadow crossing me and heard breathing, panting almost. "Stephen?" I went to turn my head, but a hand caught my neck and then before I could even react, I was pinned down, cheek pressed against the floorboards and the weight of someone leaning heavily on me. I could feel breathing now as well as hear it, a ragged, uneven breath.

"Nosey *Cow*." A voice hissed in my ear, but I couldn't place it, it could have been anyone. My head was lifted slightly, until there were several inches between it and the floor and a sheaf of paper was shoved into the space. My eyes couldn't focus on it properly but I recognized the suspect list. "Nosey, nosey cow!" the voice was unnervingly creepy and unpleasant.

I couldn't move, but I could and did scream. I screamed as loud and hard as I could considering my position. Whoever was above me swore loudly but they let go of my neck. I turned my head but too late, not even a glimpse of their feet. I tried to sit up, but my arms and legs were equally shaky. "Stephen!" I sobbed, and as if in answer I heard his voice from the corridor and his fists banging on the door.

Why didn't he come in? I managed to clamber to my feet and stumble across the bedroom. The handle wouldn't turn. Stupidly I twisted it again to be sure, but it was…locked. And the key was gone. Whoever it was had locked me in.

"Stephen," I tried to make myself heard through the thick old-fashioned door. "I'm locked in! He took the key!"

"What? Who took it? Are you OK?"

"No. Yes. Please, Steve, get the door open please."

There was silence for a few minutes, then I heard Caroline.

"Paula? It's OK, pet. You're OK now. Stephen has gone to get Leslie." I heard David Howard's voice chip in "She has master keys Paula, to every door. She'll have you out in no time. Hang on!"

I leaned my back against the door, trying to breathe more evenly. Nothing was out of place in the room, except the papers Doyle had given us which were spread across the bed and on the floor. Guiltily I realized I had no memory of seeing them while packing. I had assumed they were still in the briefcase from the night before. Someone had gone through our room and discovered them.

On impulse I grabbed them all and stuffed them back into the satchel and clipped it shut. A minute later, there was the scrape of a key turning in the lock and Stephen, white with fright, almost fell into the room.

"Paula!" He hugged me tightly "What the hell?"

Caroline, Leslie and David were at the doorway, and I sensed rather than saw that there were others in the hallway behind. Full details could wait until we were alone, I decided. I caught Caro's eye over his shoulder, and she nodded slightly.

"I don't know," I explained. "I came up to pack, was almost finished and then someone grabbed me. I started to scream, they ran out the door and locked me in!"

"Oh my god!" Leslie gasped. "Oh, I'm so sorry! Was anything taken?"

"I've said it before," David broke in angrily, "Anyone can walk in or out, some lowlife thought he could rifle through the bedrooms."

From the hall I heard Diane Howard exclaim, "Oh! He could have been anywhere. My jewellery." This had the effect of scattering the audience, to go check on their own bits.

"I'm so sorry," Leslie said again, "We've had a few people try to wander upstairs when we're busy but never like this."

"We need better security," David snapped.

"Do you mind?" Stephen retorted. "Could you discuss your security lapses elsewhere and let me mind my fiancée?"

David flushed. "Of course, I'm so sorry. Truly. It's just, of all the people for this to happen to! I am annoyed at myself too, for not preventing this. We are a bit complacent down here, it's rare to have any kind of burglary."

Caroline intervened tactfully. Murmuring platitudes like "It's easily done," and "At least there's no harm done, and it doesn't look like anything was taken," she succeeded in herding them from the room, shutting the door firmly.

Half an hour later, I was feeling much better. Stephen had been fussing over me (which I admit I thoroughly enjoyed) and a stiff brandy had been sent up by Leslie.A soft knock on the the door signalled Caroline's return, having persuaded the others to call the local station and report an intruder.

"Honestly, they acted like I was trying to drag Howard Castle through the gutter press, the way they reacted. In the end, David insisted. I'll say this much for him, he is genuinely upset for you." She perched herself on the armchair at the dressing table. "Now, if you're feeling better, tell me exactly what happened? You put the heart crosswise in me, screaming like that."

I bit my lip. I'd already told Stephen, but it was hard to get the words out again. When I described him shoving the suspect list under my nose, Caroline gave a sharp intake of breath.

"That's all of it. I didn't catch a glimpse of him, I didn't recognize the voice – it was rough sounding, with a Dublin accent but…well, it could have been put on. I don't know. It sounded fake. Someone's been through our room, Stephen, and they found those files."

Stephen hugged me again, cursing softly under his breath.

"It's my fault" Caroline replied flatly. "I should never have taken them from Doyle. I should never have let him mix us up in any of this. Bad enough we were there when they found Frank Clarke's body – that's enough horror for a lifetime. I should have handed him back those files and told him to feck off."

"No." I surprised myself. A minute ago, I was thinking that I was a fool to have brought them, and for thinking we could help an investigation. But somehow, hearing Caroline say it, something rebelled inside.

"We were right to help. And even if Doyle hadn't asked, Derek Fields had already asked us to be on the alert. Whoever attacked me, they are rattled. What made them search our rooms anyway? How did they know we had anything worth searching for?"

Stephen nodded. "I have to say, Paula's right. We have had a very nice, sociable weekend. So why suddenly be suspicious of us?"

Caroline answered slowly, "I might have said something. To be honest, I just said it on impulse because he was being so…well, so Murrough. He gave me a lecture about how my politics are wishy washy. He's a right wing, all immigrants are bad, the gays are coming to marry your kids, type. He was trying to bait me, so I ignored most of it but I couldn't resist asking him, had they ever figured out what was wrong with the clock?. The one in the Bank lobby, that was wrong for the first time since Sean O'Dwyer was a baby."

"And what was his reaction?"

"He didn't show much but it rattled him. I wonder, did it rattle him enough to start snooping around our rooms?"

I was doubtful. "In fairness we've been wandering around all day asking people questions and bringing up the murder."

"True, any one of them could have been spooked. But at least you're sure it was a man?"

That was the one thing I could say with confidence. The person who had assaulted me was definitely a man.

Stephen strode out of our room, calling over his shoulder, "Have you checked your room yet, Caro?"

I ran after them both, and into her room. At first glance nothing looked out of place, but Caroline frowned. "The bags, they're out of order." Her make up case was on the floor instead of neatly stacked on the wheelie case. "Hang on," she opened first one then another and confirmed, "Yup. Someone has had a good old riffle through them. Nothing missing, but there's something out of place in each."

Unlike me, Caroline is a military grade packer, trained spies couldn't search her bags without her noticing something a millimetre out of place.

"Okay, Murrough begins to wonder if there's more to us than just Ireland's best PR team. He starts with your room and then does ours. And when he finds Paula alone, he…I'm going to kill him," Stephen finished grimly.

"We don't know that!" I pointed out "And whoever took the papers took them between this morning and now, because I know they were in the case last night. Would Murrough have had time?"

Caro shrugged, "Honestly haven't a clue. I reckon he did, but I can't be sure."

"And," my brain was finally back up to speed, "we still have this Bank of Leinster meeting looming. We can't go thumping a board member because he may or may not have been the intruder."

"Bless you," Caroline said warmly, "Only you would put a Jordan PR contract ahead of your personal safety."

Stephen laughed reluctantly. "OK. But if it turns out it was him, I'm taking my 4 iron to his skull."

"Fair enough,"

"So what now?"

"We do nothing. We go with the intruder story. I saw nothing, they were disturbed in the act. We were lucky they ran off. We don't rock the boat and we leave whoever it was guessing why and what we are up to."

"Great, back to lying to the cops," Caroline said gloomily.

"Only local cops," Stephen said comfortingly. "That's nothing. Sure, aren't we used to lying to the Special Crimes Squad?"

Chapter Seventeen

S Doyle

DI didn't hold out much hope that Caroline and the gang would have much to tell me when they returned but it was worth a shot and, in the meantime, I had my own inquiries to pursue.

The incident room was quiet, for once. Powers waved at me from across the incident room. Excitement radiated off him; a pleasant faced man around his own age, with a mop of dark hair and round gold-rimmed glasses, was sitting beside him looking equally eager. His desk was a confusion of computer monitors, keyboards and a dozen add on pieces of tech we had long ago learned not to question. As Graves put it, we had plausible deniability in case he was running some kind of elaborate hacking operation from Special Branch.

The SCS was formed within Special Branch to deal with "sensitive" crimes, which is cop speak for the crimes that involve the kind of people who have the Minister for Justice on speed dial, and call her "Lilian, *Darling*." Our current Justice Minister was a tough, professional politician devoid of any trace of idealism. If an influential citizen was discommoded by our inquiries, Lilian Roche wasn't above making sure that particular excrement rolled downhill to us.

Realistically, any tools that enabled us to do our job, without having to directly confront and annoy people was a godsend. Powers brought a keen mind, youthful enthusiasm and a relentlessly cheerful attitude to the table but redeemed himself by being able to understand computers. And other tech. And social media and all the rest of it.

"Doyle!" he pushed a chair towards me and gestured at his companion. "This is Noel, a friend of mine from college. Noel works for Systems Ireland Computing but he's on secondment to the Bank of Leinster."

"System Ireland has the contract to fix the problems in the IT department," Noel interrupted, grinning. "Darren asked me to show him the systems and talk him through it."

"Marie Flynn was there too. You know, the receptionist? She was able to show me all the scheduling and admin stuff." I've no idea why Powers grinned at me as he said that. I ignored the fatuous eejit and addressed myself to Noel.

"So, you understand how this famous clock organizes everything? I understand it's all to do with time keeping for security logs and -" Noel was openly laughing.

"I take it I'm talking nonsense?" Noel and Powers exchanged smug looks.

"Yeah," said Noel, "they're very proud of the fact that all the bank computers are set by the analogue clock. 'We're as reliable as our clock, was as reliable at the founding of our state as it is today' blah blah . . . it's all bollix mate, sorry."

"But it does do something. Otherwise why bother changing it?"

Noel and Powers looked at each other again and Noel gave a tiny nod.

"We-ell," Powers launched himself into an explanation. Experience had taught me not to interrupt him. Powers had his own way of giving information and derailing him just meant he'd start again at the beginning.

"At first glance it's all very standard. Except their data protection is crap, I'm glad they're not my bank I can tell you. It would be fairly easy to achieve a massive data breech…but anyway, that's not our problem."

He dragged himself back on subject and continued. "Once upon a time, like fifty years ago, the bank had a single large mainframe computer. By large I mean it physically took up a lot of room, like half an office floor, but it wouldn't have the computing power of the phone in your pocket. Every morning its RTC would be set from the -"

"RTC?"

"'Real Time Clock'" and it would be set by the big wall clock in head office.

"There were two clocks?"

"Sorry, yeah. You know every computer needs a clock? The RTC is the clock in the computer. These days though, there are thousands of computers in the organization, and many of those aren't physical computers, they run in the cloud, and in fact these days a lot of them aren't event virtual computers, a lot of the work is done in service fabric layers and lambda functions-"

"Powers, the clock?" I know where these asides can go.

""Right, yeah, the clock. Right, so all those computers talking together, all the time, communicating together . . . knowing how long each request asking for information takes – from one computer to another, when it was requested, when it arrived, when data was sent to a database, when was it saved, when was it updated, when who logged in, who asked for which data and when . . . all of these computers have to be running on exactly the same time, or as exactly as we can make it".

"And by exactly, you mean to the millisecond?"

"Yeah, or better if we can. If these were all out by as much as one hundredth of a second, the whole system would break down." Noel interjected. "So believe me when I say that the entire system is more certainly not run by that old yoke."

I chewed this over for a minute then gave in. "Okay what am I missing?" Cos this pair of grinning loons were far too pleased with themselves for that to be the full story.

"Noel here did a deep dive for me. We know what the clock couldn't do, but somewhere in the mess that passes for a system in the Bank had to be the answer to what it *can* do. What we were looking for were any basic systems linked to that clock, not the high-tech stuff. And we found it. Some bright spark made a decision years ago to link the vaults overnight security to that clock."

He looked at me expectantly but sighed at my blank face.

"The clock controls the vaults from 8 pm to 8 am. Literally, you can't open them without individual codes, and only a handful of people have access to them. You need two people, with separate codes to open the system again. Once it would have been possible to over-ride but a few years ago they tightened it up again to prevent tiger kidnapping."

It made sense – tiger kidnapping had become an all too familiar part of the Irish crime landscape in recent years. Thugs would break into a bank official's house, threaten their family and hold them hostage until the official opened up the bank safe and got the contents for the kidnappers. Banks had become increasingly careful about access as a result and most had systems that refused entry overnight, or limited access at all times.

"Now, that's fairly normal." Noel said. "In most branches where actual cash is stored, there are lots of similar fail-safe methods. But the HQ doesn't have cash in its vaults. It has a safe deposit vault, full of all kinds of things. I asked around and according to some of the older generation, the ones there since before we were born, this vault is something special. It's where all the boxes from older branches, boxes that have been abandoned or the person died or the branch has closed down, are stored."

"There are boxes down there going back 180 years, Doyle. Boxes they took over from old private banks that are long gone, bought up by Leinster Bank." Powers said. "There could be literally anything down there. Marie pulled up records going back donkeys' years but the majority of old boxes – about three hundred of them - were placed there somewhere between the end of world war two and the seventies. There are some that not even the bank knows the contents of, and some that were handed down in families, until the last heir died. Anyway, access to them is controlled by the clock system now."

"That's not all, Powers, tell him."

"It also controls access to some of the secure areas, including an office where old mortgage deeds, valuable papers, loan agreements, that sort of thing are stored. There are some very important records in there, from what we can see. And none of them computerized, from what we can see."

"And the whole system controls…" Noel consulted a sheet of scribbles, "…the three steel security gates between the lobby and the vaults, and the secure areas. The cameras and other security measures are on different, independent systems. But they're accessible through the main system. I figure whoever disabled the CCTV cameras accessed them that way. But the rest, the security doors and the vaults, that was done by disabling the clock."

I stared at him doubtfully. "That's a very old clock," I objected but he cut me off impatiently.

"What you see when you look at the clock is a façade, the old analogue clock face, giant second and minute hands turning around – behind that is quite a modern mechanism, linked to various parts of the system." He was speaking slowly and clearly, obviously dumbing it down for the dinosaur here. "It was very sophisticated and cutting edge ten, even fifteen years ago although it looks antique now. But it's effective. From eight pm to eight am, the only people who can access those areas for any reason are Board members and anything they do is logged with individual codes."

Light began to dawn. "What you're saying is, if Sean O'Dwyer decides to check out a deed held as collateral by one of his developer buddies after hours, he needs another Board member, and both codes, which are immediately logged by the system?"

Something was taking shape in my head.

"OK, if the clock is disrupted…"

Darren grinned at me. I felt like a slow but hardworking pupil who has finally managed to grasp the subject. "Bingo! Disrupting the clock means no codes are logged, and no one can tell who accessed the vault. It took a bit of digging, but it's all there in the system records. If there's a power cut, for example, the clock is offline for a while until a backup battery kicks in. The power source for that is safely tucked away in the Records Office at the end of that corridor. Between the main source going and the back up kicking in is about thirty seconds, all told. Now, Marie and myself did a wee experiment-"

"Marie Flynn?" It was well for some, playing games with good looking women as part of their investigations.

"Yeah, Marie. She stood by the first steel door, on this corridor here,"

He thrust a diagram at me, that looked less like a floor plan and more like kindergarten art. There were three "x" marks at intervals along the corridor, the corridor itself running straight for about three-quarters of its length, with two X's and then turning sharply right. At the end of this shorter length was small foyer, and a final x marking the steel door that led to the vaults, and their cache of security boxes.

"If you stop after the second X," Power explained, "There's a door leading the Records office, there's a clerk there during the day and that's where the records of land deals and so on are kept. At night it's locked but just an ordinary Yale lock. Before you ask, it was forced. "

"Once we knew what we were looking at, Noel disabled the vault doors so we could see if it was possible to get them wedged open in the time." I carefully avoided asking if that was strictly speaking, legal. Or a firing offense. Sometimes you had to be practical about these things.

"Now, when we timed it, Marie got from the first steel door to the last in under 20 seconds. Say, the clock was put out of commission, the power cut to the system. Each of those doors clicks "unlocked" but don't actually move unless you push against them. If someone ran from one end of the corridor to the other, pushing each door as they went and placing something in front of them, a wedge or similar to hold it open, they can open all three doors. Access to everything, no records."

"And then, on the way out, they remove each wedge…." I said slowly, "and each door slammed shut as if nothing happened."

"No traces. Except, if you also temporarily disable the back up, you've plenty of time to remove anything you need, then set the whole system off again. The only tell-tale sign is, the clock hands stopped turning while you worked, and when you reset, the clock is a tiny bit slow. As long as the back up is disabled, the clock hands don't turn," Fellows finished triumphantly.

"The mystery of the perfect clock. At least we've cleared something up. Well done, mate. That's the first actual damn break we've made in this case.

Finally, something!"

He flushed. "Thanks," trying to sound gruff and nonchalant, he shuffled the sheets of notes and calculations.

"This is your baby, Darren. Find out if there's some way of determining which they were after, the offices or the vaults. Or both. And Noel, thank you. We owe you one. And I'd appreciate it if you'd keep an eye out in there, anything else you notice that might help would be gratefully received."

"Already on it. Oh, by the way, Marie was asking after you."

Oh.

"Yeah?" I made a stab at gruff and nonchalant myself. "What about?"

Noel shrugged. "Not about anything in particular, I think. She just asked how you were. She said she would be calling into the hospital later to see how Tomas Warskowski is doing. His fiancée is due in tonight."

"Fine, thanks. I might try to catch her there then. In case she's remembered something." It was lame, even to my own ears and Powers shot me a skeptical look. But it couldn't hurt to call in. It didn't mean anything.

Chapter Eighteen

Even under harsh hospital lighting and obviously tired, Ms. Flynn looked pretty. She had a face that was interesting, as much as anything, with angles and cheekbones and her eyes were a warm amber brown. She had dark hair worn in a professional looking bun thing – what my ex used to call a chignon, if I wasn't mistaken. It was the first time I'd seen her out of uniform, she looked cool and edgy and much younger. I sighed. No point in kidding myself, she was exactly the type of woman who wouldn't look twice at an awkward gimp of a fellow like me.

Anyway, it was highly unprofessional to even think that way about a witness in a murder case. All my life I've seen guys hit on women when they're vulnerable, exploiting every insecurity or heartbreak. Yes, Marie was lovely but Jaysus, I refuse to be that guy. I stuck a professional expression on my face and approached her, choosing the next seat but one to her on the row of anchored together, plastic bucket chairs.

"Ms Flynn? Hi, sorry to intrude…"

"Oh! Hi, you're not intruding. She started to stuff something back in an over-sized bag, a slightly embarrassed air to the action. It was a brightly coloured, woollen item, with at least three different coloured strands of yarn attached to it and a large pair of wooden knitting needles stuck firmly into it.

"My knitting," she said, seeing me look. "I bring it everywhere. Well, anywhere I know I have to wait any length of time. Better than staring a phone."

"My mother knits," I blurted out. I tried to save it by adding, "Not that only old people knit or anything. Just she happens to knit. Lots of young people knit."

I'm not sure that improved it. But at least she laughed. "Oh, knitting is huge right now, I know so many people who knit and crochet. It's definitely not an old folk's hobby any longer. Having said that it's inspiring to see what older knitters can do, they can make stuff in their sleep that would take me months."

"You like...what's the word? Crafty stuff?"

"I love it," She was unself-consciously enthusiastic, shifting a little in her seat to face me and holding up her two hands to show off an array of silver jewellery. A delicate snake coiled itself around one finger, while another boasted a knuckle duster of a ring, that covered from base to knuckle. One ring was set with an amber stone and yet another had an intricate design that people lumped under "Celtic" art. She had a few silver bangles as well and shook her head to show her earrings. They were attached to the top of her ear by a cuff, and from the lobe a trio of tiny silver bells dangled.

"Listen!" She leaned forward, and I caught a light fragrance from her skin. There was the tiniest tinkle of sound from the earring bells. "I'm a silversmith. I make jewellery."

"That is seriously impressive. They're amazing." It seemed churlish not to share in return. "I actually, um, do a bit of carpentry."

"Oh wow! Do you have any pictures? I love carpentry but I'm no good at it myself. What had you made?"

Feeling a bit foolish I took out my phone and flicked through some photos until I found a good shot. "It's not professional quality, not like your jewellery, but this turned out well."

A year ago, I had found the time to build a cabinet for my parents, a sort of wedding anniversary gift. They were married 45 years, but both insisted that anniversaries and birthdays were silly things to fuss over and we – my sister Deirbhle and I – rarely gave them gifts. I only made an exception that time because I wanted an excuse to make a cabinet and it wouldn't suit my rather soulless apartment.

"Oh, that is gorgeous," She smiled at me. "You're being far too modest."

I stuck the phone back in my pocket, trying to remember that stern professionalism was in order, not exchanging hobby preferences. Although I was too curious not to ask, "Tell me then, what are you doing stuck behind that desk in the Leinster? You should be making your rings and things."

Somewhere in most social conversations I become aware that I've put my foot in it, or said something too blunt, but I don't usually make people cry. To my horror, Marie's eyes filled with tears, and she looked so sad, I could have thumped myself.

"Sorry!" I began but she shook her head vehemently.

"No, no, don't be. It's not your fault. I'm sorry, it's so stupid. I'm just a bit down tonight and it's – well, it's a sore subject. I used to be a jeweller. I had a workshop, I sold online, and I was getting into some of the very good shops. All my own designs, and all handmade…Oh! I loved it. But, well, I also used to be married and when it broke up, I had to find regular paid work. Temping was the fastest easiest way."

"That's rough." I filed away the nugget that she'd been married. She seemed so young to have a divorce under her belt already. It had to be hard, most people in their thirties here were only settling down and she had to go through a breakup. As it still took almost 5 years to get a divorce, it was never an easy experience.

A wan smile. "Yeah, it was. Declan, my ex, he was a gambler. And a drinker. And if we're going to be completely honest, a cheating lying low-life." She looked away, memories obviously catching her attention. "He left me with a load of debt. Signed my name everywhere, ran up a credit card bill you can't even imagine. I lost the workshop, the stock had to be sold off to pay some of the debts. We lost the house, he stopped paying the mortgage on it. I sold everything, including my car. And now he's shacked up with a young one down in Waterford, living the life of Reilly on her trust fund and I'm working as a temp receptionist and there are dead bodies in conference rooms and work colleagues in hospital."

Without thinking, I patted her shoulder. Normally I wouldn't touch someone without asking but I felt like she was a friend. Then I caught myself and had a vision of Graves or Locke and the faces on them if they had seen me. "Sorry" I muttered.

She smiled, a real one this time. "It's OK. I should say sorry, for dumping all this on you. I honestly do not usually vomit personal information on people!"

"It's the hospital," I assured her, a bit pleased that she felt she could tell me things. Most people have the opposite reaction unless we're in an interrogation room and I have evidence. "It makes people feel vulnerable. I've noticed it before. How is Tomas, any word?"

"He's no better, but then again I suppose he's no worse. Milena is flying in tonight -well, she's probably at the airport now. I offered to meet her off the plane, but she asked me to stay with Tomas, she is terrified something will happen and he'll be all alone."

"Jesus. The poor girl. I'll have to have a word with her, but maybe tonight's not the time."

"I dunno, wait til she gets here," Marie suggested, "She seems like a sensible, capable girl to me. I think she'd sooner get it over with and help if she can."

"I'll wait then."

Marie took out the knitting again and started to click-click, needles flashing, brightly dyed yarn feeding out of the bag at her feet. There was something companionable and soothing about the sound. We kept up an easy flow of chat, another thing I wouldn't usually enjoy but she was good company. And even prettier up close, when she was animated and smiling.

Good job I was a professional and completely immune to things like that.

The light faded quickly outside and the lights of the city were visible from the waiting room windows. It was a blustery, cloudy night and the wind kept up a keening wail that lent an eerie, otherworldly feeling to the place. I was happy enough to be indoors, chatting in murmurs and admiring the progress of Marie's work.

The sound of raised voices cut across the relative peace of the Intensive care ward waiting room, and a dark-haired woman entered through the swinging doors, short and plump with a sweet face, dressed in jeans and a jacket that looked too big for her. She looked like a child playing adult dress up from a distance. The nurse at the nurses' station gave her a hard stare, obviously thinking along similar lines. She discovered her mistake when the girl said in clear, forceful tones, "I am Milena Zielińska, I am here to see my fiancé, Tomas Warskowski. I am to speak to Dr Mahmud, Dr Nasim Mahmud."

"Milena?" Marie jumped up immediately. The other woman turned sharply then smiled and held out her hands. "Marie? Oh, thank you so much, so much." She flung her arms around Marie and hugged her fiercely. "I cannot thank you enough! My poor Tomas, he would have died if you had not gone to check on him. Dr Mahmud tells me so, and it is true. He said Tomas only has a chance because of you." Marie flushed and tried to demur, but Milena swept on. "You are his guardian angel. I am so grateful to you."

"Milena, I – I don't know how much they told you but, well, it's very serious. Tomas was very badly hurt. He might not…well, it's still touch and go."

Milena shook her head firmly. "No. I am here now, and he will get better. I couldn't come earlier because of my poor mother, but my cousins have come, and they will mind her. She told me, go to Tomas so he will get better. I'm here now." The nurse met my eyes and shook her head sadly. My heart ached for the poor girl; she was so certain that her Tomas would recover through her sheer force of will. And she had left her dying mother only to visit a man who would probably pass himself soon. What a choice.

Marie hugged her again. "You go into him, Milena. Have you your bags?"

Milena indicated the small hold-all she had carried into the waiting room. "That is all I need."

Marie picked it up. "OK, well you have the address – here's the spare key. You come and go as you need, and I'll catch you in the morning."

Milena disappeared with the nurse, into the darkened hush of the ICU.

"She's staying with you?"

Marie nodded. "It was the least I could do. She's awfully nice, anyway. We've been chatting on the phone a lot, so I feel like I know her."

"I'll give you a lift then." I was rewarded with a huge smile and to my surprise, a sort of quick arm hug. I am usually allergic to touchy feely people, the huggers and kissers of the world, but Marie Flynn was as genuine as they came, so it wasn't cringy.

And I am, I reminded myself, a hardened professional.

We drove through Dublin evening traffic (not quite as horrendous as Dublin all day traffic but close) until we reached her home, a small, terraced house in one of Dublin's less leafy suburbs. A solidly working-class area, with a mix of community minded, reliable hard-working people and a minority of drug dealers and hard men who gave the area its bad name. I grew up for a while in a slightly nicer version, in a country town, where my dad was the local sergeant before his promotion. Same kind of houses, mass built in the nineteen sixties and seventies by the local council or corporation. Same shops, same graffiti, same air of neglect.

It wasn't where I would have placed Marie Flynn.

"This is me," she said cheerfully. "I'd invite you in, but the flat-mates are probably smoking dodgy cigarettes in the kitchen."

"That's OK, I can see how a detective strolling in would cramp their style!"

She burst out laughing. "Does nothing phase you at all? I'm only joking about the hash, they're a pair of strait-laced serious hipster types, it's all vegan food and environmentally friendly cleaning products in there. But they're nice and they don't seem to mind sharing with a geriatric like me, which is rare indeed. I looked at about 20 places before I finally got a room here."

"If you don't mind me saying, it seems very unfair. Your ex-husband shouldn't expect you to pay his debts."

A wry expression crossed her face. "I suppose I could have pushed back, fought harder, you know? But I hadn't the heart. It was so depressing, all the years together just thrown away. I just wanted to get out and I couldn't bear thinking about how many people he had cheated. People I know. I had friends who lent him money, invested in his schemes and they haven't spoken to me since the break-up. They can't believe I didn't know."

"Karen – my ex-girlfriend…" Once again, I found myself volunteering personal information to this woman, "she told everyone after the break-up that it was my fault, how useless and difficult I was to live with. I'm not the best but I know I didn't do half the things she claimed. Like, the evenings I came home and cooked for both of us, only for her to ring from a pub saying she'd popped out after work. I never complained, because I don't think anyone should have to get permission to go out, from their partner. But one night I asked her could she text me, just to let me know before I cooked. She told everyone I was rigid and controlling. Friends said to my face that they could imagine me behaving like that. I gave up arguing. I just wanted her to move on and leave me alone, by the end of it."

That was the longest I'd ever talked about myself or a relationship to another person, besides my sister. And I'd blurted out how my ex found me controlling. What a player.

"Ah, the old reverse accusation," Marie nodded wisely. "Derek did that too. Accuse you of something they're guilty of, and make it look like you're the one with the problem. Gas-lighting, it's called. You're well out of that."

I laughed shortly. "Yeah, that's for sure. You too. He sounds like a complete eejit."

"Well, if you ever want to compare horror exes again, give me a ring," She closed the door and gave me a thumbs up. "Ring me anyway."

Ring her.

Did she mean that, I wondered, watching her let herself into the house, or was it a polite convention that people said, without thinking? I made a mental note to ask Paula. She could usually translate for me.

Chapter Nineteen

Paula Hughes

Monday morning, just over a week since the murder, and even the weather was against us. We were back in the office, rain pelting off the windows from a sky that was a sea of rolling grey clouds. Autumn was taking hold on the city, despite the occasional sunny days. After the lovely weekend weather, it was a shock to the system, and we all felt it. Caroline was due to meet Derek Fields and some political cronies in the Huguenot, a new and very posh restaurant on Baggot Street, so she had opted to meet us in the office first.

"Look at that," she said disgustedly, pointing at the rain. "I've to go out in that. It's a cosmic joke."

I hadn't an ounce of sympathy. She was at least off to discuss interesting current events with Derek whereas I was facing into a couple of hours in the company of the obnoxious JJ McDonnell, to try to nail down this benighted In-House Magazine, or as Stephen termed it, "the Best Budgets Vanity Project."

If they'd gone the e-zine route it would have been an interesting project. Hell, I could have coped with the old-fashioned glossy magazine if it hadn't been for McDonnell. While he had restrained himself from making more overt sexual comments since our last lunch date, probably out of sheer fear of Caroline, he was picky, capricious and a general pain in the hole to work with. He wanted no input from us into content, and God alone knows what rubbish he'd fill it with. Every suggestion for launching and promoting it was met with sullen resentment and a counter suggestion of such inappropriateness that I was often left speechless.

When we communicated by email, it was bad enough but face to face left little time to find the right, tactful, words to massage his ego and I felt as if I was floundering badly. It was depressing, considering the number of far bigger, more public events I had managed perfectly well. His constant nit-picking was getting to me.

Caroline would have waded in on my behalf if I'd asked but that felt a bit too much like admitting I couldn't cope.

Stephen was sympathetic but he'd never had to deal with this. Men don't generally compliment other men in a sleazy way, imply they are useless at their job, and then patronize them with a backhanded compliment. When I repeated the exchanges between us, they felt trivial even to my own ears, let alone anyone else. Stephen must have thought I was being fierce sensitive.

"When you dislike someone, everything they do and say grates on your nerves, pet," My mother said when I told her. "You just have to shrug it off. Sure, you've dealt with gobdaws like that before."

So, with a knot in my stomach, I set out to meet McDonnell in the Best Budgets Head office, a grey and uncompromising building in a large industrial park on the outskirts of South Dublin. Parking was a nightmare; some genius had placed the car-park a quarter of a mile from the building and then carefully removed any trace of shade or shelter from the area. The cars baked in summer, so you got hit by a wall of heat and in bad weather you got soaked just getting from the car to the front door.

The building had a revolving door at the front and then another glass door a few feet away – making it even more difficult to get in especially with numb fingers and an armful of marketing materials. A man was peering in the door, obviously as lost as I had been in the grey concrete industrial estate; luckily for me he leapt forward and held the doors steady, flashing me a wry smile.

By the time I half fell into the lobby, losing the battle with the revolving door, I was wet, cold and already tired of the whole business. I marched up to the reception desk and had just started the mantra, "Jordan PR for JJ

McDonnell," when my brain caught up with my eyes.

Marie Flynn stood behind the desk, and for a horrible moment I thought I had driven to the Bank of Leinster by mistake. Considering we were all consumed by the upcoming Bank pitch, it was a distinct possibility. Then I remembered the ten-minute trek across the concrete clutching my files and case.

"Marie?"

"Oh hi!" She seemed genuinely pleased to see a familiar face. "It's Paula, isn't it? I mean, Ms. Hughes."

"Call me Paula, for heaven's sake. What on earth are you doing here? You've left the Bank?"

She flushed. "It's more the Bank left me. I got a call from my agency last night, telling me that I wasn't needed there anymore and to present myself here instead first thing this morning."

"You're kidding?" I mean, I knew the Bank employed people on terms that were a national disgrace, filling positions with temporary staff and using every loophole possible to avoid unionization, but this was high handed in the extreme.

Marie lowered her voice, despite the tiny foyer being empty besides ourselves. "It's not just me. Milena told me they terminated Tomas' contract too, and him still in a coma."

"Oh my god. That's cold. You're probably better off away from them, but it's a nasty way to treat people. Especially after what happened,"

"I think that's why. I think they want us gone, like we're reminders of it or something. Distance themselves from us."

I thought about it. "Yet they're calling in Jordan PR for a pitch and half promising it to us…"

"Well, that'll keep ye on side, won't it? They can't silence you, but they can get rid of Tomas and me. To keep you sweet, they offer you a chance at the contract."

"Jesus wept." A happier thought occurred to me, "Marie, are you interested in a full-time position?"

"Interested? I'd kill my own granny and sell yours for a permanent job."

"Okay then. Look, we desperately need a receptionist and office manager. The money would be OK, and as we grow it'll get better. We aren't hiring until we secure this Bank contract, but if we get it, what do you think?"

Her face lit up. "Oh please, if there's any chance, please consider me. I can email you my CV if that helps? Literally, I will do anything you need. I'm a decent hand at general admin, I can use a computer, I can handle any graphics packages and photoshop, and I'm good with people."

"I need to run it by Caroline," I fished a slightly damp business card out of my pocket. "Here, email me your CV, but all going well I think you'd be ideal."

Marie promised to get the email to me that evening, then buzzed JJ to come collect me from the lobby. "He's some prize isn't he," she whispered. "I've already had to quote the Sexual Harassment in the Workplace act to him twice this morning."

JJ bustled up to the desk, ignored me completely and smirked at Marie. "Well, hello again! You missed me already, eh?"

"Ms. Hughes from Jordan PR," she replied primly.

He glanced at me over his shoulder. "You're late," he pointed out.

"Sorry, the traffic-"

"I don't need excuses," said the man who had been over 45 minutes late for our last meeting. "Come on."

From this ungracious opening, I guessed JJ wasn't in his best mood. An hour passed in interminable wrangling over tiny details, details I knew I would have to run past him at least once more, and in writing, to be sure he didn't deny agreeing to them. Finally, I closed my notebook firmly and stood up.

"Well, we're nearly there," Fake positivity was a good way to ignore his behaviour. "Thanks for your time, JJ, I'll get this into a memo and email it over to you this afternoon. You need to decide on a venue, if you could look at the suggestions in my last email? Thanks."

Before I could make it to the door, he asked sullenly, "Is this how you treat all your clients? Not even a bit of chit chat before you run out the door?"

Choking down an "*Oh, sod off*," I managed what I hoped was a polite smile.

"Oh, I'm so sorry, JJ. I have another meeting in about fifteen minutes and traffic is horrendous today. Let's have lunch next time, in town? There's a lovely place opened up near us, let Jordan PR treat you."

He "harrumphed" but appeared mollified. "Well, I'll hold you to that." The leer was back, and it made my skin crawl a bit, but at least he wasn't likely to renege on everything we agreed just for spite.

Marie was busy dealing with a call as I exited but she gave me a happy wave as I passed. The more I considered it the more I liked the idea of hiring her. Please let us get this bank job, I prayed to the gods of PR. The difference it would make to our finances was impossible to overstate. And I had a kind of fellow feeling with her, as someone who had witnessed that appalling scene. That reminded me, I had promised Stephen to tell Doyle about the incident at Howard's Castle. Even leaving aside my own nasty experience, we should update Doyle on the weekend, especially our suspicions about Murrough.

It would while away the next hour in traffic, at any rate. I stuck the hands-free set on and listened to Doyle's number ring out. Then his recorded voice barked out,

"DS Alan Doyle, leave a message."

"Janey Mac, Alan," I winced. "You'd want to change that voicemail message, it doesn't exactly encourage people to ring you. It's Paula here, give me a ring when you have a chance."

Two sets of traffic lights later he rang back.

"Is it that bad?"

"It is. Change it. Say something like DS Doyle, I'm sorry I can't take your call but if you leave a message, I'll get back to you…that class of a thing."

"Thanks." There was a slight pause. Dear god, I realized, the man was writing it down. "OK. Anyway, what's up?"

"Want to hear about my weekend?" Caroline found Doyle exasperating, but I liked talking to him. He was surprisingly open to things a lot of guys didn't like to discuss, and despite his lack of social graces, he was a decent, caring person underneath. I wished Caroline could see past the brusque manner. We emailed regularly, and Stephen was always after him to come over for dinner some night.

"Hit me. Wait, this is Howard Castle Hideaway, right? OK, in that case I *am* interested."

I rolled my eyes so hard I'm surprised he couldn't sense it down the line.

"Well, where to start…" There was no point burdening Alan with descriptions of the castle, or details of the exhibition, so I skipped to a character sketch of each of the main players. He interrupted occasionally to ask questions but mainly I talked, and he took notes. I was almost back at the office, when I got to my adventures with the mysterious intruder.

"For the love of – next time lead with that, Paula. Are you OK?"

"Yeah. Like, it was a fright, and to be honest I'm glad we were leaving that evening. I wouldn't have liked to stay on wondering if someone was about to jump at me out of the dark. And a lot of that castle is dark, let me tell you."

"But you're not hurt? I'm sorry, it never occurred to me those files would put you in danger."

"Caroline thinks it might have been her comment to Murrough Loxburg about the clock."

"Hmm. Mr. Loxburg bears close watching. Anyway, thanks, that's all helpful. What did you make of Simon Prendergast?"

Simon? "He's very jealous, hates anyone being praised, watches Charlie Loxburg like a hawk. But he has nothing to do with the Bank surely?"

"He has close ties to Sean O'Dwyer and his party." Doyle said. "Banking, Politics, this arty crowd. They're all tied up together. Of course, he knows Peter O'Dwyer well."

It took me a moment. "Peter? Leslie Howard's boyfriend?"

"Yes." He sounded surprised. "Didn't you know? Peter is Sean O'Dwyer's son."

No. We had no idea. I thought back to the hand pushing my face into the floor, the rasping voice in my ear. Could it have been? He certainly spoke so rarely I might not recognize his voice easily. But he seemed so nice.

"Peter wouldn't like us nosing around his father's business." We'd seen first hand what a son of a powerful, rich man could do.

"Don't leap to conclusions," warned Alan, "If it makes you feel better, Peter and his father are not meant to be on the best of terms. At any rate, don't worry about it. I'll have a word with the locals who answered the call to Howard Castle, see what they've come up with."

"Thanks. I'd better go. Oh! I've an event in a few weeks, that trad band you like is playing at it. The long haired ones with the electric fiddle." To me they sounded like scalded cats, but Doyle assured me they were the future of Irish music. "Will I put your name at the door?"

"Oh. Ah yeah. I'd like that." He paused. "Um. Can I bring someone?"

Chapter Twenty

Caroline Jordan

I was certainly paying for having taken the weekend to go to Howard Castle.

Derek had a mountain of queries, plus a load of small but crucial nuggets of information to impart and top of the list was Bank reform. Hence this lunch at The Huguenot, one of the most exclusive eateries on the south side of the city, almost opposite the tiny cemetery for seventeenth century Huguenot refugees. It was an open, airy space with polished wood surfaces, linen tablecloths and heavy, folded napkins. Crystal glasses and shiny silver cutlery, and an air of post -funereal cheer. The Maitre D' eyed me with contempt but allowed me enter. I am reasonably sure he counted the silverware on the table though.

Derek arrived with the Minister for Finance, Una Linehan and Peadar Moriarty, an economist who was constantly quoted in articles on the state of the nation's bank balance. I'd quoted him myself a few times, when his pronouncements happened to coincide with the required narrative. Una was young for a Minister, and very sharp. She had a keen sense of optics too and had carefully constructed an image for herself of an attractive, intelligent woman who was above all, a safe bet. *"Conscientious, reliable, and trustworthy,"* one of our leading journalists had termed her.

Peadar had a reputation as a bit of a maverick, usually bucking whatever was the current trend. He prophesied doom and gloom usually, and of course eventually he turned out to be right and everyone applauded his foresight.

In fairness to him, he was among the more upright of our political pundits, some of them would write anything for a decent sized cheque. His brutal honesty had earned him a number of enemies, which frankly endeared him to me. Derek had a high opinion of him. O'Mahony respected him but had been known to roll his eyes at the inevitable "I can't advise tax cuts," response from Peadar to any degree of fiscal generosity in the budget.

"Bank reform," Derek had waited until the pleasantries were over before launching into his pet project. "Una, would you like to start?"

Linehan's eyes lit up. "Bank reform is so long overdue, Derek, so long." After that, words like "fitness and probity" and "transparency of procedures" and "monitoring compliance" were bandied about. It was clearly a topic on which she was well informed. Her enthusiasm for the reform programme seemed genuine.

"Accountability is key!" Una finished up, her salmon and cream cheese still untouched on her plate. She smiled suddenly and acknowledged, "I know I get on my hobby horse about it, but let's be clear, it's the single most important issue for our economy at present. We need to repair the damage of recent years."

She talked in soundbites but managed to make them sound sincere and convincing. She would make a great client, if I could get her on board.

"And Peadar, you're unusually quiet?" Derek caught my eye and there was the ghost of a wink. "I take it you're optimistic about this reform package?"

Outraged, our nation's Most Serious Economist put aside his Hake fillet with rosemary and dill salad and sat upright. "I wouldn't say "optimistic" Derek!" he exclaimed in horror, and then went on to explain how while Una was right in everything she wanted to reform, there were a million or so reasons why those reforms might or might not work.

I wished I had had the foresight to order a vodka and sprite rather than a mineral water.

"We are facing an antiquated system, Derek, and an almost sinister code of Omerta among senior banking officials."

Steady on, Peadar, I thought. That was some allegation. I glanced at Derek, but to my surprise he was nodding. "I agree, Peadar, there is a rotten culture at the heart of banking in this country. We need to pull them under the direct control of the Central Bank, with stringent measures and penalties in place. That's what they'll resent the most and it will be real reason they oppose reform." Derek touched Peadar's arm in a fatherly gesture. "We rely on you, Peadar, to expose that in the public arena. No one can explain better than you why Bank reform is in the best interest of the ordinary person."

Peadar puffed up a little. "Well, I like to think I have something to contribute albeit small," he demurred modestly.

"You're key to our success, Peadar, and we will *be* successful." Derek said firmly. "We have been lucky enough to receive an overwhelming vote of confidence in the last election, and we shall not waste this opportunity. There are a lot of things that we need to reform in this country. We're starting with Banking, but great changes lie ahead in every way."

Both the Minister and the economist nodded enthusiastically. It might not last until they got back to their comfy offices but right now, they were revolutionaries fighting for the common good. Even my tarnished soul felt it.

As the talk turned to less weighty topics, I thought of something. "Minister," I turned to Una who interrupted me immediately to say "Call me Una."

"Una. In these proposed reforms, has anything been mentioned about Bank Vaults? Historic ones I mean, the old ones that are abandoned or waiting on heirs to come forward? Or left over from closed branches. That kind of thing."

She looked faintly surprised but said, "Well yes, now you ask. It's only a footnote I suppose, it's not a huge issue - but yes, we're planning to make provision for them."

"Do you mind my asking, what kind of provision?"

"Opening them, in short. That's what it will boil down to. A lot of them need to be opened, the contents examined, and attempts made to trace ownership. Heaven alone knows what's in most of them. I've been told there are boxes dating back 200 years. Apparently, officials have just ignored them, people inherited entire estates without being informed of the existence of a bank vault or security box!" She was warming to the subject, "There are supposed to be paintings, gold, and it might be fanciful, but it's possible there are confessions."

"Confessions?"

"From the Civil War, maybe even the War of Independence. Men and women did things that were necessary, but they believed endangered their immortal souls. Some of these things were State secrets. They wouldn't break the oath not to reveal them, but some wrote confessions on their death beds and they or in some cases their family, deposited them in security boxes. Imagine the contribution to history?"

Peadar interrupted. "Now you mention it, I know for a fact that my uncle took confessions from old IRA men and women, in the 60s and 70s. He said he put them in safe keeping, which probably meant his monastery but might have been a bank deposit for all we know."

"There you go. No doubt those vaults are full of things like that."

"How many do you think there are? Abandoned boxes and vaults I mean?"

"Thousands," Una waved her hands, "Thousands. I bet there's illegal stuff too – my researcher claims there are rumours about guns and cocaine stashes, left for decades as the owner cools their heels in prison. Or maybe dead, and no one knew where they stashed the stuff."

Derek and I walked back to the Department of An Taoiseach, it being only ten minutes from the restaurant. Una Linehan had accepted an invitation from me to lunch the following week, which was a positive development. Derek was in great form, the prospect of a good fight always appealed to him.

"By the way, Caroline," he asked suddenly, "What was all that about Bank Vaults?"

"Something. Nothing. Probably nothing. I have to tell you about our weekend in Howard Castle, Derek."

He gave a short laugh, "You met Murrough Loxburg, I take it."

"Full marks. Yeah, lovely bloke. Sinister, right wing racist homophobe with questionable taste in women."

"Tell me all,"

By the time I'd recounted the story, leaving out the endless planning meeting about the Exhibition but including Murrough's romantic tryst in the gardens with Diane Howard, Derek was silent and thoughtful.

"Well, it's not much, but for what it's worth, that's my impressions of them all."

We had reached the Offices some time before but had lingered outside to continue the conversation. Derek nodded, slowly. "It's valuable, Caroline. I knew Murrough had some links to what we might euphemistically term "conservative" elements but not that he was so openly vocal about them. It's also interesting that Simon Prendergast is not on good terms with him – there might be hope for that young man yet."

"Emily's a dark horse, too. Very opaque. She's political though, from what I heard. And she's got a strange relationship with both Murrough and Prendergast. An uneasy truce, I'd call it."

My phone pinged and I automatically glanced at it, in case it was important. It was from Paula, and read simply, "Peter Dwyer is Sean O'Dwyer's son."

"Derek, did you know this?" I showed the text to him.

He smiled. "Yes."

I rolled my eyes. "Every day's a test, eh?"

"Yes, Grasshopper." He opened the door and held it open for me, politely. "All things are connected, I keep telling you that."

Chapter Twenty-One

C*aroline Jordan*

"And Doyle said he'd check it out with the local cops," Paula finished recounting her trip to Best Budgets and chat with Alan. "What do you think about Marie Flynn?"

"Never mind Marie Flynn." My patience was not at its best. "You and Doyle, what's all this ringing each other and exchanging information?"

Paula rolled her eyes at me. "Honestly, Caro, will you give it a rest? Alan Doyle is a nice guy. Stephen and I happen to like him and," she added pointedly, "we're grateful to him even if you aren't."

"I am," I protested. Like, I feel genuinely awful about it, but I find him hard to take. The idea that my two best friends were on such close, personal terms with him was disconcerting. "He's always so...so rude to me. So snarky."

"No, Caro, he isn't. He's just not someone who smiles a lot and says meaningless pleasantries. He isn't full of bull either and he tries so hard to be friendly and nice to you. Okay, I'll admit it doesn't always come off right, but if you would only look properly, you'd see he is trying. Can you say the same?"

I stared at her. This was the second time she had inferred that I was wrong about Doyle, if by "inferred" you meant "told me outright."

"Look, Caro." I recognized her tone of voice as "patient," the one she usually kept for our difficult clients. "You think Doyle is weird because he doesn't think like you, he doesn't interact with other people like you. Ever think maybe, you're just as weird to him? You don't think or behave the way he does. Who died and made you the judge of what's the right way?"

That sneaky inner voice hissed "She has a point," and added *"PR Boss turns out to be wrong,"* for good measure but I wasn't ready to admit defeat yet.

"I think you'll find I'm in the majority," I answered, trying for an air of lofty certainty. "I am not saying Doyle has to change but he should maybe try conforming to what most people consider polite."

The words were no sooner out of my mouth than I regretted them. Having spent a large portion of my life from early teens onwards bucking against "the norm" and "conventions" that entire point of view on Doyle sounded hypocritical to say the least. Paula just laughed at me, which was fair enough.

"Cop yourself on," she said kindly. "And think about what I said. If you gave Doyle half a chance, he'd be a good mate to you."

Hmm. I would admit that I could make more of an effort and be less of a cow about it, but "mates" might be pushing it. Still, Paula was pretty much the best person I know so if she said try, I would give it a go.

"Well, back to Marie Flynn then," I sighed. "You think she'd fit in?"

"Don't you? I really like her, what I've seen of her. She's smart and creative. I reckon she could be an asset."

Marie had emailed her CV over before Paula had reached the tiny Jordan PR offices in the heart of the city. I clicked it open and read it again.

"It's some change though, from jeweller to receptionist. Wonder what the story is there? Her temping work has been mainly admin based, at least." I looked up and nodded. "Call her. If we get this contract, we'll offer her a 6-month trial and go from there."

Paula was delighted. But "I know what will wipe that smug grin off your face," I warned her. "Best Budgets 's finest, JJ McDonnell, has just emailed to say he wants you to bring over the amended proposal in person as soon as it's ready."

I realized she looked stricken. "Oh God no."

"You OK? Honestly, if he's being inappropriate…"

"No, no. I can manage. Just, he's difficult."

"Difficult? He's a creepy lech with the creative brainpower of a caterpillar."

Paula snorted, "It's okay, I can manage. Just, I thought Bank of Leinster were going to be a tough sell, but I would sooner deal with David Howard any day."

It surprised me again, how much she seemed to like Howard. "He's no different, not in reality. Just smoother," I remarked.

"That's unfair, Caroline," Paula took me more seriously that I had intended. "David was incredibly nice to me this weekend, when he didn't have to be. He's nothing like that - that pig McDonnell."

It wasn't like Paula to get so heated and after our recent conversation about judging people like Doyle, it made me uncomfortable. Maybe I was just a bitter cynical auld cow. Well, OK, *obviously* I'm bitter and cynical but maybe my judgment was a shade too harsh in this case.

"OK," I sighed dramatically, "You can have Howard. But come the revolution, when we smash the patriarchy to its knees, McDonnell is going to be first in the arena to face the lions."

Paula giggled. "Oh definitely. And wolves. Lions and wolves."

"Lions, wolves and Trained Seagulls, I'll train those evil devil seagulls from the mean streets of Dublin to attack men like JJ and peck at their willies." It would be a great investment of time and breadcrumbs, frankly.

Paula wandered back to her desk still laughing. Much as I wanted to concentrate on the Leinster pitch, it was hard not to mull over the events of the last week or so. Murrough Loxburg had got right under my skin; I'd bet my last euro he was as crooked and ruthless as – well, as the next crooked and ruthless banker. But did that mean he was a murderer and thief? Surely a man with his position in the Bank wouldn't be hanging corpses from chandeliers.

I forced myself back to work, armed with a lot of insight from Derek Fields on upcoming problems the Bank might face under new reforms, and permission to hint at them in the meeting. By the time we hit 6 pm I was satisfied. If we did get the summons on short notice, everything was in place. Murrough would doubtless expect a favour in return, but such was life. He could expect all he wanted.

Paula popped her head around the door, looking worried. "Caro, I've a woman on hold. She's from the Evening News, and she's dead pushy. Margo

Kealy."

I groaned. It was too much to hope that we would have avoided the press interest completely but by being completely unavailable since the tragedy, most had given up. My reputation and the fact they were afraid that I would hold a grudge and never let them inside Leinster House again, had helped. But this one had rung a few times, and bitter experience had taught me that a journalist like that would eventually write something, anything, if they didn't get their own way.

On her own head be it, I thought, signaling to Paula to put her through. I have a reputation for holding a grudge because I often hold one.

"Yes?" I aimed for curt and hit it.

"Oh. Is that Caroline?" she sounded surprised. My finally answering her call had caught her off guard. "This is Margo Kealy. We met once or twice, I don't know if you remember."

If I though hard, a faint memory came back to me. If I was thinking of the right woman, she had been covering the commission on public spending for the Economics page of the News. A tall, good looking brunette, early thirties, nicely dressed but not flashy and quite pleasant. I wondered when she had transferred to Crime.

"I'm sorry, Ms. Kealy, I meet a lot of journalists."

"Oh. Yes of course, I'm sorry. Well, I'm with the Evening News, I write for the Business and Economics section. I've been at a few Press calls in Leinster House, and so on. But sure, that's beside the point." She laughed nervously. "Look, I'm awfully sorry to just ring you like this but we – I mean, I feel and the others too, because there are a few of us, you understand – we try to make contact with anyone that might be affected, come into contact with, him."

I looked at the phone and shook my head.

"Ms. Kealy," I tried not to sound as impatient as I was. "You lost me at Hello. What is it you want to interview me about?"

"Interview? Oh. No, no, I don't mean to interview you. Look, I'm not doing this very well. I'm better with numbers, to be honest." She sighed and tried again. "OK. As a woman, I'm sure you've come into contact with your far share of creeps, right? And if you could warn someone off, save them the same hassle, you'd do it?"

"Yeah," I said cautiously, wondering where on earth this was going. As a political handler hearing the words "creep" send warning sirens off in my brain as I tried to think which of the knuckle draggers in the Party might have been harassing journalists at press conferences. The list was embarrassingly long. Maybe it was someone in the opposition party, I prayed fervently.

"There's a few of us who have had encounters with a certain person, and we try to make sure we give a heads up about it to other women. I volunteered to ring you because I had met you. And we know people in common, so you can ask around about me and you'll see I'm not some crackpot."

"I see. Well, I sort of see. What I don't get is, who's this creep you're talking about?"

There was a long pause. "I have to ask first, will you treat this as confidential? None of us want to have any trouble. We can't afford to be seen as troublemakers, that's the God honest truth."

"If you want it kept quiet, I won't drop anyone in it." Curiosity was killing me now. "Who are we talking about?"

Fifteen minutes later, I called Paula in.

"Guess who has a whole fan club of women whose sole desire in life is to join us in training killer seagulls?"

By the look on her face, I could see she wasn't even remotely surprised.

Chapter Twenty-Two

Paula Hughes

"It's on!" Caroline was already shrugging on her jacket and stuffing her laptop into its bag. "Sean O'Dwyer wants us in the Bank at half past two."

Stephen and I were way ahead of her; the moment Stephen patched the call through to Caroline's desk we grabbed the presentation and were on stand-by at the door ready for action. There wasn't another word spoken until we were all in Stephen's comfortable Toyata Avensis, and even then, it was a stilted, terse exchange of information. I had a nervous ache in the pit of my stomach. Caroline was grim-faced and even Stephen looked worried, which added to my anxiety as he is normally the calmest of all of us. For once Dublin traffic was obliging and we pulled into the car park ten minutes early, but by unspoken accord, we just sat there staring at the front door.

"This is it," Caroline began but then stopped, shook herself and laughed. "Ah, what are we like? No, it isn't. If we win this, brilliant and if we don't, we will win the next. We're letting them wind us up."

A band of tightness eased in my chest.

"Damn right," Stephen straightened his tie and fixed a grin on his face. It made him look like a tightly wound Jehovah's Witness. I could see him asking the Board "Are you prepared to accept Jordan PR as your marketing saviour?"

"Pretend we're in a movie," Caroline said, sticking out her chest and tossing her curls. "Let's walk in like the car has exploded behind us and we're packing

Uzis. Or Bazookas. Whichever does the most damage."

I have no idea what we actually looked like, but in our heads, we swept through the car-park and up the steps like we were directed by Tarantino. It worked; by the time we reached the reception desk I felt as if we were larking about and not at all as if my future financial well-being depended on the next forty-five minutes. The receptionist was a sharp-faced, brusque woman in her mid-forties; considering what Marie had told me about the working conditions there I forgave her the grumpy attitude. Our introductions produced a minor shift in her manner, and she favoured us with a brief wintry smile before click clacking across the marbled foyer to Meeting Room 3. We winced in unison as she opened the door and exchanged sheepish looks when all that confronted us was a standard bland corporate meeting room. I exhaled a breath of relief and as half my nerves settled, I realized we had been unconsciously preparing ourselves for yet another disaster.

Almost as soon as we were seated, Monica Delahunt appeared at the door. She wore the same uniform of expensive blouse, pencil skirt and designer scarf tied in an intricate knot, as when we last met. Apart from that I would have had difficulty recognizing her. Pale with only the barest concession to make-up, she looked like she'd been on a three-day bender – dark rings under the eyes, puffy face, nervy twitches.

"Monica," Caroline smiled. "How are you?" Her warmth was genuine, we all felt a bit of fellowship with anyone who was there that awful morning. Monica didn't make eye contact I noticed, and she mumbled some greeting. "If you would follow me, the Board room is upstairs."

Sneaky gits, I thought. Classic move to put us off our stride. "Of course." We picked up all our paraphernalia and trooped out again. Monica led us to the lifts, discreetly tucked away around a corner from the reception area, hidden from view. The Bank of Leinster certainly didn't want anyone accidentally finding their way upstairs. She pressed the top button then produced a small key, inserted it into a tiny lock and turned. The left jerked upwards, another relic from the last time the building had been renovated in the nineties. The Board took their privacy seriously, I had met rock stars whose penthouses were more easily accessed.

"How are you doing," Caroline tried again. "I hope they've been minding you, after that shock. We're all still a bit shook ourselves."

Monica stared fixedly ahead. Was she snubbing us? Marie had described a real tartar, a woman who acted as if the Bank was her personal fiefdom. Was she just that cold and unaffected by the brutal events at our last meeting? I glanced at her hands, tightly clenched. Maybe not. She looked as if she was suffering.

The lift doors opened to reveal a plushly carpeted area with a polished mahogany desk to one side of large, gleaming, paneled double doors. Pushing Monica's troubles from my mind, I stepped out with the others and followed Caroline's lead. "Thanks, Monica," she said, then nodded at the young man seated behind the desk. "Are they ready for us?"

He grinned. "Hello, Ms. Jordan. Yes, please go through."

Stephen stepped forward smartly and swung the doors open with a flourish. If we were going to be playing games, his expression said, let's play our way. We – and I say this as a woman who has never before managed anything approaching this – we *sashayed* into the room. There was no denying how impressive a space it was, with an acre or so of more plush carpeting, a gigantic table of yet more shining mahogany surrounded by chairs with studded leather detailing on the seat, backs and armrests. There was artwork on the walls that cost more than a mortgage.

Each chair housed a well clad bottom, belonging to an assortment of powerful people whose expressions ranged from disinterest to hostility. In a way, for me at least that made it easier. Jordan PR was used to being the underdogs, a bit of opposition tended to bring out the fighter in us. I smiled brightly and at a glance from Caro seated myself in one of the three carefully arranged chairs at the bottom of the gigantic table. Stephen chose the furthest chair leaving Caroline enthroned in the middle.

Sean O'Dwyer was at the head of the table directly opposite us, a solitary but imposing figure, grey haired and sleek in a dark pinstriped suit with a plain waistcoat and crisp shirt. He was aging but handsome in a way popular 30 years ago. He smiled, a shark's rictus with no trace of warmth in his blue eyes. I stared at him, searching for a look of Peter but the son obviously favoured the mother. Or the milkman, for all I knew. It was hard to reconcile this urbane tiger with that tall, lanky young hipster.

Caroline was mid introductions before I spotted Murrough Loxburg, seated two from the top on O'Dwyer's left. Opposite him sat David Howard and to my left, Emily Cleethe. She gave a slight nod, but otherwise looked blank and bored. I risked a glance at Howard, and he smiled back, raising one hand in a gesture of recognition. I smiled back, gratefully; at least we had one real friend in the mix.

We had rehearsed so much I could repeat the presentation in my sleep. I knew to the minute when I was needed to chime in. In the meantime, I kept one ear on the presentation while I scanned the faces staring at us and tried to pick out which ones to target. Cleethe started to look interested as Caroline began to expand on the wonders we were prepared to achieve for the Leinster, so that was a good sign. The man to her right, a corpulent, nervy looking individual, took occasional notes which meant he would be asking us detailed, but largely irrelevant questions later just to show how clued in he was. But at least he was engaged. Murrough's neighbours looked as if they were asleep; and the only other woman on the board, a stern looking blonde whom I'd seen before on television giving out about the state of the country under Taoiseach O'Mahony, was glaring at Caroline. I could tell she was only waiting for Caro to stop talking to jump in with objections.

Caroline waved a hand in my direction and gave me my cue. I focused on the faces that looked encouraging and blanked out the rest. The words flowed out, and a surge of pride welled up. Pride in myself, in Caro and Stephen, in our little firm. Hang it all, it seemed to say, win or lose we're here batting with the big firms. Enthusiasm for the campaign began to win over nerves. We had some brilliant ideas, and a solid plan to build customer confidence. We had the facts and figures, and we had some cards in the background we weren't sharing yet so we could pull them out when the cross examination started. Might as well enjoy it.

As I drew to a close, Murrough Loxburg surprised me with a nod of approval and a faint smile. It was a moment of cognitive dissonance as pleasure at winning over an influential vote warred with the knowledge that he was an absolute gobdaw. Plenty of time to sort it out later.

Stephen stood and as if he was already best friends with everyone in the room, gently but firmly outlined where previous campaigns had failed the Bank in its hour of need, so nicely that it barely sounded like criticism while stripping bare their inadequacies. By the end, if Duggan and Fines PR themselves had been in the room, they'd have agreed it was all their fault. He contrasted the previous mistakes with the proposed new campaign, emphasizing not only the need to make up lost ground but to positively recruit new, young, customers. Looking at him, confident and quietly resolute, my heart turned over.

(*We're getting married in 6 months,* I thought. *I swear I will stop stuffing myself and start walking. I can't stuff this up, he's the best thing ever happened to me.*)

Then it was over. Stephen sat down and smiled at me. Caroline leaned forward slightly, ready for the inevitable barrage of questions. I counted to five in my head and the nervy man with the notepad kicked it off before I hit four.

"What share of market spend do you expect to assign to print ads?" As little as possible, I thought, it would be social media all the way if we could. But the age group facing us considered newspapers to be essential, along with glossy trade magazines, which conjured up JJ's smug face. Pushing it away, I nodded gravely

and spoke about cultivating positive press and not being too overt with advertising, and twice used the word "curating" in cold blood. He seemed happy enough, having used up 10 minutes of the available time. Cleethe was next, with some thoughtful queries. I was impressed. At Howard's Castle she seemed to be second fiddle to Charlie Loxburg, easily overlooked as the jealous, slightly insecure consort. Here she was in her element, and it was clear she knew her subject.

We seemed to be working our way up the table. Howard avoided questions but made some very encouraging comments about our proposals. He also made a point of saying how much he had enjoyed working with us on the exhibition, which seemed to interest the two sleepy members more than anything said so far. Murrough also chimed in with some very complimentary remarks although his sardonic delivery was hard to read.

That just left O'Dwyer.

He had the same expression now as at the beginning of our meeting. Either he had the best poker face I've ever encountered, or he was botoxed into immobility.

"Thank you, Ms. Jordan, and your colleagues. That was most...*impressive.*" Somehow it didn't sound like a compliment. "You've certainly given us a lot to digest. We will be in touch once we have had a chance to discuss the points raised. I'll have to ask you to be patient for a week or so while we confer."

An impatient gesture from Emily Cleethe made the sleepy gentlemen jump. "We need to move on this, Sean. I for one am not willing to let this situation run on any longer. We are all here, so we should debate it now. I see no reason why it can't be decided today." She added "With all due respect, of course."

"I agree," Murrough said smoothly. "We've heard from several firms at this point. Surely, we can come to a decision today. The situation warrants some urgency, you'll agree, Sean?"

Without waiting for O'Dwyer to reply, Caroline stood and nodded at him. "Well, thank you Mr. O'Dwyer and whatever you decide thank you so much for your attention today. We do appreciate the opportunity to present." With much smiling and nodding and murmurs of general well wishing, we extricated ourselves from the room, Stephen making sure those double doors were firmly shut behind us. The young clerk at the desk watched us curiously but confined himself to a friendly goodbye. It wasn't until the lift doors closed and the ground floor button was pushed that Caro spoke.

"Jaysus wept. The tension in that room... I had to get us out, O'Dwyer would never forgive us if we'd witnessed anything more."

"He looked genuinely grateful when you stood up," Stephen laughed. "I think he went from absolutely hating us to just disliking us intensely."

"Well, we did our best and frankly that was a belter of a presentation. I couldn't be prouder." She hesitated but added, "In all honesty I'll be surprised if we get it. I think O'Dwyer won't want us for political reasons. Cumann na Laochra will never forgive him if he chooses their rival's favourite PR firm. It'll depend on how many votes he controls."

"Is that why Derek wanted us to pitch?" the words were out without thinking. I reddened as both my friends stared at me. "It's silly, sorry. Just it occurred to me, how like him it would be. If we get the contract, he knows O'Dwyer is losing his grip. If we don't, he knows the status quo remains intact."

Caroline threw back her head and laughed. "Oh, I'm *so* slow. I bet you good money…yup, that sounds like him."

She was still laughing to herself as we took our leave of the grim-faced receptionist and trotted towards the doors. A new security guard was on duty I noticed, looking very self-conscious. He nodded to our group but as we went to pass, stuck out an arm and said quietly, "Please, Ms. Delahunt would like to see you." He looked around nervously. "In the room 3, please. She says please go in."

Caroline groaned. I could read her mind, the last thing we needed was another complication. And I also knew, she couldn't have passed up that invitation for hard cold cash. Into Meeting Room three it was, then.

Chapter Twenty-Three

aroline Jordan

Delahunt was looking rough, there was no polite way to sugar coat it. When she had escorted us upstairs, I thought she looked sickly and tired. Under the lights of the meeting room, it was clear that things were worse than that. Her eyes were red-rimmed and her skin puffy from crying. Or drinking, I thought, noting the shake in her hands as she placed them on the table, palms down. I glanced at the others; it was clear they were just as shocked.

"Monica?" Paula said gently, sitting down beside her. "Is everything OK?"

The woman shook her head and to my horror, burst into noisy tears. Paula patted her back and made soothing noises while Stephen and I tried to look sympathetic while avoiding eye contact with anyone else. Stephen glanced uneasily at the door. I shared his feelings, the last thing I wanted was for someone to walk in and find us sitting around looking at Monica Delahunt bawling her eyes out. Just the fillip needed to push our bid over the line, I thought grimly. Paula worked her magic though. The episode passed as suddenly as it had started, leaving her hiccoughing and sniffing but able to talk at least.

"I'm sorry," Her hands clutched each other. The knuckles were bone white beneath the skin. "I'm not myself. It's just that – It's just so awful. And poor Frank, it's just not right!" Her voice began to raise again but Paula hushed her gently. "He was such a nice man," Monica continued a trifle more steadily. "He worked so hard, he lived for this place. And his uke group. He was an excellent uke player. He never did a bad turn to anyone. He was the only person in this place that was nice to me. And now he's dead…" A fresh wave of tears broke, and I tried not to look as frustrated as I felt. I'm not unsympathetic, I swear, but this was a truly embarrassing situation.

And if I'm being honest and strictly between us, I couldn't warm to Monica.

"Yes," Paula said gravely. "It was awful. I'm so sorry for your loss. But the truth is, we didn't know him at all. We're terribly upset about it, obviously but…"

"You!" she pointed a finger at me, almost accusingly. "You were mixed up in that political murder, the Fitzpatrick case." I bit back a sharp reply. The mess that was the murder of my previous client, Minister Fitzpatrick follows me everywhere. "It was you, right? You know that cop too, the one who was here – Doyle? He said you were friends."

"We're not-" I began but conscious of Paula listening I amended it to "We're friendly, yes."

"Well, you need to do something about it. Frank was murdered, right here in the bank and no one seems to be doing anything."

"Well, do you know anything?" Stephen surprised us all by interrupting. "I mean, we're all sorry about what happened but we don't work here, and we didn't know the man. You did. If you want us to help, tell us something. Tell us who hated him or if he was mixed up in anything. Give us something, anything. Otherwise, what can we do?"

Instead of breaking down again, his words seemed to have a bracing effect. She sat up a little straighter, her words coming more clearly and coherently.

"Frank had just been promoted to Head of Marketing, after that stupid banking app mess. They fired Peadar Murray over it. Which wasn't strictly fair, but it was a good move for Frank. He was so pleased. He'd worked so hard to get ahead in here and it was such an uphill struggle for him. He wasn't one of the boys, you see."

She looked at me defiantly. "I know what everyone says about me, but if you're not in with "The Boys" you haven't a chance. Not unless you work twice as hard as everyone else. I made myself indispensable, that's how I got ahead. I started in Secretarial, did you know that? I barely had my leaving cert, but I worked like a dog. Frank was the same. He came from some bog in Sligo. He hated it there. He wanted to have a career and the Leinster was everything to him."

"He knew he'd never be on the Board, people like Murrough Loxburg and Sean O'Dwyer won't let a pleb like him in. It's all who you know and what posh school you went to. But they couldn't ignore him forever. That promotion was owed to Frank, for years. And when he finally got it-" Monica gulped back another wave of crying. "It's so unfair. And they'll get away with it if no one does anything."

Paula shot me a glance, one part sympathy for Monica and nine parts telling me to step up. I sighed. Where we never to be shot of this mess?

"Monica," I tried for calm and reassuring, but even to my own ears it sounded far closer to frustrated, "If you were close to Frank, you should have told the Gardaí. I know for a fact they're finding it hard to get a handle on him, his life in Dublin, who he saw outside work. And if you know anything at all about why he was killed, you have to talk to them. You obviously cared for the man. He was your friend. Don't tell us all this, tell the cops."

Horror and yes, fear, flooded her face. She resumed her hand wringing, and kept her eyes fixed on the table. "I can't."

I may have sighed at this point. Her head shot up and she hissed at me, "It's all right for you. You hobnob with them, the Loxburgs and the likes. You're in with all the politicians aren't you, and the Gardaí. No worries for Ms. Jordan, eh? If they come after you, someone will protect you. Well, I can't afford to lose my job. If I go running to the cops, they won't have me in to talk to the Board. They'll have me out on my ear."

"Did someone threaten your job if you spoke to the police?" Frankly it sounded incredible. "Really, Monica?"

She flushed dark red. "Yes. *Really*, Ms. Jordan. I was told in no uncertain terms that if I talk to anyone, I'm out on my ear. I've been here 15 years and they'll fire me in a heartbeat if they hear I was talking to you let alone that detective sergeant and his lot."

"But who?" Stephen asked, frowning, "Who threatened you?"

"The Board. Well, O'Dwyer and them. Cleethe, Murrough, Howard. First, they sent round a public email saying they expected us all to cooperate fully with the investigation. And then they called me in, privately. They said they were concerned about the Bank's reputation in all this and then they made it clear, anyone shooting their mouth off would be let go immediately. They fired that Marie Flynn, did you know that? And they would have done the same to Tomas, only he ended up in hospital first. All they had to do was tell the recruitment company not to send them here anymore. I'm permanent staff, so they couldn't do that to me. But they have a thousand ways to fire you, if they want. I know. I've seen them do it."

She looked up appealingly, "I'm sorry I was rude to you. I am. But I'm scared and – and I miss Frank."

Even my hard heart was touched. Who knew there was a soft side beneath the designer blouse?

"Okay. We don't have much time; I don't want them seeing us together any more than you do. Tell me, is there anything at all you know about what happened to Frank. And by "know" I mean, suspect, think or even have the faintest damn inkling about?"

She twitched, literally had a whole-body shudder. "Yes, I think so. I don't know anything for sure, but – about three weeks ago Frank and I went out for a drink after work. It was most unusual; he rarely came for a drink at all, let alone suggest it. He was upset, he'd been upstairs with some of the Board members just beforehand. He came down in a right state. He asked me to meet him across the road in Finnegan's, but when he arrived, he made me leave with him. We ended up in some place near town, a nasty dingy little dump. He was absolutely paranoid. He was talking about avoiding anyone from the Bank, and how he didn't want them to know he was talking to me. He- he said he didn't want to get me into trouble."

She looked directly at me again, and said, "I didn't take it seriously. God forgive me, I thought he was being over dramatic. I didn't pick up on how serious he was. He was scared, I can see it now. Genuinely scared."

Paula went to speak but I cut across her, I couldn't help it. "I know what that's like, Monica. I had a friend, a best friend. He tried to tell me something and I didn't listen properly, I didn't pick up on it. He ended up dead too. So, honestly, I do understand."

A quick sympathetic glance from Paula almost unnerved me but I pushed on. "Anyway, what had him so scared. Tell me everything you can remember."

The door opened right at that moment and the security guard popped his head around the door, looking worried. "People are coming, Ms. Delahunt. From upstairs."

Like a scalded cat, the woman jumped to her feet. In seconds her face rearranged itself into something approaching professional poise; I had to hand it to her she was strong-willed. "I have to go! Look, can you meet me later? Can I call to your offices?" She was pushing us physically out of the meeting room door at this point. "Please, go! I'll call to you after work, about seven o'clock."

We were out in the lobby, with the door slammed in our faces before I could respond. The guard was back at his station by the door, and the receptionist was chatting to two suited men. It was a relaxed scene with not even a hint of sinister undercurrent. But she had gone to ground for now, and there was little point in trying to force the situation. It would have to wait until later.

Good job I had no life outside work, then.

Chapter Twenty-Four

aroline Jordan

C It was a long wait, between catching up on the work we had shunted aside to prepare the Bank presentation and staring wild eyed at my phone every time it pinged, in case it was news about the same.

"They'll never have an answer today," Stephen repeated for the tenth time. "It'd take that lot a month to agree on what brand of tea bag to use." I knew he was probably right but looking at it from the flip side, if they had done as promised and debated it right then, they would have called already. But as we hadn't heard anything, it looked like we had failed.

I told the others to go home, get a nice meal and forget about it all for the evening but they refused. "Let's wait until Monica comes at least, Caro." It was part curiosity and part the ongoing extra care they had been giving me ever since the events of last year. Nothing like almost dying to gain sympathy and make your friends paranoid.

While we waited, Paula drew a large folder out from her desk drawer and began to write notes in it, muttering things like "Board members" "scared" "Why did they get rid of Marie and Tomas?"

"Paula?" I asked. "Are you, truly, compiling some sort of dossier on this?"

She looked up; her cheeks red but her tone defiant. "Yes, I am. I have the reports Doyle gave us, I have a basic synopsis of what has happened so far, and I'm updating it now with what Monica said. Why?"

"No reason. Oh wait, I do have a reason. It's pure mad! We're not detectives, you do know that? Like, I don't mind giving info to Doyle if it helps him and he can't get it himself, but I draw the line at starting an office folder on it."

"Oh yeah?" she folded her arms and gave me the stink-eye. "So why are we all here waiting for Monica to show up and tell us what she knows? Why didn't we just pass her on to Doyle, then?"

"If she'd managed to tell us anything important, I would have passed it on," I protested. "We're only here to get the information because she won't talk to him." But Paula had a point. We were getting drawn into this, between spying for Derek Fields at Howard Castle and probing Murrough Loxburg about art robberies, we needed to take a step back.

"This is it," I warned. "We talk to Monica, you can compile a report in triplicate for your DS Doyle, and then we concentrate on work. Like, how to persuade the voting public that our beloved Minister for Justice isn't a goose-stepping wannabe-Nazi, with her new "three strike" policy. The woman thinks she's in a Western or a Mafia movie half the time."

"And now you mention it, where is Monica?" Stephen pointed out, "She's pretty late." It was 7.30 already. Even in the worst traffic, at this time of year a trip from Ballsbridge to the Christchurch area in the city centre wouldn't take this long. I tried to ignore a niggling sense of unease but when fifteen minutes more crawled by, it was time to worry. "She probably changed her mind," I offered. "But maybe we should ring Doyle and tell him?"

Paula had started dialing before I finished. "Alan?" (Alan? Right so, they were that chummy.) "Have you got a minute?" She filled him in succinctly and he took it seriously enough to promise to check on the absent Delahunt. By then I was cross and exhausted and deflated.

"What a day, what an utter *bog* of a day. You two head off, for goodness's sake. If I hear anything about the Bank presentation, I'll ring. And if Doyle gets in touch about Monica, ring me, OK? I'll lock up here."

Twenty minutes later I winced as the lift creaked its way to the basement – our building was only ten years old but had been flung up by the cowboy developers that blighted Ireland for decades, and it was showing its age. In the same spirit, the basement car-park was darker than it should be, with every second light either broken or glitching rapidly, giving the whole dank place the air of a zombie movie set. It was also quiet, almost empty, and I felt in my bag for my can of mace. Mace is not legal or recommended in Ireland, so don't tell anyone, but I carry it everywhere now. I also have two cans by my bed, one openly on the bedside table and one hidden in the drawer. Belt and braces. I liked the feel of it in my hand, it was comforting as I walked rapidly to my car, the only sounds the drip of water from some faulty pipe, the hum of those infernal light fittings and the clicking of my heels on the concrete.

"You're fine, you do this every evening. The odds of anything bad happening are slim to non-existence. You are perfectly safe. If anyone moves at you, mace them 'til their eyes bleed."

My grief counsellor had given me a set of affirmations that I had adapted to my life. I'm not sure I was using them as intended but they worked for me. It was a relief to reach the safety of my car, though, my lovely Jaguar with its soft luxury and reassuringly quick door-locking speed. As I beeped it open, my phone rang, the sound echoing around the concrete box of a car park, surprising an embarrassingly loud yelp from me. I muttered crossly, fishing it out, and then as I saw the caller ID, I yelped again. Murrough Loxburg.

"Murrough," I managed to sound normal, while my heart pounded against my rib cage. His voice, with its bored drawl, set my teeth on edge. Probably ringing to tell us we'd been passed over.

"I'm ringing to let you know – and I am delighted to be the bearer of good news – the Board has voted to retain Jordan PR as our new Bank of Leinster PR team."

The lovely man, I thought, isn't it a pity he's so misunderstood!

"Murrough, thank you so much. That is excellent news, and it goes without saying, we deeply appreciate the opportunity."

"I'm sure. And I'm sure it also goes without saying, you won't let us down." In my mind's eye I could see his smug grin. "I should also tell you, although it's not usually our policy to disclose this, it wasn't a unanimous decision."

"I take it Mr. O'Dwyer still had reservations?"

Murrough hesitated. "Yes, and one other. But as I say, I shouldn't tell you that. The main thing is, you're hired and the majority of us are excited. We have been stuck in a very unproductive place in recent years, and the image of the Bank has suffered. We need new ideas."

"We have lots of ideas," I said firmly, "We are going to bring a whole new attitude to the Bank."

"I look forward to it. We shall get contracts out to you immediately. Let me know when it's all signed and sealed."

I rang off with suitable expressions of gratitude and tried not to wonder too hard why the man had such an interest in the well-being of Jordan PR. Monica had been adamant that he was buying us off, keeping us quiet. Never mind, it was a great opportunity for Jordan PR. I was mid jubilant text to Paula and Stephen when the phone rang again, this time the caller ID flashing "Git face."

"DS Doyle," I answered, making a quick mental note to change his caller ID before Paula saw it. "Alan. What's up?"

"We are having difficulty locating her," he said tersely. "Left work almost two hours ago. She should have made her meeting with you in plenty of time."

I sank into the car seat and clicked the doors shut securely. "Hang on, I'll put you on hands-free. I'm in the office car park, let me get out and on the road." My headlights swung in an arc as I navigated the narrow, badly spaced rows of vehicles and ramps leading to the exit. As I turned into the last ramp, something caught my eye, an odd bundle of what looked like clothes and other bits, hard to determine in the dim light, lying across the entrance to the downward slope.

"Doyle."

"What?"

"Stay on the line. I'm getting out of my car to check something. There's… it looks like someone is lying on the ground, across the exit ramp." It looks like a body, I thought, but it isn't. It can't be. "Hang on."

"Caroline, stay in your car! If you think it's anything sinister stay -"

Ignoring him I stepped out. He was still on the hands-free system so I could hear him swearing, his voice amplified by the car speakers and expletives bouncing off the concrete, as I approached the shape. From a foot away it was still hard to tell for sure. I forced myself to edge a little closer, cursing all passing gods and bent down.

"Please don't be Monica," my inner voice chanted away. Trying not to touch anything, I peered down and then with a shock recognized it for what it was, what I had known it would be from the moment I got out of my car. A dead body.

I stumbled hack into the car, Doyle's voice was silent now. "You still there?"

"Caroline! Yes, I'm still here. What's going on? What was it?"

"It's a body." The words came out flatly. "It's another body. It's a dead person, lying across the exit ramp of our building car park, Doyle."

"Okay. Caroline, listen to me. Don't touch it, OK? Just stay where you are. Block anyone from going past you. Just stay right there. We're on the way. Is it- is it Monica Delahunt?"

A strangled kind of laugh passed my lips. "No. No it isn't Monica. It's Sean O'Dwyer."

My new client, I thought. Peter's father. Frank Clarke's Boss.

All of us, together, in one tangled web.

Chapter Twenty-Five

DS Doyle

Caroline looked like she had recently been sick, her face slick with a veneer of sweat and her hands trembling slightly. Her usual air of confidence had disappeared, and it disconcerted me. I had become used to thinking of her as indestructible; even her recovery from near-death at the hands of a psychopath had been phenomenal. She takes her hits and bounces back, Graves had said once. But the girl in front of me didn't look like she'd be rebounding any time soon.

"Sit in the squad car, we'll move your Jag."

"No. Thanks but no. I'll sit in my own car." She eyed the squad car. "No offense, like."

"None taken. I'd sooner not get in it myself. Your jag is far more comfortable. Sit in it, while I get things sorted here. I'll be over in a few minutes."

She walked away, pausing to wave at Claire MacPherson, who called out a greeting before returning to the task at hand. Securing any crime scene was tricky; a public car park, where the body may have been dumped rather than killed in situ, and where it's damp and dark in equal measure, required the best efforts of techs and cops alike.

Dr Lorraine O'Toole had told me once, the men and women in forensics hated TV shows like CSI for a reason. As they donned paper protection suits and prepared to work in a dank, smelly car-park, the idea of a swanky, state of the art laboratory wasn't a bit funny. Plus it could take weeks to get evidence processed by the laboratories we used. They were private companies with contracts and other clients to please. There wasn't an ounce of glamour about it all, not that I could see. Then again, my day wouldn't measure up against Miami Vice or even the Sweeney.

To add to the fun, my phone was already burning up with messages from Superintendent Looney, who was having an epic meltdown at the thought of another high-profile murder. His expectations of us were unreasonable at the best of time; he would now be the single biggest hindrance to a proper working of this case. Graves had a policy of ignoring him, which meant Looney moved onto me when he couldn't raise my boss.

I would ignore him as long as I could, but after me he would contact David Locke and God alone knew what David might blurt out.

Dr Lorraine was on her knees, her face set in grim lines. She gave terse, if polite, instructions to her team, all dressed like her in full body white Personal Protective Clothing, all moving in a sombre dance around the remains. She caught my eye and nodded at what used to be Sean O'Dwyer.

"He's not long dead," she said. "I don't like guessing but for what it's worth, we're talking an hour, tops."

Graves and Locke were deep in conversation with the few personnel on duty that night in the car-park. A teenaged girl, who alternated between scared and excited and an older man, mid-fifties if I was any judge, who was busy explaining the CCTV system.

"It's bleedin' useless," he said with typical Dublin bluntness. "It's a feckin' shambles. They put it in twenty years ago, and then promptly forgot about it. It's been looked at once or twice when a car got stolen, but that's about it. Never been updated, and it's wiped every couple of months."

In Dublin "couple" meant anything from two to five, as in a "couple of pints." "You're welcome to look, but it's grainy and you can't see anything but the entrance and the pay stations."

"Sure, we'll look anyway," Graves said amiably, his soft Clare burr a contrast to the true-blue Dub accent of the car park manager. "It's better than nothing."

"You're the boss, Guard. While you're at it, you could ask the hotel for their footage. If anywhere has cameras that work, it'll be them. Their car-park overlooks our entrance, so ya never know, yiz might get lucky!"

David Locke shot me a look that said SCS would never get that lucky, but he trooped off to bother the staff of The Dubliner Hotel, an institution in the Christchurch area of Dublin. Conscious of Caroline sitting in her car, huddled over the steering wheel looking miserable, it seemed a good time to interview her; maybe we could at least let her get home. I was surprised Paula hadn't already arrived, or at least Stephen. She might be a right wagon at times, but she certainly inspired loyalty.

Her Jaguar was warm, and comfortable; and at least it wasn't a squeeze for a man of my height. I settled myself in the passenger seat. Caroline ignored me, she seemed to be staring at a fixed spot on the car park wall. Like someone on a boat staring at the horizon trying not to be sick. I gave it a few minutes before tapping her on the arm.

"How are you doing now?" I asked.

She turned her head and I flinched. Whatever vulnerability I had witnessed earlier had vanished; the eyes that looked back into mine were blazing with a fury I'd only ever seen before in steroid-fuelled pub brawlers.

"Was he murdered?"

"Yes."

She swore, long and colourfully.

"In the car park of my building. We were sitting here worrying about Monica Delahunt and instead it's poor old O'Dwyer. He was pretty much seventy, did you know that? An elderly man. What the hell is going on, Doyle?" Without waiting for an answer, she held up her hand and started to list, "First it's Frank Clarke. We are due to meet him, he ends up dead. Next Tomas gets battered and left for dead. Then we are drawn into this art thing, Loxburgs and Howards, all connected together through the Bank as well as the art world. And just as we secure the Bank contract, Monica gives us a dramatic performance, persuades us to wait for her here and O'Dwyer ends up dead. Have I missed anything?"

"Nothing much. We think we know why the Bank was robbed. Your pal O'Mahony, our beloved Leader. He and Derek Fields are hot on this bank reform bill. It'll drag all kinds into the light from shady land deals to those vaults of abandoned deposit boxes you told us about. Someone wanted something from the Bank. And before you ask again, no we can't just check the interior CCTV cameras there either. They are, to quote our friend Anto over there, bleedin' useless."

She sighed. "I take it from that there's no working cameras here? Anto is okay by the way. He's a decent sod, and he's conscientious."

"I'll bear that in mind. We won't beat him with rubber hoses just yet then." She managed a half-hearted smile but still gave the impression of vibrating with anger.

"Okay. Walk me through everything, from Delahunt calling you in to chat right up to finding O'Dwyer." I already knew a lot of it, but in my experience, people need to tell the story from start to finish, otherwise they miss details. Caroline gave an admirably clear account, including the conversation with Monica.

"Can I ask you something?" she said when I had finished taking notes. I nodded.

"When did it come to this?" she said. "I mean, people being murdered in the city nearly every day. Stabbings, shootings, muggings, beating. Was it the boom? Did we all lose the run of ourselves in the Celtic Tiger and now we can't cope? It wasn't like this when I was growing up, it wasn't. Your dad was a cop too, wasn't he? He'd know. It's got worse, it has."

"In fairness it's not every day. It's maybe every third day on average. Though honestly, we can go weeks without one, unless you count gangland killings."

"Are you joking about this?"

"No. Yes. A little. Sorry, no one gets my sense of humour. Look, yes people get killed. And life may seem a bit more violent than when we were kids. But there are so many factors behind that. We grew up in a time when things weren't reported the way they are now. We weren't exposed to a lot of things that were happening. Everyone kept things hidden. Suicides, Domestic Violence, Child Abuse – they all happened, we just never talked about it. And if you factor in terrorism, we had a more violent society back then. Organized crime has taken up some of the slack there."

As I talked, she looked at me curiously, it was hard to know what she was thinking.

"But yes, the boom years didn't help. You have some people getting richer and richer, and entire communities being left behind. Not everyone in this city had a boom, people forget that. For loads of folk, the cost of living got higher, rents especially. They were only hanging on and then when the bubble burst…down they fell. We let them fall. Homeless everywhere. Kids going to schools that have barbed wire fences and alarms. Young kids being recruited by drug dealers. People are just trying to survive and it's hard."

I pointed at the huddled body. "People like O'Dwyer didn't help. Banks like the Leinster…well, don't get me started. But it's still a good city. I've seen policing in other cities, across Europe. I'll take Dublin every time. We still have communities, even in the so-called rough areas. People are still pretty decent, overall."

"How can you be so optimistic," Caroline shook her head. "You see things like this all the time. I'm on body number three and I think I'm having a nervous breakdown."

Optimistic? It was a new idea of myself, to think I was "optimistic." If anything, people told me I was sour and suspicious. Which was fair enough. But if pressed I would have to admit that I believe in people, generally. Most people want roof over their heads, food on the table and a bit of security.

"You'll survive. I don't mean that in a bad way. You're strong, I admire that about you. You have Paula and Stephen." I hesitated but ploughed on. "You have me too. As a friend, I mean. We're not exactly soul mates but at this point we've been to enough crime scenes together to call each other ." This got a genuine smile.

"So as a cop, you don't think we should go all right wing and war on crime?" She spoke lightly but her eyes were serious. "I had a conversation recently with someone who thinks progressive politics are ruining the nation."

"Only people who talk about a war on crime are the ones with something to gain from it," My father's old mantra, from his own days in the force. "It's a mirage, something to dangle in front of voters. We need solid reforms, of the Force as much as anything. And the Law, and Banking and housing policies, all of it. Otherwise, we're just cleaners, running around mopping up the mess."

"Thanks. I needed to hear that. For a dark moment there, I began to think we should be rounding people up and throwing them in jail just for looking like they might be criminals."

"Problem with that, Caroline – the biggest criminals look a lot like your client list."

"Cheeky git." But it was said without rancour. "Oh, here's Paula." A familiar figure gestured anxiously from behind the police cordon and Graves waved her through

"Grand. I'll leave you in her capable hands. She can ply you with vodka and let you rant about the ruination of Irish society."

"At least she won't interrogate me," she retorted. As I swung my legs out of the car, she grabbed my arm. "Thanks. I mean it. I know we don't always get on but – I'd like to be your friend. I mean, I think we *are* friends."

I nodded to Paula. "Take this one home, and make sure she doesn't stay up all night googling crime statistics." Paula raised an eyebrow but jumped into the passenger seat and hugged Caroline fiercely. "Caro, you poor pet!" I suspected half our détente was due to our mutual affection for Paula. But it felt good to have reached that point with the redoubtable Ms. Jordan.

Chapter Twenty-Six

Graves tipped his chair back.

"Someday he's going to go head over heels, and I'll laugh my bum off," Claire remarked pointedly, but he just grinned.

"I've plenty of padding back there, I'll take my chances. Where are we now?"

"In the deepest possible pile of -" David Locke didn't finish the sentence. Superintendent Looney had gone into full rage mode about twenty minutes after we finished processing the scene. An angry summons had been issued to Graves, who had reluctantly had to detour to Looney's office instead of doing what he was meant to do – investigate the murder. The roars out of Looney could be heard from the far side of the building; Vice sent up a junior officer to see what was going on, and the Drug Squad rang me twice (once to ask what the row was and the second time to offer some valium-like tablets they said were guaranteed to knock Looney out for a few hours.)

Graves was as near to being truly angry as I've ever seen him, when he finally joined us. But nothing could knock him for long.

"Don't be so negative, Locke. It's what my daughter and her pals call "toxic." Be positive, son."

"I'm *positive* we're screwed," Locke replied.

We rewarded this with a snigger, but truth be told, we were all feeling too depressed to deny it.

"There's too much going on," Claire said. "You know those cases where there's no leads, no suspects? This is the worst opposite. There's just so many possibilities and no real way to narrow it down. We know – well, we guess – the night of Clarke's murder was a robbery gone wrong. We're sure they disabled the clock and opened the security doors. But where did they go? The Bank swears nothing was touched in the Deeds office, and there's no real way of knowing what was taken from the Vaults. *Apparently.*"

She shared my conviction that if there was a comprehensive inventory, the Bank wouldn't share it anyway. In fairness to them, if a security box had been opened and emptied, they couldn't know. But if one was missing – I couldn't believe there wasn't a list somewhere of the actual boxes.

"Then we have the security guard, Tomas – why was he there? Was he involved? No way of knowing exactly where he fits in, and he can't tell us!" She thumped her hand, palm down, on the desk. "And now O'Dwyer."

Graves shook his head. "Well, I agree, we have too many possibilities and not enough solid leads. That's why Looney is releasing some uniforms to us, they're joining us today. I want ye to turn over all the nitty-gritty stuff to them, get them to chase every single item. Check every alibi, badger the bank for a list of the security boxes. Find every call or text or email Dwyer ever sent, go back as far as you have to. You know the drill, take two uniforms apiece and give them your lists to follow."

Powers whistled under his breath, and I eyed Graves with fresh admiration. Any man who could walk into one of Looney's legendary tantrums and come out with ten extra uniformed Gardaí to help with the investigation deserved respect.

"How?" I asked, "How did you manage it?"

He grinned again but ignored the question. "Powers, I want you back in the Bank. No more softly-softly. I have the paperwork; you're authorized to examine the whole system. Get in there and find me some proof of what went down that night. Claire, you're on the Clarke end. Monica Delahunt mentioned a musical group, some class of a Ukulele lovers club. It's the nearest to a friend group we've been given – get in there and check it out."

Locke volunteered, "I have an idea Boss, but it might be a mare's nest."

"Shoot."

"Well, the only thing outside the Bank that connects every player is this Loxburg art scene connection. My girlfriend – okay, settle down. Yes, I have a girlfriend – she's a lecturer in NCAD." The National College of Art and Design, a prestigious third level institution for art studies. "She was talking about the Loxburgs, and then got onto some old rumours from the eighties and nineties, about how Charlie Loxburg and the Howards were mixed up in some scandal. And Prendergast's name came up too."

"I am aware of the connection," Graves said drily. It was an old sore point, that unsolved art theft.

"Well, yes, but guess whose name also came up? Emily Cleethe. Member of the Leinster Board. No alibi for Frank Clarke's death."

"Cleethe would only have been…what? 14 or 15 back then."

"1985," Graves interjected. "She would have been 16."

"Sweet sixteen. It's all in her file, born in the UK, went to college in Dublin -NCAD, which is how Fionnuala knows about her – and after various jobs around the world she settled back in Dublin, took up with Charlie Loxburg and now rules the arty world. But what it doesn't say in here is, how she came to live in Ireland as a teenager." He looked around us smugly. "Her mother married again and relocated her, bringing Emily and her brother to live with their stepfather. In a big house in Carlow…Bellingham Hall."

Graves sat up so quickly he almost fulfilled Claire's prophesy. "The Kinsella robbery. Are you – oh!" He rubbed his face with one hand. "The stepdaughter. I remember her now. She was very shy, hair hanging in front of her face, looked – what was that fashion? Dark clothes, gloomy faces? Goth, that's it. She was a Goth. Lots of eye makeup. No wonder I didn't recognize her."

A ripple of excitement moved through the room. It felt as if we were on to something, although what exactly I couldn't tell you. But it was another connection and when you start making them, they usually lead somewhere.

Emily Cleethe was around at the time of the robbery that persistent rumours linked to Charlie Loxburg. "She was only 16 though, and he would have been 30. Are we suggesting a link between them at the time?"

"Find out," Graves said shortly. Gone was the placid, dogged detective I knew. Instead, he was animated, a bloodhound who was warming to the chase. "That's one too many coincidences for me. Doyle, you take this with Locke. Let's nail down exactly how these people are linked; see if you can connect it to the Bank case. If you can't…well, we'll leave it aside for now, but we might get lucky."

"Caroline Jordan said from the beginning that they're all hand in glove politically as well," I said slowly. "O'Dwyer and Cumann na Laochra, Murrough Loxburg too. He's the face of their right wing, from what she tells me. His father isn't political, but he mixes with that set. The Howards are involved too, Miriam Howard is a County Councillor for Cumann too. Those families are all linked from years back."

"Didn't Philip Howard run for local government too? Before your time, I suppose, but he used to be a bit of a figure in Carlow and Offaly."

"I dunno, but I know a woman who does." I could only hope Caroline's goodwill towards me could survive calling in another favour. "I'll go see what I can find out in Carlow. Locke, you reach out to the NCAD crowd, find out anything you can that links these people. I'll ask Caroline Jordan to talk to Derek Fields. If anyone knows about Cumann na Laochra it'll be him."

Graves rubbed his hands together. "Right. I'm off to interview the O'Dwyers. We need to know what got Sean O'Dwyer killed. And find Delahunt. I want to know what that woman was about to tell Jordan."

"On it," Claire was already hunched over the computer, "I may have a lead."

"Keep in touch everyone," Graves said. "Back here at 6 pm, unless something breaks earlier."

It occurred to me to ring Caroline rather than visit in person but the walk from Kevin Street to Christ Church wasn't arduous and I thought a personal call might be more tactful. Also, in fairness she had had some fright the night before. I knew she was in work, because it was Caroline and only grievous bodily harm would keep her out. I texted Paula to make sure she was in the office, rather than wrangling politicians in Government Buildings, then set out. It was a good choice; the air was crisp and clear, in fine Autumn sunshine. Wandering past the Viking glory of Christ Church

Cathedral, with its archway over Winetavern Street and the eccentric sprawl of it outwards around the hill on which it was built, always lifts my spirits. I read somewhere that the exterior is mainly Victorian in design, due to restorations over the years, but it looks the part to my plebeian eyes. By the time I'd reached Caroline's office block, part of the regeneration of the area in the Celtic Tiger Boom, the pressures of the case had lifted a bit. In the lift the music was generic pop but catchy and I was whistling it as I pushed open the doors to Jordan PR.

Expecting Paula behind the desk I sang the last line of the boy-band era tune, "AND HERE I AM, LOOKING FOR YOU!" complete with jazz hands.

"And good morning to you too," Marie Flynn grinned.

Chapter Twenty-Seven

aula Hughes

P When Doyle burst in doing his best pop star impersonation, I was on the phone to the dreaded JJ. I hung up as soon as decently possible, as an act of pure human kindness – Doyle was purple faced and tongue tied. He seemed to have lost his voice in the process, too. A sort of strangle yelp was all he managed in reply to our new receptionist.

I have to admit, Caroline had played the game magnificently that morning; she was on to the Board of the bank at 8 am. I am fairly sure she woke Murrough Loxburg up to discuss the situation. He was full of polite shock about the demise of Sean O'Dwyer, but insistent that the Bank needed our services more than ever. And while we were truly, genuinely shocked at the fact of his death, the news that we were still hired came as a relief.

I texted Marie Flynn as soon as we knew we still had the contract, and she arrived at the offices at the same time as the bike courier carrying the paperwork from the Leinster. "It must have been drawn up yesterday afternoon," Stephen said thoughtfully, "It makes you wonder. They're fierce eager to have us locked in."

"Their paranoia is our luck," Caro said. But she had the contracts emailed to our firm's solicitor immediately. I could hear her on the phone to him in her office, double checking the various terms and conditions. And now here was poor Alan Doyle, looking sheepish and trying to recover his usual stoical poise.

" Well now, you're a Boys R Us fan?" Marie asked. "I had you pegged for more of a traditional folk music man."

Doyle blushed. "Yeah, I mean – I am more into folk." He rolled his eyes and said, "It was catchy, OK?" She giggled. He grinned. They stared at each for a while.

The penny dropped. When he has asked for a plus one to the Trad Festival gig, I had imaged him turning up with one of his work colleagues, or at a pinch, some mate from school. That it would be our funky and cool new receptionist – a witness in his murder case, no less – hadn't crossed my mind.

Whenever I see a prospective couple my mind does a quick analysis, imagining them together doing mundane things like shopping, cooking, watching TV. This was something else though. It was hard to imagine Alan doing those things by *himself*. He had such a laser focus on his work, and it was so hard to get him to socialize, it was a shock to think of him having a personal life. Watching him flirt was stress-inducing.

However, Marie seemed to like whatever it was he was doing (talking random nonsense about the weather while looking at a point somewhere left of her ear.) She looked delighted with herself, frankly.

It was a shame to break them up, but it had to be done.

"Alan, any news on Sean O'Dwyer?"

"Um. Yeah. I mean, I'm here to ask Caroline some questions. And see how she is, of course." He smiled shyly at Marie and added, "I had no idea you guys finally got a receptionist."

"Office Manager," I corrected him. "Marie will be doing the bulk of our admin from here on in. It's a dream come through, frankly."

"Their files are a disgrace," she said. "It'll take me a month to get them in order. But I'm hoping the celebrity clients make up for the boring admin."

"Yeah. That star stuck feeling will wear off, once you've seen them throwing a tantrum or two."

"Does Michael T ever come to the offices?"

"Sometimes. But if you want to meet him, you can come to one of the events he attends, help us keep his best face forward to the public." I was half joking but her eyes lit up.

"Oh please! My mam is a huge fan, she'd be dead impressed."

Doyle beamed at me, and let me tell you, watching Alan Doyle smile like that is a fascinating experience, a bit like watching a shark turn into a dolphin.

"Grand so. Is Caro off her call? Go on in, Alan." Caroline hadn't volunteered much about the previous evening but had gone out of her way to say how nice Alan had been. DS Doyle had come a long way since the day she had cornered him in the police station to berate him for being a sexist pig. It was a relief to see them get on; I could only hope whatever he wanted today he managed with a modicum of tact.

I turned my attention to Marie, ready for a good gossip about her thoughts on Alan Doyle. She held up a finger and pointed to the headset. "Come on up," She said into it, then to me, "Sorry, a courier in reception. He's on his way up."

A leather clad figure with motorcycle helmet appeared at the door, but Marie gestured at him. "Helmet off!" He shrugged but complied and carried in a massive bunch of flowers.

"You mustn't let people up willy-nilly, and it's always helmets off," she said. It took a minute to realize she was talking to the security desk again, through her headset, not to me. "Sorry, Paula, they're divils for letting people through. Poor Alan, if they'd stopped him and rung up it might have spared his blushes."

"He's a cop, they have a habit of just going where they want." I was more intent on the flowers. "Are they for Caroline?"

Marie fished a tiny card out of the centre of the arrangement. "Um…Oh! Paula, they're for you. "To Paula, Just to say I'm here." No signature, but it must be Stephen? How romantic." She sighed happily. "I don't think anyone has ever sent me flowers like that. Declan used to say romantic gestures were all fake. He wouldn't even buy a Valentine's Day card, the tight git."

The flowers were beautiful, but definitely a departure from Stephen's usual style. He always went for solid, traditional arrangements, with roses and baby's breath and ferns mixed with other similarly hued blooms. This was a modern eclectic mix, with bold colours, in a fabulous white vase. I couldn't imagine what it cost, certainly far more than we had in our budget. But it was absolutely gorgeous, what my sister Anne called "top tier."

I texted him, *"The flowers arrived, they're amazing. It's too much but thank you. Love you XXX"*

"And speaking of romance…" I'm as subtle as a brick through a window, but I was dying to know. "What do you make of our DS Doyle?" The arrow hit the mark, as Marie went bright red and buried her head in the paperwork mountain on her desk.

"He seems nice."

"Nice – no. Alan Doyle is many things, a lot of them good, but nice isn't the word for him. G'won. Try again." My flowers were pretty fabulous, I thought, and the smell was divine. "Be honest."

She glanced at the closed door of Caroline's office. "Well. He's fierce impressive, I think. He was lovely and kind to me at the hospital the other night, and he's easy to talk to. And so funny." Fond as I had become of Alan, this description of him made me snort, but seeing her hurt expression I tried to pass it off as a cough. "He is dead talented too. Have you seen his carpentry? He just gets it, you know? The whole creative vibe. But anyway, he's not interested in me."

"What on earth makes you think that?" Had she not seen the state of the poor man, trying to string two words together at the sight of her?

"Ah, I dunno. I mean, he's probably just being professional right? He's naturally kind. Like, calling in to see Caroline. I expect they're…close friends?"

"Caroline and Alan have a…" I chose my next words carefully, "a mutual respect and they get on in a kind of bickering, eye-rolling way. They aren't what you'd call natural friends. But they do have a good relationship, on the whole. But he's not interested in her, if that's what you mean. And she isn't remotely interested in him. It's not a love/hate kind of thing."

"Honestly? Cos, like, if there was even a slight chance of standing on someone else's toes, I wouldn't dream of going after any man. I mean it. I've been on the other end of that. But if you're sure, then – well, yeah. I like him. A lot."

Score one for Alan. "You know he can't ask you out while the case is on-going? You're a witness, for a start." Also, possibly, a suspect albeit an unlikely one, but I didn't like to point that out. "I think you will both just have to lie to yourselves and each other and hang out as mates until all this is sorted out. Then you can jump him some night."

She laughed, blushing even more. "You won't say anything to him?"

"Not a word. But if I find random reasons to have the pair of ye in a room together, preferably outside working hours, I can't promise not to meddle."

My phone pinged. "It's Stephen." I read the text, with an uneasy lurch in my stomach. "Oh. He says they aren't from him." His exact words were "Flowers? Who sent flowers? Not from me, sorry. Whose name?"

Marie took another call and launched into a very professional rendition of *"Jordan PR! How can I help you?"* so I sloped back to my desk. Three emails in my inbox all from JJ McDonnell; I had learned that he would send a flurry of contradictory emails until finally settling on something he had rejected in the first one. I ignored them. There were several older emails to be dealt with, regarding various events and promotions as well as a long list of things to be done for the Loxburg Exhibition. Top of the list was arranging a meeting with the Twins, who had kept up a hilarious email exchange since the weekend.

Another email pinged in from our JJ, and close on its heels a text from David Howard congratulating us on the Bank Contract, with suitable expression of sorrow over O'Dwyer. It was bizarre, I reflected, when you realize how even a murder didn't put a dent in the corporate machine. Life rolled on; business as usual. It made me shiver a little.

The giant flower arrangement loomed over me as I sat at my desk. Probably a client and some careless florist left the name out by accident, I thought. Silly to feel worried, after all it's just a bunch of flowers.

I put the card in my pocket. There would be time enough to figure it out later.

Chapter Twenty -Eight

aroline Jordan

CMy call to our solicitors had ended and I was staring at the latest email from Margo Kealy, an eye-watering account of yet another professional woman's experience at the hands of JJ McDonnell. It was obvious something needed to be done about the bold John James but at the moment, a murderous campaign against our newest clients had to take precedence. "Later, JJ, later," I promised silently.

Doyle popped his head around the door and to my surprise, asked if he could come in. That was probably the first time in our entire history that he had managed a nod to polite convention. Well, if he could make the effort so could I; I waved at a chair and smiled.

"How are you today?" No preamble, but he was definitely trying to be more sensitive. "Last night was rough."

"I'm okay. Murrough Loxburg was on, reassuring us that nothing would derail our appointment as the Leinster's new PR team. He had contracts couriered over first thing."

Doyle whistled. "Well, that's cold."

"Yeah. I mean, I'm glad we're still hired but even I would have waited a day out of common decency. Murrough is acting Chairperson by the way."

He nodded. "We've sent Powers into the Bank, armed with warrants for access to the system. Let's see how they like that." A vision of fresh-faced Darren Powers earnestly questioning Murrough about the ins and outs of the alarm system made me smile. Powers was polite and self-deprecating, but I'd seen him in action, and he was relentless.

"I've been thinking," He looked at me warily. "Is it coincidence that Emily Cleethe, David Howard and Murrough Loxburg are on the Board of the Leinster and also running around the art scene with the likes of Simon Prendergast?"

"You're here to ask me to find that out, aren't you?"

He shook his head ruefully.

"Yes,"

My inner voice tried to reason with me, it knew I should resist getting involved, but the deep rage I was feeling shouted it down. I had spent eighteen months trying to get over the events surrounding the death of Minister Fitzpatrick, and now I was stuck in yet another murder. The idea of it made me shudder but the fear of this going unsolved, and unpunished, was stronger than fear for myself. The previous evening, watching them work the scene around the huddled remains of a once powerful, vibrant person, had almost tipped me into a dark, bitter place. Doyle's compassionate view of human nature, as surprising as it was, had helped pull me back.

"Okay. What do you need?"

"We need to know exactly what the link is between the art crowd and the bank. We don't know if it's even relevant, but we're working on next to nothing right now. What were they after in the bank the night Frank Clarke died and why kill him? Is there anything in those vaults or the records office that can link any of them to that night – I've Powers working on finding the inventory for both. A mysteriously missing inventory I might add. That in itself is suspicious."

"That's high-level shenanigans," I knew from experience powerful people will shred evidence in a heartbeat, alter files and even leak information if it kept them out of trouble. "It might have even been done after the event, if the Bank – maybe O'Dwyer himself – thought it was better to sweep something under the carpet."

"Good thinking. Also politically, what's the story with them? Who owns who?"

"Cumann na Laochra," I groaned. "Charming bunch. Be happy to dish the dirt. A lot I know, but Derek Fields will know everything. Give me a day to get it together. What's so funny?"

"Sorry, I can never quite get over how casually you mention Fields, and O'Mahony. I've never known anyone that close to the powers that be before."

"Hah. The gloss soon wears off, let me tell you. Anyway, yeah, it's all a big clique. I'd give a lot to know what was in the bank vaults. I was talking to Una Linehan. She reckons there are drugs, jewels, art works, confessions, all sorts."

"Confessions?" Doyle's cop instincts homed in on the obvious. He added "Minister Linehan, eh?"

"Calm yourself. Civil War Confessions. Deathbed ones, written to assuage the consciences of dying men and women. Tragic stuff."

"But nothing to stop it being a different type of confession," Doyle said thoughtfully. "Or incriminating evidence of some kinds."

And that's when he told me who Emily Cleethe really was. Okay, she hadn't exactly been in hiding, but she wasn't advertising the fact that her current lover had been a suspect in the robbery of her stepfather's home. But so long ago? Would it even matter anymore? Doyle had no more answers than I had, beyond remarking grimly that there was no statute of limitations per se on crimes like that.

"We're grasping at straws," he said wearily. "As MacPherson says, too many leads, too many possibilities and no way of narrowing them down."

A hazy picture had been forming in the back of my mind ever since my lunch with Derek. "Let me poke around. I think you're right. There are too many coincidences. Something binds all these people, and it has to do with the past. Maybe the proposed Bank reforms are the problem. There are plans afoot to open those defunct vaults, examine the contents. There is also going to be a spotlight on shady deals, mortgage arrangements – all the nasty little practices that brought this recession on our heads. Maybe whatever they're hiding is enough to kill for."

"You have someone in mind who might know?"

"A couple of people. Peter from Howard Castle for one and Simon Prendergast for another. Two men who hate Murrough Loxburg, and who are both intimately connected to him."

Doyle nodded. "Graves is out talking to the O'Dwyers, let him take point on that. As for Prendergast, I'll leave you to it, but anything you think might help, you pass it on to us immediately." He looked at me and said pointedly, "No heroics, no holding onto secrets, and no putting yourselves in danger."

"Aw. I promise faithfully, I'll be careful."

"It's not you I'm worried about," he grinned. "I'm awful fond of Paula and Steve. Do nothing to upset them."

He took his leave, muttering about the traffic on the motorway. Derek Field was expecting me at the offices of the Irish premier, our glorious leader Michael T O'Mahony by 5 pm. Peter would probably be at his family house, but I was happy to let Graves take charge there. It would hardly do to intrude on a grieving family. Besides, he just always seemed genuine to me, and I liked Leslie a lot – the idea that Peter was involved just sat wrong.

That left Simon Prendergast: I made a quick call to make sure he was in his art gallery on Merrion Square, a prestigious address near both the heart of Irish politics and the Art Museum and tourist trail. I could drop in, using the Loxburg Exhibition as an excuse, pump him for information and then go see Derek before our evening meetings.

Paula was mid phone call as I left, Stephen was out with a client and Marie Flynn seemed to be building some kind of fort out of our admin files, so I just waved as I went. There would be time enough to fill them in later. I made my way across the city from Christ Church to Merrion square in record time, a victory over the hideous Dublin traffic and bewildering one way system.

Standing outside Prendergast Fine Arts, I tried to gain a sense of the man. At Howard Castle, he had faded into the background; the overpowering egos of the Loxburgs, father and son, had made him seem insignificant. But here, I reminded myself, was a man who was rumoured to have forged art, avoided charges, set up his own gallery at a comparatively young age and then became the foremost broker for artists of a certain genre. Derek's warning to be careful of him was enough to prevent me underestimating him.

In the windows of the gallery were a pair of bronze pieces – interesting rather than beautiful, reminiscent of bulls about to charge but without anything so vulgar as actual shape – and a single painting, a colourful abstract that reminded me violently of my Aunt Audrey's sitting room carpet, circa 1990. What the pieces lacked in classical elegance they compensated for with energy; it wasn't to my taste, but I could see they were out of the ordinary.

As I stepped inside, a poster mounted on card and standing on an easel, caught my eye. The Loxburg Exhibition, coming soon and a rendition of Howard Castle by Charlie Loxburg, in the style he had made famous some twenty years before. I felt a swell of pride; Paula had produced the perfect publicity image. It stood out against the stark minimalism of the gallery. Interestingly there didn't appear to be an actual Loxburg on the walls, despite Simon's close associations with the artist. Instead, the work on display was a mix of abstract and colourful, obviously by the same hands as the window display, and two intriguing offerings at the far end of the long narrow space. They appeared to my untutored eye to be a pair, similar muted tones in both, and a mix of heavily applied oil paint, fragments of fabric and other materials – twigs and leaves and possibly mud. I'm not sure I would have it in my house, but there was something about it.

"That's a Melanie Murphy." I turned sharply, to find Simon Prendergast directly behind me, a tight little smile on his face.

"The name means nothing to me, I'm afraid." I learned a long time ago never to pretend to knowledge on art or music, if you were likely to be caught out. Far better to admit your ignorance and let the other person graciously teach you. "Is she very famous?"

Simon blinked rapidly. "No, not famous exactly. But she will be. Her first solo exhibition is early next year – if all goes well, you won't buy a Murphy under five figures."

"That's impressive. And you discovered her?"

"Well, yes. I know her lecturer at Limerick College of Art. When she graduated, she submitted a few pieces to me, and we've sold them steadily ever since."

"That's even more impressive. You must have some eye for talent! I didn't realize you promoted new artists too."

He frowned. "You thought I was just some kind of glorified agent for Charlie Loxburg, is what you mean."

"Not entirely. I'm afraid the ins and outs of the art world haven't been my area – until now. This collaboration with Leslie Howard has been eye opening. Every time I mention the art exhibition to a client, they are desperate to attend the opening. Even the political crowd, and let me tell you, there are few natural art lovers in the bank benches of our government. Or the opposition party, for that matter. But they want in."

"But that's excellent! I said to Charlie, right from the start – we should be targeting the movers and shakers in this city. No offense to him, but he is obsessed with his legacy. Getting through to him that it's a business too, not just a massive vanity project, is hard going."

"I can see how reliant he is on you," I nodded. "He doesn't have much grasp of the logistics involved in all this, the planning and the financial side of it doesn't seem to interest him at all. I thought Emily might be more clued in, but she doesn't seem interested either. If it wasn't for you, we'd be charging tuppence a ticket and providing free drink."

Flattery is a wonderful tool in the PR woman's arsenal. Simon absolutely bloomed in front of my eyes. Stood straighter, adjusted his tie, puffed out his chest. "Charlie likes money, but he looks down on people who openly work for it." He smiled, which softened the barb. "I'm terribly fond of the old man, but even so, he can be hard to take."

"Say no more. I totally understand." We launched into a sotto voce bitching session, delicately agreeing that Emily was strange, Charlie was unreasonable and egotistical and Murrough was overbearing, in quick succession. "It's obvious, he has no *feeling* for Art," Simon added. "Great at measuring a space but everything atmospheric about the exhibition, everything artistic, came from your team!"

I accepted the compliment, but added "And you, Simon. If you hadn't backed us up, we would be looking at a few paintings slapped on a whitewashed wall." Our new friendship firmly cemented; I turned my attention to the matter at hand.

"Of course, this terrible business with Sean O'Dwyer might set things back a few weeks. Leslie will know, of course. Poor Peter! He must be devastated."

Simon shuddered. "It made me quite ill hearing it on the news this morning. Quite ill. I assumed it was a heart attack at first, but they seem sure it was violent."

"First that poor man, murdered in the bank, and now this…"

He pricked up his ears. "Of course, you were there when they found that man, Clarke – and they still haven't caught the murder."

"Not yet," I dropped my voice again, "Obviously this is just between us." He nodded eagerly. "One can't help hearing things, in my position. And the Bank of Leinster is under such scrutiny these days…now Jordan PR is handling their public relations, we're in the loop. From what I understand, the police are making a lot of headway. I can't tell you details, obviously, but they're looking into past events, shall we say. Some very shady dealings."

Simon stepped back hastily, as if I had pinched him. His face whitened and he flapped his hands. "Past events, what do they mean past events?"

"Who knows? I mean, there were a lot of rumours about Charlie at one time, bit of art forging, back when he was young."

"Oh. Well, I know nothing about that. I can't see how that would have any bearing on the murders." He looked around, nervously I thought.

"Ah well, it'll all come out. I wonder if there's anything in the rumours, though? Imagine the story, "Famous artist once forged masterpieces!" The press would have a field day. Are you all right, Simon?" His face was covered in a film of sweat. "You look a bit off-colour."

"No. I mean, yes. I'm fine. Listen, Caroline, I have to get on. Was there anything else? It's been lovely chatting but -"

"Oh of course, you're very busy, I'm sure. I was hoping to photograph a couple of Loxburgs hanging in the gallery, but we can manage without. I don't suppose you'd have any old images of them, from when you last sold one?"

"Um, possibly. Oh wait! We have the catalogues from previous sales. Let me see – yes! Here's one from a few years ago, we had three Loxburgs hanging. "Death of a Hound," and "Felicitous" and then an older one, from his early Colour Block period, "Miss Clever."" He pointed at the catalogue images.

"Yes, they're perfect. Could you send the original images? Thank you so much. Oh! "Miss Clever," that's the one that's in the National Art Gallery?"

"Yes, they acquired it at that sale. Before then it was in a private collection. The National Gallery bought several pieces, if I recall. A very rare Gainsborough and a Jack Yates. And some sketches by various artists. This was their first Loxburg."

"How wonderful that must feel," I enthused. "Selling something that hangs in the National Gallery now, seen by thousands of people. Especially a Gainsborough!" Even I knew who Gainsborough was.

Some of his buoyancy had returned and he launched into a detailed explanation of how the famous painting had come into his hands.

"It's called Lady in Waiting. The pity of it is, it was originally one of a matching pair, but the other was stolen. It was in a private collection, and it disappeared in a robbery. It's probably been destroyed, no one could fence it. It's far too famous. Not even the most avid private collectors would risk it." He sighed. "I could have trebled the price for the pair."

We parted on the most amiable terms, but as I waved goodbye, he was already frowning and chewing one fingernail. It wasn't clear to me yet how it all fitted together, but I was sure another piece of the puzzle had fallen into my hand.

Chapter Twenty-Nine

D S Doyle

"I don't understand." The old man was querulous and anxious. "You say my step-daughter sent you?"

My companion, Garda Sergeant Phil Boscoe, from the station local to Bellingham Hall, repeated himself patiently. He reminded me of Graves, a big solid man with an air of calm.

"No, Mr. Kinsella. Emily didn't send us. We are here to ask some questions *about* her."

Kinsella stared at us; his face creased in lines of worry. "She's not coming here? She's not allowed to come here!" He appealed to the lady standing behind him, a middle-aged woman in the blue and white of a home-carer. "Miss Pearl! Tell them."

"You be calm, now," Miss Pearl soothed him. She patted the gnarled hand that rested on the arm of his chair. "These men are policemen. They won't let that one near you, not at all." Her expressive brown eyes shot us a warning. "And no one is going to upset you about her either."

He smiled up at her, with the trusting air of a child. "She's not allowed, is she, Miss Pearl?"

"No, sir, not at all. We told her, if you want to come to this house, you need to ask permission."

Phil Boscoe nodded. "That's right, Mr. Kinsella, we won't let her bother you." He elbowed me in the ribs. "Isn't that right, Detective?"

"Absolutely. Emily is not allowed to bother you."

The old man smiled at me. "I met a lot of Detectives, when we had the robbery. What a day! My poor Jennifer, she was so upset. She loved those paintings. It went straight to her heart, that did. Those buggers took every painting she loved. Left some on the walls that were more valuable. Took the ones poor Jenny liked."

"She had great taste," Miss Pearl said.

"Yes, indeed. Well, it showed, didn't it? Left more famous ones, but the ones she liked, they went for those. Emily laughed about it. She was a horrible child, spoiled by those English aunts of hers. So unpleasant as a teen. Laughed at her poor mother that day."

"Tell us about the robbery," Phil prompted gently. "It must have been a dreadful shock."

"It was terrifying." Old Kinsella said bluntly. "I was afraid they were going to kill us." I glanced at Phil in surprise. This was the first I had heard about any violence involving the family. "They hurt poor Adam, hit him hard. Down! He went. I tried to swing for the one nearest me, but he was too strong. I wasn't that young, you know. These were fit young men. He hit me. Then one of them grabbed Jenny and that was that – I told them to take what they wanted."

Phil prompted, "And they left ye all tied up."

"Yes. Yes. Until morning. Miss Pearl, I am hungry – when is dinner? Have I eaten it?What was I saying? Oh yes, tied up. Emily came home from her friend's house. She'd been sleeping over, some teenage party. She found Adam in the hall, called an ambulance. Then untied her mother and me. Unsympathetic brat. She was more upset over Adam than her own mother. Of course, we didn't realize then. We thought it was all teenage huffs."

His eyes were cloudy, and his voice trailed off. Miss Pearl shook her head at Phil. "We'll take our leave," he said, "thanks for the help, Mr. Kinsella."

I nodded to Kinsella and his watchful nurse and went to leave. Before I could follow Phil out to the hallway, Kinsella called out, "Detective!"

I crossed back to him and crouched down. "What is it, Mr. Kinsella?"

"We were afraid for her, Emily I mean. We thought he was a bad influence, arrogant young pup! I didn't realize at the time. She was the one to watch, not him." He leaned forward, until his face was almost touching mine. I could smell the sourness of his breath, the smell of old age that clung to his clothing. "She is the one, you see. And she laughed at her mother." He sank back and shut his eyes. Miss Pearl looked at me reproachfully.

"I'm away," I told her, and hurried after Phil.

Ten minutes later we were sitting in seats in a tiny café in the grounds. There were fewer visitors this time of year, but local dog walkers and garden enthusiasts kept the place in business. Phil ordered for us both, two coffees and slice of some local cake he highly recommended. I mulled over what Emily Cleethe's stepfather had told us.

"Well now, does it fit in?" Phil raised an eyebrow in exaggerated curiosity. "Any further on?"

"I'm not sure," I said slowly. "It puts our Miss Cleethe in a different light. He makes it sound like she was the dominant one and Loxburg was her tool."

The sergeant shook his head. "She was only sixteen. He was a grown man. If there was anything between them back then, it was his fault."

"Oh, I agree. But the old man is scared of her. I want to ask that nurse what happened if anything, to have her banned from the house."

"Ask her now," Phil pointed out the café window, "Here she comes."

Miss Pearl strode into the café, scanning the clientele. When her eyes lit on us, she smiled and made her way through the cluttered tables and chairs until she reached us.

"Please," I indicated an empty chair. She sat down and huffed for a moment.

"I ran after you as soon as I could, I hoped you'd be here," Her voice had the lyrical lilt of the Caribbean, a singer's voice my mother would say. "The mention of that girl's name upsets him so much, it's easier to talk away from the poor man."

A waitress appeared with a cup of tea and smiled at the nurse. "Early break today?" Miss Pearl smiled and accepted the tea with thanks. "They mind me something fierce in here," she said, the Irish idiom sounding both familiar and new in her lovely voice.

"We'd be grateful for any information, any insight at all. Why is he so upset with her?"

"Well. Where do I begin? I wasn't here when she was a girl, obviously, but I've heard all the local gossip. I've been Mr. Kinsella's nurse for almost five years now, and at the beginning, Emily used to call quite regularly. Her mother had died, and I assumed she was fond of the old man and calling to check on him. They weren't what you might call "warm" with each other, but they seemed on good enough terms. Kinsella is a nice man, you know. He wouldn't say a bad word about anyone." She sipped her tea. "When she came, she would dismiss me. I mean, absolutely dismiss me out of the room, like M'lady Muck. And I would leave them alone, at first. But I notice, and the other staff agree, he is very upset after every visit. I'm no fool. One day, I make sure to walk back into the room, no knocking."

She sat back in the chair and sighed. "That woman, she is leaning over the poor old man, and she is like a cat, spitting and hissing. Asking him over and over, where is it? He was almost crying and shaking, and he says to her "I can't tell you." And that woman, she raises her hand, and she goes to smack him. I tell you; she was about to hit that sick old man."

"Jesus wept," Phil said. "What did you do?"

"I grabbed her arm and I pulled her out of that room, like a bold child. She was raging, of course. "You're fired," she says, only she adds in a word or two I won't repeat. But I say to her, I am employed by Mr. Kinsella not you and if you come near him again, I will tell everyone that you bullied and threatened him."

"How did she take that?" From Paula's description of Emily Cleethe, I couldn't imagine her giving in without a fight.

"She stalked off, and Mr. Kinsella told me he didn't want her in the house again, and I promised him. She didn't show up for a few weeks, then one day back she comes, bold as brass. Banging on the door, demanding to come in. O'Neill, that's the man who runs the estate and the guided tours, he went out to her and told her to get away with herself. It happened maybe twice more, then she stopped."

"When was all this?" I asked.

"End of March, that's when I told her to go. Last time she turned up was about 6 weeks ago." Miss Pearl stood. "I have to get back now, but so we are clear – Miss Cleethe is a bad woman, and a terrible daughter. Ask Linda here, her mother was working here when Emily and her mother first came. The mother was a lady, by all accounts. Not at bit like Emily. Talk to Linda, that's my advice."

I thanked her sincerely; if only every witness was as forthcoming my job would be much easier. I thought of my own aging parents – if they ever needed nursing, I hoped it would be someone like her. Miss Pearl waved Linda over before leaving and introduced us, adding "You tell them everything you know, Linda, like a good girl." The young woman smiled at us and sat down.

"I've only a few minutes, mind. But I'll tell you what I can."

"Thanks, Linda, we appreciate it." Phil said. "We're after some sense of what happened around the time of the robbery, especially where Emily and her parents are concerned."

Linda rolled her eyes. "Miss High and Mighty Cleethe? Well, for a start she never fitted in around here. My mother worked here when Mr. Kinsella remarried. Jennifer Cleethe was a lovely lady, everyone liked her. My mother felt sorry at first for Emily, she was a sour little madam by all accounts, but Mammy felt it was because she was lonely. Thought it was her parents' divorce and the move over here from the UK."

"But every time anyone tried to do anything nice for Emily, she threw it back in their faces. She was a right wagon, my Dad says. She had endless temper tantrums, she sneered at everything, was always trying to get the other kids into trouble. She'd egg them on to do something, especially the younger ones, then tattle on them. Mam, God rest her, used to try to talk to her about it, explain that it was wrong. Then one day, Mam gets called into the office by Mr. Kinsella."

She had two red spots on her cheeks, and her voice shook with anger. "Some items had gone missing, small knick-knacks but valuable. Mr. Kinsella was apologetic but said he had to question her, because Emily had sworn she saw my Mam take them. He said if they were returned, there'd be no charges pressed, and she could even keep her job. My Mam stood up and roared at him, she was so angry. She said the Kinsella's could stuff their job, she was no thief. And that Emily was a dirty little liar."

Phil clucked sympathetically. Linda drew a shaky breath and continued. "Like, my Mam wouldn't take a penny off the floor that wasn't hers. Everyone working here knew it and fair dues to them, they stood up for her. The Kinsella's were decent, they were awfully upset but I suppose they felt they had to believe Emily. It was a standoff, until one of the young lads working on the estate confessed."

"He had stolen the bits?" I asked.

"Yes, and no. He and Emily had stolen them. He showed Mr. Kinsella where they had stashed them. He said they were seeing each other, and Emily had asked him to hide the stuff, as some kind of prank. She denied it, but Mr. Kinsella knew she was lying. She was made apologize to Mam, and it was all smoothed over, as some kind of teenage rebellion. The young fella left the area: his parents wanted him away from her. Mam stayed on working, but she steered clear of Emily after that."

"Did she ever talk about the robbery, your mam?"

Linda nodded solemnly. "Yeah, of course. Everyone was *obsessed* by it, still are to be honest. A Dublin gang, they said, but the rumour was they had inside help. There was all that business with the artist too."

I tried to sound as nonchalant as possible. "Artist?"

"Yeah, there was this man here at the time painting a portrait of Jennifer Kinsella. It was a birthday present, or a wedding anniversary or something. Anyway, he was practically living here for months. At first everyone liked him, even my Dad, but Mam said he was tricky. Full of charm, but tricky. And then there was a huge row one night; Mr. Kinsella and the painter guy, shouting at each other and throwing punches. No one got hurt, but it was a real scrap. My Dad came up from the town when my Mam rang him and helped separate the two of them." She leaned forward conspiratorially. "Mam was doing a late shift, prepping for an event the next day. She heard a commotion in the hall, and when she went to check, there was the artist half naked, being hauled down the stairs by Kinsella. Mrs. Kinsella was screaming but Emily was standing on the staircase, laughing her head off. Kinsella kicked him out of the house and was chasing him around the yard when Dad arrived."

"They took your man down to the pub to cool off, and Dad stayed with the Kinsellas. But he couldn't make head or tail of what it was all about and no one was talking. Mrs. Kinsella locked herself in her bedroom, Mr. Kinsella was so upset Dad had to sit with him a while. Emily just danced around the place, laughing and singing to herself – my dad thought maybe she was high."

"And this was when?"

"Two weeks before the break in. Now, here's the weird bit. During the robbery, someone went into the room that had been used by the painter, and the slashed the portrait of Jennifer Kinsella to pieces."

She looked at me, her grey blue eyes meeting mine with a direct stare. "What kind of gang does that? Ignore the silver and the jewels, takes a select list of paintings and stops to destroy one single, unfinished one?"

I had an idea but didn't share it. Instead, I asked, "Would you know the name of the artist? Or would your Dad remember?"

She smiled. "Sure, I know the name. Isn't he mad famous now? He was on the Late Late Show a few months back. Dad recognized him immediately." I knew before she told me, Charlie Loxburg. But it was good to have it confirmed.

We took our leave, both of us deep in thought. Boscoe pointed at the imposing walls of Bellingham House as we made our way to the car-park.

"Some set-up, eh? He's a good employer, Kinsella. Most of the kids for miles around start working here, summer jobs and so on. The estate generates a lot of business for the area."

"I can imagine. Poor old man, he seemed decent."

Phil nodded. "Not many have a bad word to say about him."

"What did you make of Linda's story?"

"Which one, Emily being a rotten little cow back then or Charlie Loxburg being caught in flagrante delicto with someone and kicked out?"

I laughed. "Either, I suppose."

"Well, I think considering both the nurse and Linda's mam had their run ins with Cleethe, I'd say she's one to watch. If it were just the teenage stuff,

I'd be skeptical. Many a horrible teen has turned into a tolerable human adult. But the fact she'd bully a sick old man has me thinking."

"Yeah, and I wonder what she was looking for?"

"As for the other story, it seems to me either he was having an affair with the wife or the daughter – or trying to have one."

More threads, I thought. More little fragments and pieces. We needed to follow them to the end and hope it all came together. I took my leave of Phil, promising to let him know what came of it all.

"Be a change from sheep botherers and diesel smuggling," He grinned. Right then I felt like I'd swap place, settle for life as a village cop.

Chapter Thirty

Paula Hughes

Marie plonked the parcel on my desk. It was elaborately gift-wrapped and bore the legend "La Boheme," a very plush and expensive lingerie boutique. I stared in confusion.

"What's this?"

"It came for you a few minutes ago, it was left at reception." She grinned impishly. "Well, someone is spoiling you today!"

I glanced at my watch. Stephen was due back any minute, and I was supposed to be on my way to the dreaded JJ's offices. He was eating up an inordinate amount of my time these days, but Caroline had promised me we would deal with him soon. Until then I could manage, but I couldn't risk being late again.

"I certainly hope these are from you!" I wrote on a piece on paper and stuck it to the outside of the La Boheme box, before leaving it on Stephen's chair. There was no way I was opening a box of lingerie in the office. He could take them home for me.

The creaky lift was an age reaching our floor, and it crossed my mind that maybe I should have taken the stairs for a bit of exercise. The wedding dress fittings were on the horizon. Tiredness got the better of me though. When the doors finally opened, I stepped into the elevator gratefully; the only other occupant, a man in a suit carrying a very hipster looking brown leather satchel, smiled at me. "What floor?" he asked his finger hovering over the buttons.

"Oh, I'm going to the car park," I pointed at B for Basement. "Thanks."

"No probs. To be honest I'm a bit lost. You got on at the fourth floor? Is that Carefree Travel?"

I laughed. "No, they're on five. Four is Jordan PR. I take it the security guys steered you wrong?"

He laughed and agreed. "They sounded dead sure!"

I made a mental note to get Marie Flynn to chase up the building management. Between helmet clad bike couriers and wandering visitors randomly getting off at every floor, we needed better security. Which made me sad, because a few years ago I thought having a security guard on duty in the lobby was overkill.

Since Margo Kealy's first phone call to Caro, the issue of JJ had been discussed endlessly. We now had a dossier of his antics, even if most of the women involved didn't want to go public with their stories. One woman had recounted how after meeting McDonnell at a seminar on trade publishing he had rung her firm, asking to speak to the "busty brunette" and implying she had made a holy show of herself. Another said he had tried to persuade her to go to a hotel with him, approximately twenty minutes after they were introduced at an industry party. When she refused, he had followed her around the venue making remarks about frigid ball-breakers. Those were the mild ones. Women who had the misfortune to work with him had even worse stories; one unfortunate woman came home to her fiancé who wanted to know where she had been that day. When she said at work, he called her a liar saying her workplace had rung looking for her, as she hadn't been in all day. It turned out JJ had rung him, as a "joke." As part of the joke, he had implied she was off with her boyfriend from the office – an epic lie but that was JJ McDonnell for you.

It was hard to be civil to him, especially in person. But Best Budgets was a solid contract and we owed them our best even if that meant putting up with McDonnell. It was every bit as unpleasant as I had feared; he made endless suggestive remarks, followed by a chuckle so he could claim "it's just a joke!" Teeth gritted and a fake smile plastered on my face, I got through the forty minutes of leering somehow and escaped gratefully. I was halfway across the massive car park when a voice I recognized called my name.

"Monica?" I replied, as I spun around. It was her all right, although she was muffled up in a coat and headscarf despite the still mild weather.

"I've been waiting here for you," She clutched my arm, her bony fingers digging in to the flesh above my wrist. "I'm sorry, I had to see you."

"How did you know I would be here, Monica?" I extricated my arm and moved a few steps away from her.

"I didn't. I've been following you." She glanced around. "Please, we can't talk out here. My car is over there-"

"No!" It came out sharper than intended but I mean it. "Sorry but no. Last time we arranged to talk, Sean O'Dwyer ended up dead. In our car-park, Monica. So no, I won't be getting into your car, thanks. Whatever it is you have to say, say it here or go tell the SCS."

She flinched at the mention of O'Dwyer. "Don't you understand? That's why I'm afraid! They killed him, because he was on his way to talk to Caroline." Her eyes were haunted and dark-ringed. "Please Paula!"

I sighed. "OK, you can sit into my car. But then you're going to tell me everything, do you hear me? No more games." She followed me meekly, still glancing around every few seconds. I waited for her to settle herself, and hoped she wouldn't notice my phone, balancing on the seat divider, recording every word. You couldn't hang around with Alan Doyle without picking up a few tips.

"Tell me about Clarke," I said.

"Frank was scared. He said he had been instructed by the Board to draw up a list of the security boxes in the vaults. That was OK, if a bit outside his job. He had been working on it for weeks, on and off. With the talk of Banking reform, he was expecting the old boxes to be opened at some point. He was trying to link the boxes with their owners, or the owners' descendants. He enjoyed it, if you can believe that. He said it was like a puzzle. He went through box files of old paperwork in the records office, crosschecking and referencing until he matched boxes with owners. None of it is computerized, you know. We only started using computer records in the mid-nineties."

She swallowed. "Anyway. He found something, that's what started the trouble. He wouldn't tell me what exactly, but he said it was strange. Later he said it was more than strange, and that when he had asked Murrough about it the man had become belligerent and threatening. Told him to keep out of it and leave well enough alone."

"But you don't know what exactly "it" is?" I pressed her.

"No. But – well, I think he might have told someone. He wanted to tell me." A sob escaped her. "When we went to lunch, just before he – before it happened, he tried to tell me, and I wouldn't listen. I was afraid to be involved. My job is all I have! I shut him down. He said he understood, Frank was like that. And he said maybe he should talk to someone outside the Bank. That's why I told you to check out his music friends. I think he may have told one of them."

"Why on earth didn't you tell Doyle this!" I shook my head in exasperation. "You've wasted so much time!"

"I couldn't," she wailed. "I told you, I was trying to keep my job! But then, they started getting rid of everyone connected to Frank. Marie Flynn, and poor Tomas. And I felt so badly about letting Frank down too."

"Did Frank ask Tomas to come late to the Bank that night?" A thought had struck me as Monica had talked.

"I think so," she said. "I don't know why, though."

"Never mind. We can come back to it. Tell me why you didn't turn up last night."

"After I spoke to you in the Leinster yesterday, Murrough Loxburg asked me to come to his office. O'Dwyer was there, looking very put out, but Loxburg was smug. He told me that the Board had decided to go with Jordan PR and that I was to draw up contracts and so on and have them couriered over."

"Was that normal?"

"Oh yes. I do all the important, confidential paperwork," she said with a flash of the old pompous Monica. "I was just leaving the office when I – well, I overheard a conversation between O'Dwyer and Murrough."

Listened at the door, I translated mentally.

"O'Dwyer said if they were going to rely on Jordan PR then they should tell you everything. That it was too risky, the Bank couldn't afford to be blindsided again. Murrough said he was being ridiculous, and that once Caroline Jordan got her payday, she wouldn't care what scandal erupted. He said she was used to lying for politicians and the like."

"Charming. You mean he wanted us to get the job because he thinks we will happily cover up anything."

"Yes. But O'Dwyer insisted, and then I heard Murrough say "on your own head be it. But it changes nothing." Then O'Dwyer stormed out and I had to – I mean, I didn't hear any more." She avoided my eyes and stared instead at her hands, clasped tightly in her lap. "I went to your building. I decided to go in through the pedestrian entrance on the car park side, so no one would see me." To enter that way, she would have to use the stairwell for four flights and cross the car park to the entrance to the fourth floor. Technically only those with offices should be able to access it, but in reality, the doors were left unlocked most of the time. "I saw him immediately. On the ground." She covered her face with her hands and gave in to the sobbing. "I was so scared I ran away."

I looked at her, torn between pity and exasperation. She couldn't help it, I reminded myself, not everyone can react bravely or selflessly. She's a scared, lonely person who is utterly dependent on her job.

"It's okay," I patted her on the arm. "At least you're coming forward now. Everything you've told me will help the cops, I'm sure of it. You couldn't help being scared."

She sniffed and looked at me hopefully. "Do you think people will understand?"

"Yes, definitely. You were afraid and you did what you thought was best at the time." Caroline's PR instincts were rubbing off on me. "But you have to come with me now and tell the cops."

She nodded and agreed but insisted on taking her own car. I wasn't one bit surprised when I pulled into the car park at Kevin Street Station half an hour later and she didn't turn up. I sat in my car for another half hour, to give her the benefit of the doubt, but eventually gave up. My phone in hand with the recording of her version of events safely stored in it, I found the desk sergeant and asked for anyone from the SCS.

Chapter Thirty-One

S Doyle

D Locke and Powers were both in the incident room by the time I returned from the wilds of Carlow. David waved me over, while Powers never raised his head from his computer screen. "What's he at now?" I asked

"He's been like that since he got back from the Bank," Locke said. "That tech friend of his has turned something up. I'll let him tell you himself. Meanwhile, in real life…guess what I found out?"

I sat down wearily. "Why don't you go ahead and tell me?"

"Cheer up, this will make your day. I got onto a load of people who knew Loxburg and Cleethe back in the day. This may shock you, but Arty people like to gossip. In fact, your friends at Jordan PR got me in touch with a pair of chatterboxes named Brendan and George. Incidentally, is there anyone in this city Jordan isn't linked to?" He didn't wait for an answer. "Right, here's the picture. If you'll forgive the pun, har har. Charlie Loxburg may be famous, but the deep establishment won't touch him. The National Gallery is reluctant to hang him, the old guard shy away from him. Apparently, it's a source of irritation to the great artist, he resents the way he's regarded, and he uses the "rebel" label to pretend it's because he's some great innovator. But the real reason he's over-looked?" He slapped the desk triumphantly. "Everyone who is anyone in the art world is convinced he was involved in some shady crap. Him, Simon Prendergast, Emily Cleethe and David Howard's late father, Matthew."

"Matthew Howard? That's new."

"Yup. Philip Howard seems to be above board. Played at politics for a while, bit of a knob by all accounts, but honest. His brother Matthew however, he ran with a bad lot. Passed a few dodgy cheques, was let go from a position in an insurance firm, all hushed up but still. He was interviewed a few times, over suspected art fraud and he had ties to a well-known fence or two."

"So probably handling stolen goods."

"Yeah. At the time of the Kinsella case, there was nothing to link Emily Cleethe to the robbery. She had a cast iron alibi, staying overnight in a friend's house. But the case report states clearly that the gang gained entrance to the estate through the main gates, which the estate manager at the time swore blind were chained and locked. The chains were found, and the padlock, in a utility room off the main house. It was assumed that the manager had slipped up."

"But what if it was Emily – she gave the key to whoever robbed the place, and they put the chains and padlock back in the house as cover."

"And the stolen paintings, there's a whole other set of rumours about them. Remember I said Matthew Howard was let go from a position in an insurance company? Guess who owned the company?"

"Ah. Let me guess. Mr. Kinsella!"

"You're a detective, aren't ya?" Locke was understandably pleased with himself. "Now we have the Howards, the Loxburgs and Cleethe all mixed up in the Bellingham House job. But when we look at the Bank, we have them pop up there again. Hopefully when Jordan gets back to you, she'll know how the Bank and Cumann na Laochra fit together, but I will bet my next pay cheque they do fit!"

"No argument here. Let's hear how wonder boy over there got on with the system in there." Powers looked up at that and grinned. "Go easy on me, will you? I don't think I could take another hour of tech jargon!"

"No tech jargon, I promise." He pointed at the screen in front of him. "The guys in the bank nearly had conniptions when I waltzed in with a warrant. Never before in the history of the Bank has such an outrage been committed, etc. But I pulled Noel in and pretended I just needed him to give me access to the system. Instead, Noel went on a deep dive, right into their deleted files, private emails, anything he could think of. Transferred it all to this-" He indicated a small oblong of metal, about the size of my thumb. I felt very old. "It's all here now, on my computer and I've been busy."

He clicked a few times and a new screen popped up. "Here it is. The inventory of "orphaned" security boxes, stored in the vaults below the Leinster headquarters." Another screen popped up, superimposed on the last. "This is a detailed cross-referencing spreadsheet, connecting the paperwork in the bank to the boxes. And here, in a separate sheet is what looks like a list of files held in the records office. I haven't finished yet, but I can tell you that several names appear on all three lists."

"Let me guess. Howard, Loxburg, and Cleethe."

"Nearly. Howard, yes. There's a box belonging to Matthew Howard. It shouldn't be in the orphaned box vault because of course, the man's own son is a senior officer of the Bank. Then there's a box, deposited first in the late 60s, belonging to the Kinsella family. Again, it seems odd that it's in this vault because Kinsella is alive, and even if he's incapacitated, Cleethe should have been able to inform that bank as next of kin."

"Assuming she knows it's there." I pointed out.

"Oh, she knows. Because, and this is the bit that stinks of fish, the last record of the box being accessed was in the late nineteen eighties, and it was accessed by ...drum-roll please!...Emily Cleethe. She had the key and a code according to the records."

"Well, well, well."

"And then we have the last piece, Murrough Loxburg. I can't find any record of a Loxburg security box, but in the records office, there is a very interesting wee document. Murrough raised a loan fifteen years ago, in 1997. I mean a whopping great big chunk of money, the records on the spread sheet didn't say what for but it did flag something. As collateral for the loan, he put up his father's personal art collection. There's a note on the spread sheet, just a couple of lines." He looked at me expectantly.

"What did it say?"

Powers smiled the smug smile of a winner. "It says, "Signature on loan papers of Charles Loxburg" followed by a question mark."

I thought about this for a minute. "Oh."

"Yup. Did Murrough forge his father's signature to get the loan approved? Can we see Charlie Loxburg staking his entire precious collection, his paintings and the ones he's acquired over the years?"

"And these files, the ones someone went to the trouble of deleting, who compiled them?"

Powers had been waiting for this moment, I could tell.

"Frank Clarke. Frank Clarke was working on them, right up until the day he was murdered."

This was it, I could feel it in my waters. Where everything fitted and who was the guilty party remained cloudy, but the structure was there. "Congratulations," I clapped Powers on the back. "You've played a blinder on this case." Powers went bright red; giving the compliment was worth it for that alone.

"Thanks. Oh, and Claire got back earlier, she left a note on your desk about that uke group. It looks promising."

A scrawled note was on my desk, secured by my stapler. In typical MacPherson fashion, it wasted no time on pleasantries but was to the point.

"Went to Rathfarnham, huge Uke group there. They knew Frank well. He played with them and another couple of groups. Very helpful but the main group are away in France at some festival. They will get the leader to ring as soon as she's back. Note: One man thinks he saw Frank out there day before the murder. Also, they rang to say they knew him, some uniform fobbed them off. Get his name for me."

I pitied the poor beggar who had dropped a vital lead, but better MacPherson gave him hell than Graves or worse, Looney.

Locke's phone buzzed and he picked up. After listening intently for a moment, he said "Send her up." Turning to me, he elaborated, "Paula Hughes is here. She's on her way up. She says she's got a statement from Monica Delahunt. Sort of."

Chapter Thirty-Two

aroline Jordan

Derek was waiting for me in his office. He occupied one beside the official office of the Irish Prime Minister, the Offices of An Taoiseach. He ran interference, between the party faithful, the opposition Leader, the various lobbyists and members of Special Committees, who all wanted to grab the ear of Michael T O'Mahony. O'Mahony himself was always a gracious figure, and rarely rebuffed anyone, which lent him an air of humility and kindliness. It fell to Derek to filter the mob, and as half the House was utterly terrified of him it worked.

Like O'Mahony, Fields worked late and weekends, even holidays. Most of our elected leaders were inclined to spend the least possible amount of time engaged in governing our country and I knew for a fact they often voted in debates for each other, the political equivalent of clocking in for your mate at work. At the other extreme, the Taoiseach and his right-hand man were hard to get out of the place. As Field's protégé and heir presumptive, I was spending more and more time there. Evening meetings with my two bosses were now a matter of course, whereas when I was employed by the late Minister Fitzpatrick while we lowly creatures worked into the night, only a national scandal kept him back late. And then only if it involved him.

I sat in the leather armchair Field reserved for favoured guests while he sipped coffee at his desk and eyed me quizzically. As ever, I felt fairly sure he knew what I was about to say and was wondering how it took me so long to figure it out. It was one reason I liked him so much.

"We have the Leinster contract. I'll be working for Leinster House and the Bank of Leinster. I should get tee shirts made." Leinster House was the commonly used name for the Irish parliament. My feeble joke raised a wry grin. "And now, I need to know – did you push us for this contract, so you'd have a foothold in Cumann na Laochra territory?"

"Yes," He said.

"And how thick was I not to cop on that you have history with the lot of them?"

"You knew I had history," he replied mildly. "Sure, didn't I tell you that myself?"

"No. Well you warned me about Murrough and the entourage surrounding his father but the words *"And you'd be obliging me because I know the lot of them are mixed up in political shenanigans,"* never crossed your lips."

"Should they have had to?"

"No. Fair enough. I should have thought it through myself. But now I need your help. Frank, honest help. Not the time for Grasshopper and mystic guru."

He chuckled. "Fire away."

I drew breath and marshalled my thoughts.

"I know there are links between all of them – to the Bank, to the art world, and politically. I know the links are shady and dirty and they don't want them out in the open. Emily Cleethe is tied to the Kinsella robbery. So is Charlie Loxburg. And probably the Howards too. Need I mention that all of these people are now my clients in one form or another? I need to get out ahead of this, Derek."

He nodded. "You're right and I apologize for not being more open with you. I had no idea this would blow up into the mess it is. Michael and I both agreed having you in the Bank, even peripherally would be an advantage – for you as well as us. We meant well."

I grinned. "I do appreciate that, Derek. But this has spiralled now."

I waited. Derek would tell me what he could, without me labouring the point. He needed time to apply that labyrinthine brain of his to the situation. Looking at him, as he sipped and stared thoughtfully ahead, you would never know that he was busily pulling half-forgotten secrets and scandals from his mental files and cross referencing them. If there was anything relevant, he would find it.

"Murrough Loxburg is hotly tipped to be the Cumann candidate for Rathdown- Dun Laoghaire in the next General Election," he remarked. "Sean O'Dwyer had aspirations to see his son Peter take on that role, he tried to groom him to enter politics. Peter rebelled and took up with Leslie Howard. All the boy wants is a quiet life, and he dislikes the far-right politics currently infecting their party." He looked at me steadily. "Peter is a nice boy. He takes after his mother, rather than Sean. She is a lovely woman."

There was a whole back story there, but I let it pass.

"David Howard is the son of Matthew Howard, Leslie's uncle, and Matthew was a ne'er-do-well from the start. Dishonest and nasty. He was an embarrassment to his brother, and the rest of his family. His wife left him when David was very small. Philip and Diane Howard raised him. I can't imagine it was a happy childhood but at least he seems to have turned out better than his dad."

A pang of guilt hit me. Paula was right again, it seemed. Poor David, what a start in life.

Derek continued, "For what it's worth, there is no proof of any of this, but rumour has it Charlie Loxburg has always liked young girls. Sixteen, Seventeen, when he was younger and now slightly older."

"I saw him in action," I nodded. Danielle the PhD student, hanging on his every word while Emily Cleethe looked on angrily. "He's what my aunts call a Dirty Old Man."

"Exactly. He had an affair with Emily when she was a teenager, and it's whispered that she helped him rob Kinsella House. She was a troubled rebellious teen back then. He took full advantage of her. Simon Prendergast used to be very close to her, did you know that? When Emily reappeared on the scene as an adult, she dated Prendergast. He was Loxburg's agent of course. Once she got Charlie's attention, she dumped Simon."

"Simon had his own troubled past - he was mixed up in a scandal about forged paintings. Not that anything was ever proven but people tend to shy away from buying a painting from someone suspected of selling fakes. It's taken him a long time to rehabilitate his reputation. Loxburg was, and still is, his main ticket and his popularity has enabled Simon to fund his gallery."

I nodded. "And he couldn't afford to throw a temper tantrum over his main client stealing his lover."

"No. I've observed Emily's career with great interest. She knows who to target and how. She has become a solid player in the financial world; even this recession has barely dented her operation. She failed at being an artist herself, but she's Queen Consort to the reigning King of the popular art world, and she has invested in a lot of young artists, all of whom are doing well. Her one weak spot, as far as I can see, is her infatuation with Loxburg."

I turned it all over in my mind. Pretend it's a public relations issue, my inner voice prompted. Imagine it's a scandal and you need to find a way to flip the narrative. How would you string it all together? Emily and Charlie, David and the Howards, Peter O'Dwyer hiding away down in Castle Howard…or was that a red herring? Go back, back to the beginning. Frank Clarke and the bank vaults, and Tomas. Why was Tomas in the Bank that night?

"I have to go talk to Alan Doyle." I stood up. Derek raised an eyebrow but nodded.

"Go. We'll catch you up here tomorrow." The door was closed behind me before the end of the sentence.

Chapter Thirty-Three

Caroline Jordan

Paula and Stephen were sitting together in the office, neither looking particularly happy, when I burst in. DS Doyle had ensconced himself in my good chair, wheeled in from my office but I forgave him, seeing as he had obeyed a summons in such short order. Marie Flynn was perched on the reception desk, legs swinging and two knitting needles, joined together by some kind of steel cables, flashing around a thin purple yarn. They all looked at me expectantly, but I took my time to get a chair and sit.

"I think I understand how it all happened. I need to hear from ye, what you found out today. Just the main points again." Both Paula and Doyle had given me garbled versions over the phone, but I need to hear it properly. The flimsiest of outlines had formed in my mind and I was afraid of losing the threads of it in the extraneous details. If they thought I was being bossy, neither showed it. Paula gave a succinct résumé of Monica's story and Doyle gave his news as if he was testifying in court, bullet points with solid facts.

As they spoke, the idea in my head took firmer shape.

"This uke group – there are dozens in the city!" I knew this from Brendan and George, and their obsession with the famous Ukulele Hooley in the People's Park in Dun Laoghaire. "Where did Clarke live?" A man as dedicated to work wouldn't waste time traveling across the city to a group. It would either be near work or his home.

"Rathfarnham," Doyle replied promptly. "MacPherson found them…

Frank played there regularly."

I turned to Marie. She was already at the computer before I'd finished and to my surprise, squealed in triumph. "I have them! Rathfarnham Super-Ukers." She pointed to the screen, "I checked Facebook. There's a post on their page, dedicated to Frank Clarke. Like an obituary, with everyone saying how sorry they were to hear it."

Three pairs of eyes swivelled to stare pointedly at Doyle. He shrugged. "Yeah, someone screwed up. We know." I shook my head in disbelief. "Any contact numbers?" Marie looked. "Yes! A mobile for a woman called Amy."

She called out the digits as I dialled. The ringing tone sounded once, twice – then a woman's voice answered saying hello.

"Is that Amy from the Super-Ukers?" I asked.

"Yes, yes. Are you ringing about tonight's classes? I'm afraid we're fully booked at the moment, but we'll be running more on the weekend."

"No, thank you, but I'm not after uke classes. I wonder, and I'm sorry to do this by phone, but did you know the late Frank Clarke?"

"Oh. Well, yes. We all did. Frank was a very valued member of the Super-Ukers. I was actually about to ring the Garda about it…Who is this, please?"

"My name is Caroline Jordan, and I was an acquaintance of Frank's. Through his work."

There was a slight gasp at the other end of the line. "Oh my god. I know who you are – it was in the paper. You found poor Frank, didn't you?"

"Yes. Look, I know this may seem odd, but I need to ask you, or anyone in the group who might know – did Frank give you anything to keep?"

"The files, you mean?" She sounded relieved. "He said someone would come for them, but when he died, we didn't like to bother the family. We have a kind of club room, you see, where we store spare ukes and amps and stuff. His friend put the boxes in there, and we forgot because we were so upset about Frank and then we didn't know what to do for the best. He made it clear they weren't to go to the Bank, you see."

A weight lifted off my chest as the last piece slipped into place.

"I'm sitting here with Detective Sergeant Doyle, Amy. He's in charge of this investigation, and he's going to send some Gardaí over to take those boxes off your hands. Was there anything else? Just boxes of papers? OK. Thanks. And don't worry, you did the right thing."

I turned back to the others. "Let me tell you a story," I began.

It all began with a troubled, angry teen-aged girl. Not your average rebellious teen; Emily Cleethe was a walking time bomb. She resented her stepfather, was jealous of her mother's attention, and of the adoration Jennifer Kinsella received from her husband. She was unscrupulous and devious. Then she met Charles Loxburg and fell for him. He was living in Bellingham House, and probably casing the joint while painting Jennifer's portrait. But he couldn't resist seducing the teenager, or perhaps he did it deliberately to get her to help him. Whatever the reasoning, the fight between Kinsella and Loxburg wasn't over Jennifer, it was over Emily.

Charles was now out on his ear, and this must have been a disaster for him. The gang who placed him there would blame him if the heist failed. But Emily was willing to do anything to help him. She gives him the key to the gates and makes herself scarce. However, the paintings stolen, under Charles' direction, weren't the most valuable but the ones guaranteed to hurt the Kinsellas most.

There's a side effect to that little act of spite – the pictures included one that was almost impossible to fence. Simon Prendergast sold the match of it to the National Gallery a few years ago. He said it himself "It was one of a matching pair, but the other was stolen. It's probably been destroyed, no one could fence it. It's far too famous. Not even private collectors would risk it." It was a Gainsborough and while the crooks would have burnt it as too risky to keep, Charlie couldn't do that. It would be unthinkable to destroy something so beautiful, so important to art.

What to do with it? Well, Emily Cleethe had access to a security deposit box. Her stepfather's. It must have tickled her pink. Hide it in his own deposit box, right under his nose. And if it ever came to light, what would it look like?

"Insurance fraud," Doyle said promptly.

"Exactly. Yes, there would be records of Emily accessing it but who would believe that a kid her age planned it? They'd say Kinsella forced her to do it, and he would be the monster who involved an innocent kid in his crime."

"But time passed, and no one went near it," Doyle was on the trail now. "And at some point, Murrough Loxburg must have moved the box in with the orphaned boxes, deep in the vaults. At the same time, we have Murrough forging a signature to gain funding for his real estate developments. Emily Cleethe was on the Board by then; she must have known whether his father had signed off on that loan or not."

"I think she knew he hadn't. She got Murrough under an obligation to her and now she had father and son relying on her silence. Everything must have looked pretty damn perfect. Until poor Frank Clarke started working on the vaults. He took the job very seriously, that's the kind of man he was. He cross referenced every single box with the old, uncomputerized records."

Paula chimed in, "As he came across the Kinsella box, and the Loxburg one, he knew they shouldn't be there. What's in the Loxburg one, I wonder?"

"I suspect some evidence that links Emily to the robbery." I replied. "Letters, probably, she wasn't as clever back then. Charlie has kept her around for years to keep her quiet and she's put up with his infidelity and open leching. They both must have something to lose if they break up."

Doyle whistled. "I feel like my brain has unscrambled. This is the first time this damn mess has made any coherent sense. But what about these boxes of Clarke's?"

"Ah. That's where we come to the murder. Frank reached out to Monica Delahunt and she didn't want to know. He had no other ally, that he knew of, in senior management. There was no way of knowing how many of the Board were implicated, because they are all so incestuously linked. Politically, financially. He felt trapped."

"In desperation, he decides to remove the box files, the deposit boxes and the paper work."

There was silence for a moment as they all digested this. Marie was the first to speak. "Are you saying, Frank Clarke robbed the bank?"

Stephen clapped his hands and rubbed them. "Of course! He knew how to manipulate the system, so that he could get the doors to open. But he couldn't possibly have made that run, through the corridors, open the doors and wedge them. Not at his age, or the shape he was in."

"Exactly. He asked the one person he could trust, an honest and loyal person. Tomas. How much he told him, I don't know, and poor Tomas can't tell us." There was a sombre moment of reflection for the unfortunate man. "But Tomas not only helped him wedge the doors and remove the goods. He left before Frank and delivered them to the club house in Rathfarnham. He stored them as instructed in the equipment room. When you ask, I'll bet you Amy will tell you Frank had a key."

"What happened next is still not one hundred percent clear," I admitted. "I think Frank ran into Emily and Murrough. They must have been horrified to realize the boxes were gone, and the records. I think they confronted him, tortured him to find out where they went, and they killed him. Frank didn't tell them. We know that because they haven't tried to recover them from the Super-Ukers."

I looked at Doyle, knowing he was already on the same page. "The problem is, we can prove a decades old crime, but we haven't a shred of evidence to prove they murdered Clarke."

He nodded, his eyes never leaving mine. "But you have a plan, don't you?"

"I do. You won't like it, but I do."

Chapter Thirty-Four

Paula Hughes

Before we dealt with the shady dealings in the Bank, there was time to fit in a few other issues. Stephen, normally the most placid and laid back of men, drew the line at having underwear sent to his fiancée. I could hardly blame him; if the situation was reversed, I know the worm of suspicion would have burrowed straight into my brain. The fact he was angry and worried that some creep was sending gifts and that he accepted they were unsolicited, was about as much as anyone could ask. But I was stumped as to the culprit.

Marie, Stephen and I held a post-mortem on the whole mess, shortly after the meeting with Doyle. I had warned them not to involve Caroline. She had enough to deal with. But with our plan for the Leinster Bank in place, it was a relief for the rest of us to deal with something else. I tried not to think too hard about the plan, because frankly it made my palms sweat, but if anyone could pull it off, Doyle and Caro could.

Now we had our own little problem to resolve.

Marie pointed at the lingerie box. "It's JJ McDonnell," she said. "It has to be."

"I can't see JJ spending one hundred and twenty euro on a pair of knickers, Marie," I replied.

Stephen frowned. "If it isn't JJ, who could it be. Have any of those women who contacted you about him said anything about presents?"

"No, not as far as I know. I feel like it would leave a paper trail, if you know what I mean. He's so sly, it seems unlikely."

Marie picked up the company landline and started punching numbers. "Paper trail," she said. "Let's see if he did leave one." Moments later, she was chatting on the phone with Sharon, from Flowers Direct. "Oh, I see. No of course, absolutely. You can't give customer info. Ah well, look it's grand. I'll have Detective Doyle get a court order – oh sorry, was that not clear? See, it's a case of stalking. The Special Crimes Unit were just in a meeting with us – yes, the ones in the paper. Yes, very exciting. But obviously if you can't help…" There was a long silence on our end as Sharon spoke rapidly and earnestly. Finally, Marie said "Oh my god, you're a star! Wow, thanks so much Sharon. They may still need to contact you to get details but that's so helpful, thanks. Have you an extension number for your own phone? Thanks!" With many murmurs of mutual admiration, they finally hung up on each other and Marie turned to us in triumph.

"I have some info! Sharon couldn't give us names obviously, but it turns out she remembers the order number for the flowers, because like ourselves FlowersDirect is a small outfit. She answers phones and takes orders but she's also a florist and she did the bouquet herself. It was a rush job; order came in last thing the evening before. Phone call, the money was paid via PayPal, the only thing she has is an email – which she can't give us. But the good news is, she thinks she recognized the voice! She's sure it was a regular client, and he just used a different name. Which again, she can't tell us. But at least it's something."

"It's more than we had a few minutes ago!" Stephen rubbed his hands together. "Right, then. Let's tackle this fancy undies place. La Boheme, right? I'll take this one."

It was the work of minutes for him to ring and ask to speak to customer services. To my surprise, instead of his usual gentle charm, he barked into the phone, "To whom am I speaking?" and when a woman's voice replied he interjected brusquely, "Jackie? Fine. Tell me Jackie, when a customer orders a delivery of intimate lingerie, is it the habit in La Boheme to just throw it in a box and neglect to add the very thoughtful, very important gift message? My girlfriend received a package today, from your company, as a very special gift from me. It's our anniversary! What? Well, thank you but that's not the point. I went to a lot of trouble to make this day special for her and she is not a bit impressed."

Cue apologetic chatter from the other end of the phone. A heavy sigh from Stephen in response. "But she's *not* pleased, that's the whole point Jackie. Where is my gift message? What was meant to be a sweet and intimate gift now looks like I just sent her sexy underwear…Yes, I'm positive I sent it. I don't have the order receipt to hand, but it was delivered to Paula Hughes, C/O Jordan PR, Christ Church Buildings…yes, that's it. What? No, I absolutely did request a card. Through the website? No, no… Read out to me exactly what it says…Right. Well, all I can say is someone screwed up. A what?" He looked at us guiltily, "No, there's no need for that…well, um, if you insist…" When he'd extricated himself he started laughing. "Oh bugger, now I feel bad. She insisted on sending you a fifty-euro gift voucher to compensate!"

"Oh nice!" Marie exclaimed.

"Never mind that," I said. "Did she give you any clue who sent it?"

"Ah. Well. Not exactly but she did read out the email."

"And?" Both Marie and I were on the edge of our seats, quite literally.

"DeadHead1@gmail etc." He said. "Sorry, not much help."

Marie looked at him oddly. "Sorry, did you say…Dead Head?"

"Does it mean anything to you?"

She dropped her head in her hands and groaned. "Oh no. No. Oh God."

I shook her shoulders lightly. "Marie, please!"

"My ex-husband. He used Dead Head as a gaming name. Declan Healy. DH. That's his bloody email."

I always thought people only gasped in bad novels and melodramatic movies, but I swear by all that is holy, both Stephen and I gasped. "Are you – that's insane," Stephen said flatly. "Why would your ex-husband be sending Paula gifts?"

"I don't know," the poor girl replied miserably. "I can't explain it. But I know that's his address."

"But I've never even met him," I wailed.

"How do you know?" Stephen asked suddenly. "I mean, do you know what he looks like? Marie, have you any pictures?"

"Sure, I've loads still in my phone," She scrolled frantically. "Here! Here's the eejit."

I stared at the picture. For a moment it meant nothing to me, a generically good-looking man, late thirties, smiling into the camera. But there was something about the tilt of his head, the sardonic twist of his mouth – a faint memory stirred.

"Marie, is it possible he has been following you?" I said slowly, trying to hold the shadowy memory in my head.

"Following me? Well, it's possible. Anything is possible with Declan." She said bitterly, "He didn't take me leaving him particularly well."

A figure in the doorway, of Best Budgets , peering in at reception. A man holding the door open for me as I exited the building here in Christ Church.

"It- it couldn't be," I said finally, "But yet…" The others were watching me closely. "I think – he was at Best Budgets s looking at you in reception. And here, at the entrance to the building, he held the door open for me." One final memory slotted into place. "The lift! He was in the lift with me!" The man in the elevator who had asked what floor, and then followed up with some innocuous questions.

"Jaysus wept," Marie was bright red and on the verge of tears. "Oh God! What can I say – I'm so, so sorry. I never dreamed he would do anything like this. He's harassed me a few times but – I can't believe he would pick on you like this."

"But why?" Stephen was still bewildered. "Like, what good would it do him to send gifts to Paula?"

"He would have escalated it," Caroline wasn't the only one who could put two and two together; my own mind was working overtime. "Either in his head I would be charmed, and he would reveal himself, and make Marie jealous. Or he would have started on Marie next and because I received unwanted gifts too, no one would have suspected him."

"But," poor Stephen was still trying to fit this into his view of reality. "But do people actually do things like that?"

"Men." Marie said bleakly. "Men do things like that. Not all men, before anyone starts. But some men."

"Enough men to make it a freaking reality." I added. "Look at JJ McDonnell. A whole dossier of women he low-key harassed, too afraid of the backlash to come forward. Look at me. I'm afraid of him. I'm sick of being bullied by him. But will I report him to Best Budgets ? And lose us the contract – because that's what will ultimately happen, they'll wait a while and then quietly drop us."

Few of us have the privilege of watching another human being adjust their view of the world in real time. Marie and I were among the lucky few, as a gamut of emotions crossed Stephen's face and a whole lot of complacency dropped away.

"I'm sorry." He added humbly, "I'm not going to say I'm surprised, because I shouldn't be. It's not like I don't know this stuff happens but – I have never seen it up close before."

"Oh you have," Marie replied bitterly. "You have, you just didn't have to recognize it. I guarantee it. That's how they get away with it. Men like McDonnell. Men like my ex-husband."

Stephen's eyes narrowed, the light of battle on his face.

"Right, then. Well, neither of them is going to get away with it much longer."

"Good man, yourself." Marie patted him on the back with a grin. "You can hold our coats while we deal with him."

Chapter Thirty-Five

Caroline Jordan

First thing the following morning, I met Doyle at the SCS incident room, where he brought the squad up to speed. As anticipated, Graves was absolutely dead set against our proposal but to my surprise it was Claire MacPherson who talked him around.

"It could work." She gave me an appraising glance. "If nothing else, we'll know who was involved. Either Murrough or Emily or both. And any other of their group. And they already think they have Caroline in their pockets."

"And I suppose the fact that it's highly irregular and reckless, that doesn't matter?" Graves said incredulously.

"Irregular – yes. But hardly without precedent," Claire said thoughtfully. "Obviously if she gets herself killed – or maimed – it'll look bad."

"Yeah, she's a civilian. On the other hand, it's not like she hasn't been in a hairy situation before." Locke contributed. "I vote we let her."

"Me too." Powers looked around earnestly. "I think she could pull it off. And we can monitor everything, cameras and mikes."

"I am actually in the room," I pointed out. "Ye can address yourselves to me."

They ignored me and continued to argue among themselves. In the end Claire won Graves over, with the argument that I was hardly likely to sue which cheered him up considerably.

"Would you sign a waiver, I wonder?" He asked me. "Stating that this stupid idea is all yours and that we shouldn't be fired if you end up hanging from a chandelier in the Bank?" Only he swore a lot more as he said it.

"I'll sign in triplicate, and might I just add, your concern for me is touching. Look, I wouldn't do it if I thought they could hurt me. Powers is right – wire me up and have cameras in place and at the first sign of trouble I'll yell for help."

"We need a safe word!" Powers was far too enthusiastic, in my opinion.

"Safe word?" Locke sighed. "Powers, it's a sting operation not an S&M club."

Powers reddened but ploughed on. "Well, a code word then. Something to let us know you need us to get in there."

"*Ill-advised.*" Graves grumbled. "There's a code word for this operation."

They laughed. I didn't.

"It needs to be something she might say, but unusual enough for it to stand out." Doyle grinned at me. "How about *"I'm sorry, I was wrong?""*

"Ha bloody ha. I wish you lot would take this a bit more seriously."

"Ignore them, Caro." Claire pointed at Locke. "What was that painter, the one Simon Prendergast sold to the National Gallery, the match of the stolen one?"

"Lady in Waiting."

"Hmm. No."

"Rembrandt." Doyle suggested. Followed by a chorus of art-based offerings from the rest of the Scooby gang ranging from "Abstraction-ism" to "Mona Lisa." Then they branched into unusual words they remembered from school.

Doyle finally announced that the word would be "Oxymoron" and made a rude comment about me googling it so I knew what it meant.

"Enlightening as this glimpse into law enforcement is, I think maybe I should pick," I interrupted. "Let's go with something relatively simple. If I announce I'm feeling sick, break down the doors and rescue me. Or at least, try not to shoot me in the cross-fire."

After that, it became a matter of organizing the various moving parts. I sat at Doyle's desk and wrote three separate emails. One each for Emily Cleethe, Murrough Loxburg and Simon Prendergast. The wording of the first two was the same; it took a while to get the right balance between threat and carrot, specificity and vagueness.

"Grateful as I am for the contract, handling the public image of the Bank of Leinster can only be compromised while certain matters are unresolved, in particular the situation surrounding the late Frank Clarke. I'm sure you are as anxious as I am to put that matter to bed, in which spirit I need to inform you that testimony from another bank employee is now in my hands, along with some paperwork that Frank was working on. Perhaps we could meet, as soon as convenient, to discuss the implications and hopefully, come to some mutually agreeable solution? I can stay late if it suits you to meet later this evening."

To Prendergast I simply wrote, *"I've come across something that concerns you; in the papers Frank Clarke was working on. I will obviously have to hand these over to the cops but I did feel you should have a chance to look over them first – I would hate you to be blindsided by it. After all, we all have pasts, it seems unfair to have these things dragged up. I'll be available this evening, if that suits."*

Claire cast her eye over the wording and nodded approval. "Nice. Now we wait."

We weren't kept in suspense for long. The first to reply was Emily Cleethe, by phone. Her habitually brusque manner masked any nerves. "What paperwork?" she snapped. "And what do you mean by "testimony?" I can't imagine what you think you're doing." I waited, silently. "Well, I suppose if you need to meet – why don't we say at the Bank, this evening. I have to be there anyway."

Claire shook her head vehemently. I nodded to show I understood. "I'm sorry, Emily, I'm in Leinster House – the real one, not the Bank – today. Big campaign coming up for the Government. I'll be back in Christ Church Buildings by 7 – we can meet in my offices. Of course, if you prefer, I can just drop everything off at the SCS offices instead. I probably should just hand it all over…"

"Your offices will be fine," Cleethe said. "It probably would be best to cast an eye over it before you pass it on the cops. Of course, I assume you've been discreet?"

"Oh completely," I assured her, "Not even my colleagues have any inkling."

"Good." And she rang off.

Powers cleaned a section of white board and wrote in a careful, rounded hand "Emily C. 7 pm Christ Church."

Murrough was next, again by phone. His caller ID didn't show up, he could teach even the cautious Emily a thing or two. Maybe this was his burner phone for his affairs.

"Caroline. A very cryptic email," He drawled. "Whatever have you uncovered?"

"Something interesting. I'll be in the office in Christ Church at 7 pm if you want a heads up. Before I take the lot to the Gardaí of course."

"Of course. Yes, it would be wise to get ahead of this, if it has any bearing on the Bank's reputation. I'll see you then."

His name was added to the board by Powers.

Simon Prendergast responded by email. *I won't pretend not to know what you're talking about. I would appreciate the chance to deal with it before the cops are involved. When and where?*

"He used his own email. Not exactly a criminal mastermind," Doyle remarked.

"It's a long shot," I agreed "but if I'm right, he *could* be up his neck in this. We have to include him." His name was duly added by Powers, and I sighed. It seemed our mad plan was happening.

Doyle was adamant that we set the scene carefully.

"You told Cleethe you'd be at the Government buildings, Caroline. Which means you need to go. In case they're watching you, we want it to look as authentic as possible. In the meantime, get Marie to let Powers and me in through the car-park." Since O'Dwyer's murder, security had been tightened and the doors from the car park were no longer unlocked. "Once we're in, we'll set it all up. You'll be covered by cameras and wired for sound. We won't risk a wire on you, there'll be no need with the mikes already in place and it reduces your risk."

"Make sure you're in situ, long before 7 pm," Claire admonished. "I don't care if the Government is in danger of collapse, I want you in that office before it's dark out."

"I'd better go then," Already my phone was hopping with emails and messages from Derek. "I'll put in a few hours and get back to the office by six or six thirty."

"Okay. Just go about your day," Graves stopped me as I went to leave. "You won't see us Caroline, but we'll be there."

Part of me toyed with the idea of ringing Derek and explaining but I decided against it. *"Plausible deniability"* my inner voice insisted. *"At least try to keep your boss and the leader of the country out of this mess."*

In fairness, the expectation that I would be at the top of my game and ready to work helped focus the mind. Especially the hour spent explaining to the Minister of Justice, Lilian Roche, that her continual ranting on Facebook wasn't helping her public image. Since we banned her from Twitter, she had tried out every other social media site available; being unable to post public outpourings of rage was making her even more difficult to deal with in real life but her approval rating had stopped its downward plummet.

If Derek was curious about the Bank situation, he hid it. Instead, we concentrated on the schedule of events and appearances coming over the Winter months. Parading poor Michael T O'Mahony in front of people to prove he was human was a necessary evil, and a difficult tightrope walk.

"No, no!" Derek snapped at the unfortunate who handed him a proposal from Ireland's least respectable production company. "The Taoiseach of this country will not be a guest judge on a show designed to exploit gullible young people." The idea of the respected Michael T O'Mahony issuing advice to starstruck young hopefuls, vying for a recording contract, distracted me from my own woes.

It was past six when I left, and the traffic was heavy; it took me well over the half hour to drive a distance that should have been done in fifteen. I went to pull into our building's car park and hesitated. Sean O'Dwyer had done that very thing a few nights before and he ended up dead, jumped by a person or persons unknown. Call me paranoid but I didn't feel like risking it; instead, I parked the car on the street, paid out for the exorbitant parking ticket and walked in through the front door of the building. There was a new security guard behind the desk, who shot me an odd look as I went past. I was in the lift before it occurred to me it was probably an undercover cop. Or possibly a hired assassin, my brain replied. At least two of the main suspects could well afford to have me killed by contract.

For the first time I questioned the wisdom of my decision. Somewhere between the rage and desire to get the murderer I may have ignored the inherent flaw in the plan.

I was about to stake myself out as bait.

Paula and the others were under strict instructions to vacate the office before I got there; it had to look like a normal working day but also whoever was watching needed to think I was alone. The darkened offices and locked door shouldn't have been a surprise, but they made my heart drop regardless. It finally hit me that I was facing this alone – facing not one but three people who may well be murders. What the hell had I been thinking?

Well, too late to back out now, I thought, might as well do it in style. There was a bottle of vodka in my office drawer and cola in the fridge; if nothing else, I could go out with a drink in hand. And as I crossed the outer office, I hit the lights. A darkened room lit only by the neon sign of the nearby hotel might be atmospheric, but a nice brightly lit office would give me a better look at whoever came in. The corridor lights outside would ensure they were visible from the outer door to the offices. In fact, I revised, if I sit in my tiny office in the dark, I can see them, but they can't see me.

By the time I had a drink in hand, and the lights carefully adjusted to ensure I was in complete shadow, but the reception and outer office were fully lit my nerve was somewhat restored. Remembering Doyle's plan to install cameras I glanced around but wherever they were, they were well hidden. Assuming they had installed them. I fidgeted with the papers on my desk, but then felt foolish, especially considering the SCS were watching me. I hoped they were watching me.

A noise from outside made me jump. There was a silhouette visible through the frosted glass door. It moved in and out of view, while I took a long swig of the vodka. Then it disappeared. I exhaled the breath I hadn't realized I was holding and tried to calm my nerves by pouring another healthy dose of alcohol into my glass. It had barely touched my lips when another figure, shorter than the first appeared at the door. I should really pay more attention, I thought. This time the visitor gave a short, decisive knock on the glass and a woman's voice, English accented, called "Caroline?"

Before I could make up my mind whether to respond, she opened the door and stepped into full view. It was Emily, looking as immaculate as ever in a dark olive trouser suit and pale cream blouse, not a hair of that sleek bob out of place. A wave of doubt flooded me. She looked a highly unlikely criminal, let alone murderer.

She let the door swing shut behind her, and looked around, frowning. "Caroline? Are you here?"

Bracing myself I appeared at the door of my own office.

"Good evening, Emily. Thanks for coming all the way down here."

"I'm not here to oblige you," she said sharply. "I'm here because of that extraordinary email you sent. This is not what I expected when we entrusted you with the public image of the Bank. I sincerely hope for your sake you can explain."

Reminding myself of the signed contracts sitting safely in my safe, I took a deep breath. "When you hired Jordan PR, Emily, you asked us to ensure the future of the Bank and its reputation. When anything crosses my desk that could impact on that brief, it becomes my business and I would have assumed, your business too. Of course, if you prefer, I can simply turn over the papers to the Gardaí and let them deal with it."

"Oh, for goodness' sake. There's no need to be so dramatic. Spit it out."

"I have papers that Frank Clarke pulled from the records office, before the attempted robbery. I say "attempted" because by the time the would-be burglars arrived, the goods were already gone. It was Frank who rigged the system to open the doors. He got there first, using the same plan his killers had intended to put into action."

Only a raised eyebrow betrayed any interest in that pale, impassive face.

"Frank sent the papers somewhere safe," I continued, watching her carefully "And now I have them, and they're very…interesting, shall we say? They raise questions that will be difficult for you – of course, I mean the Board – to answer." It was not my imagination; a twitch of the mouth, that's all, but enough to know I was landing some hits. "Anyway, I thought you'd like the opportunity to address the situation. Before we have to involve the authorities of course. Nothing like getting your story straight before being asked awkward questions."

Like "*how did this stolen painting come to be in your possession, Madame?*"

Emily smiled suddenly. "My. It all sounds fascinating. I must admit I'm still not sure what exactly Frank thought he had found, but you're right of course. We need to be on the same page. We don't need the media running with yet another Bank of Leinster scandal."

I matched her smile. "Exactly. It would be so damaging, on a professional level. And of course, for you personally."

Her smile didn't drop but it did freeze in place. "For me? I don't let the Bank's issues affect me personally, Caroline. You should cultivate that, as a woman in business."

"Oh, I do try to. But when my clients are exposed, and Frank Clarke had every intention of exposing you, I feel a certain responsibility."

"You mean Clarke would have exposed the Bank."

"No. I mean he was about to expose you. Oh, don't bother Emily. I don't care. Youthful indiscretion and all that. We all have our past. You were young, Charlie Loxburg seduced you and you were sucked into his sordid little crimes. It might interest you to know Frank Clarke was very thorough. It's a pity someone killed him, he was very good at his job. Bit wasted in marketing, I would have thought? Such attention to detail. I particularly admired how he cross referenced everything in the records concerning you, Murrough and Matthew Howard with the deposit boxes in the vaults."

She was leaning against the door frame now, her face a mask of polite indifference. But behind her I saw movement, a tall thin figure entering quietly into the outer office. Simon Prendergast. From his face I knew he'd been listening avidly. He bit his lip and hovered near the reception desk.

"The boxes are full of interesting things," Emily drawled. "I'm quite looking forward to seeing them opened, once the reforms go through."

"Hah! I bet you are. How will you explain the presence of the Kinsella box among the orphans?"

"Why should I explain it? It must have been placed there by mistake. I'm sure my stepfather will be delighted to hear it's been located. It'll be removed and placed in an active centre."

"Of course. And how will you explain that you were the last person to access it and that you did so regularly, until it was hidden in the Vaults?" My polite inquiry was rewarded with a narrowing of eyes and a sour turn of the mouth. "Honestly Emily, when I say Frank was thorough, I mean it. He noticed the Kinsella box, and the Loxburg one. Not to mention various little transactions and underhanded deals. Oh, and Matthew Howard's box. That was a real find too. All of you, all with boxes hidden safely in the vaults. After the whole Y2K scare, you couldn't access them any more out of working hours – not without leaving a paper trail. I quite agree, by the way – it would have been a dead interesting event, watching all that come to light with a selection of Central Bank officials and legal experts as spectators."

Emily's head had drooped while I laid it all out for her. For a split second I thought, she's going to cave. But as she slowly raised her eyes to mine again, something else looked back at me; something cold, reptilian, utterly self-absorbed. I'd seen it once before, in someone else. It was just as scary the second time.

"Quite impressive." She tossed her shiny hair and smiled. "What an exciting story. Simon, why don't you stop hovering out there and join us like a good boy?"

Prendergast started but trotted up to her obediently. "Hi Emily. I didn't expect to see you here."

"Nor I you." She eyed me suspiciously. "Why would you invite Simon here for this? Or are you in it together? Come on, Simon, I know you're spineless, but blackmail seems a little crude for you. I expected better."

Prendergast stared at me and muttered, "I don't know why I'm here either." He shrugged. "Obviously I misunderstood. I thought – I mean, I was told this was about -" The poor gormless creature couldn't finish the sentence without incriminating himself. His guilty conscience had leapt to the conclusion that any secret I uncovered was about his own shady antics, as a young art dealer.

"It's all right Simon," maybe I could head him off before he confessed on tape to art fraud in front the whole Special Crimes Squad. "I know you got the wrong end of the stick. Unless you have a box stashed away in the Leinster vaults too? It seems to be all the rage."

"I- no. I have no connection to that. I think I should head off now," He backed away from Emily, who sighed. "Such a worm. Stay where you are, Simon." She looked back at me. "I'm sorry about this. For what it's worth I do believe you would have worked wonders for the Bank. But we can't have a leech sucking the blood from us, you must see that."

"I would like to point out, I never *once* said I would blackmail you," I complained. "Just for the record, you jumped to that conclusion all by yourself. People have such a bad opinion of PR consultants."

"You can't keep me here," Simon shouted suddenly. He strode to the main door but as he reached it another figure loomed against the glass and he squealed in fright. The door swung open inwards, forcing him back a few steps. Murrough Loxburg filled the door frame, fixing us all with his usual sardonic expression.

"Well, quite the gathering." He waved Simon ahead of him. "Don't leave yet, Simon. Stay and be sociable. I'm sure you're as enthralled as I am with this tale."

Emily favoured him with a shark smile, and he smiled back with something approaching warmth. It crossed my mind, if Murrough was seeing Diane Howard behind everyone's back, maybe he was involved with Emily as well. Well, the suspects were all in place now; it was time to do my best unmasking of the killer speech.

I couldn't help but feel it was easier when it was Poirot or Miss Marple. The suspects in books didn't talk back quite as much or argue the toss with you at every turn.

"Murrough. Thanks for joining us. I'm going to go ahead and assume you know exactly what Frank Clarke stole from the Bank Vaults. I was just telling Emily here, he was very thorough."

"I *confess…*" he smiled and finished, "I confess I've been listening outside.

It seemed prudent in the circumstances. How enterprising of Frank. It never occurred to me that he would have that much gumption."

"The poor man was terrified. He was desperate. He assumed if he got the evidence, it would save him. He could at least put it beyond your reach. And now I have it."

Murrough ushered Simon into my office, which was beginning to feel crowded. He now stood between me and the door. I was fairly sure I could have taken Emily in a scrap, but Murrough was a different proposition. Something told me, I couldn't rely on Prendergast for any help; he slumped against the far wall, shrinking as far away from both Emily and Murrough as he could get in that tiny space. It was still lit only by the lights of the outer office, which Murrough largely eclipsed; I felt for the lamp on my desk and clicked it on before anyone could object.

"That's better. Now we can all see each other. Oh, do stop looming, Murrough. You don't know where I've stored everything and I'm not going to tell you so you may as well make up your mind to be civil. You too Emily. You're twitching like an outraged cat." To be honest, that was unfair because she was as imperturbable as ever, but I thought it might irritate her. From the look she shot at me I was right.

"Now. Before we get to the business end of things, I want answers. You both hid boxes in the vaults, hoping they would sit unnoticed among the abandoned ones. Yes?" Murrough hesitated, weighing up his options. Finally, I got a terse "Yes. It was my father's box, and I felt it was safer there."

"I bet. Come on, Em. Spill the beans."

"Fine. Yes, I moved my stepfather's box there. He's a sick old man and it seemed safer. I was afraid he would take out valuables and lose them."

"I thought we'd established you were the one with the key. He would hardly be in danger of doing that. Or did you just "borrow" the key, and replace it? Oh," a thought occurred to me. "I bet you did. I bet you replaced it but then, he lost it and you had to go bully an old sick man, trying to force him to remember where he put it!"

She pursed her lips. "I see you've been talking to that cow of a nursemaid of his."

"Maybe. I'm surprised Charlie isn't here tonight, by the way. Murrough, where's your dear auld dad? I thought he would want to know where his box is."

"I represent his interests," Murrough purred smoothly. "My father is an artist, with an artist's worldview. If he thought he was going to be punished for past crimes, he's perfectly capable of deciding to confess and indulge in some public atonement. Or hop a plane to the Bahamas, either is equally likely. Someone has to look after him."

Emily turned on him, the first real emotion breaking through the façade. "Shut up! What would you know about Charlie? Protect him – that's a laugh. You've never put anyone first your whole life. I'm the one who protects him. I'm the one who makes sure he's safe." Her hand shook slightly as she brushed a stray hair from her face. "I'm the one who looks after him."

Simon moved slightly. "I don't understand any of this," he complained. "What have some stupid boxes got to do with me?"

"Nothing," I said. "I do apologize. I thought maybe it was you helping Emily. She didn't haul Frank up on the desk and torture him all by herself. She had a wee helper. I figured it was one of you." Prendergast winced at the mention of torture. I grinned at Emily. "Don't get any ideas, you won't be torturing me. I've taken a few precautions of my own. If I end up dead, a letter detailing everything I know from those boxes will be winging its way to the Gardaí. No. We're just going to have a nice chat and come to a pleasant, sensible, working arrangement."

Murrough shook his head. "I don't know whether to be disappointed or impressed, Ms. Jordan. What exactly is it you want?"

"I told you. First, I want the truth. I'm not the enemy here, guys. Your continued success is my success, as we say in PR. This is a mess and I want to clean it up in a mutually beneficial way. Or we will wake up one morning to a scandal that will end the Bank, not to mention your individual careers."

"Hmm." He made a skeptical noise but moved slightly, his posture losing some of its tension. "I remain unconvinced but…as you appear to hold a great many cards, I will admit – I hid my father's deposit box, in the vaults, along with some other valuables. All legitimate ones I must add. My father has had a chequered past in many ways. Now he's reached a stage in life where he's accorded a certain measure of respect…I was anxious to preserve his reputation."

You also forged his signature and put his personal collection up as collateral for a loan, I thought loudly but prudence and a desire not to give too much away made me hold my tongue. Instead, I pointed with my glass at Emily, hoping I looked non-threatening and slightly tipsy as I did so. As I was in fact, slightly tipsy, I felt I had a good chance of pulling it off.

"And Emily here stashed some shady stuff in her stepdad's vault. Tell us, Em. Was it proof that Charlie Loxburg broke into Bellingham House? Or that he forged paintings with our Simon here? Is that the secret to your happy, long-term relationship?" I sniggered. "You must have something juicy on him, to keep him tied to you. Especially with all the Danielle's of the world throwing themselves at him."

And there it was at last. Like a porcelain mask shattering, the calm immobility of her face gave way to a snarling wildness.

"Shut up! You stupid bimbo. None of you understand Charlie and me. He loves me. He'd never leave me, not for some tart of a student."

"Calm down," Murrough spoke with authority, his usual sneering drawl forgotten. "If you're trying to pretend you don't have something to dangle over my father's head, save your breath. I've known for years that he's afraid of you. He's obviously terrified you'll expose some sordid secret."

"He loves me," the woman shrieked. "He loves me. He's loved me since I was sixteen. I didn't blackmail him – I protected him. He was going to be arrested. My stupid mother, she was going to report him. She couldn't bear that he loved me, not her. He painted her, but it was me he wanted." She drew a long shaky breath. "She was jealous. And that husband of hers, he was a clod. A philistine. He crawled out of a bog and made a fortune selling tractors. What did he know about art? Why should he have a Gainsborough, and a Yeats and yes, a Loxburg."

"Why shouldn't he?" Simon shouted back at her. "People are allowed to love art even if they don't understand it! Even if they don't know one painter from another. You stuck up cow…you sneer at everyone but look at you. You've hung on Charlie's coat-tails for years now, without him no one would pay you a bit of attention."

Well, this was an unexpected development; I looked at Prendergast with a newfound respect. Emily scared the life out me; watching Simon shout at her was like watching a shark being attacked by a rabbit.

"Be quiet," Murrough instructed Simon, but without any real heat. "Emily, go home. I will deal with Ms. Jordan here, we will sort this out between us. It's just business." He stepped aside as he spoke, reaching for Emily as if to usher her past him. His expression changed from superior to shocked in a matter of seconds, as she moved towards him; a flash of silver, a bloom of red, and Murrough Loxburg clutched his stomach in shock.

"Jesus!" I stepped forward, only to narrowly miss a swipe of the blade myself. "What have you done?"

"What I should have done years ago," She snapped. "Stay where you are, Simon. One more step and I'll gut him and then you too."

If we'd been in the outer office, there might have been less danger. In the claustrophobic space of my tiny office, with a knife wielding woman between us and the door, Simon and I backed obediently away.

Murrough had slumped to the ground, still with that shocked wide-eyed grimace on his face. He looked at me blankly and then back at the expanding band of red on his shirt. "She *stabbed* me," he complained.

"I know, Murrough," I replied. "We were all here. Be quiet now, like a good man."

Probably the SCS were scrambling into action at the word stabbed but in case anyone was still listening, I pushed on. "Is that what you used on Frank? Nasty bit of kit." She held up the blade, an elegant piece with a sturdy hilt and cruel looking edge.

"This? Yes. It was a mercy killing. He was stupid and disloyal – I enjoyed it." The matter-of-fact tone and flat statements chilled me. It was something I'd heard once before, and it meant there was no mercy or remorse to be had. "You figured most of it out, clever little Miss Jordan."

"Ms." I said automatically, "Ms. Jordan."

"You can have whatever you like on your gravestone. Or you can tell me -quickly - where those files are? Where is my deposit box?"

"Hidden."

"Stop being a smart arse," Simon hissed.

"Yes, stop, please. I find you irritating. Perhaps I should finish Murrough off – would that concentrate your mind?" She stooped to the unfortunate man as she spoke, and he shrank back with a nearly hysterical cry.

"He's nothing to me." I picked up my vodka and sipped, praying Doyle had the sense to hold the troops back a few minutes longer. "I wouldn't touch him with yours. Stab him, Ireland will be one corrupt banker less. Or you can stop being melodramatic and we can talk business."

She turned and stared at me, that flat reptilian gaze again. Just as earlier her face had cracked apart to reveal the woman beneath, now it smoothed itself back into her usual pale, unreadable mask. The first had been a shock, but this was truly unnerving. She even smoothed her sleek bob back into place, only a slight twitch at the corner of her mouth betraying the effort it took to reassemble Emily Cleethe out of the shrieking harridan of a few minutes before.

"What do you want?"

"I want to know what happened. My traffic is in knowledge, Emily. It's my currency. I know you killed Frank and I know why: I assume the Kinsella box contains the Gainsborough stolen from Bellingham House, and other interesting but too hot to shift items? Good. Thank you. And in the Howard and Loxburg boxes, should I pry them open, there would be similar embarrassing items? A pact of mutual destruction no less. I want to know who it was that beat Tomas Warskowski into a coma. Not to mention Sean O'Dwyer. Someone stabbed that man to death and left him on the floor of a car park." I glanced at Murrough. "I take it your interest in all this is just in your dirty dealings, and the paper trail they left?"

"I never touched Frank, or Sean. Please. Emily, let me go! I'll tell them it was Simon. I'll tell them anything you want." He groaned, "Kill them both if you want. I'll back you up. For god's sake woman, I'm dying here!"

Well, well.

"You'll be grand, Murrough. Hang in there, like a good man. Don't be letting the side down, eh? Simon, I take it you didn't help string up poor Frank and torture him?"

"No! I thought when you emailed me, you had some …some details about, well, things that happened years ago. I used to hang around with Charlie and Matt Howard and their friends. I was much younger than them and I – I got caught up in some things" He swallowed hard. I cut him off before he could finish.

"No one cares about that stuff." Or at least I hoped not, for his sake. "Obviously you came here to see if you could help in any way. Or something."

Emily gave a snort of derision. I smiled at her and asked sweetly, "Tell me, does Charlie know it was you who carved up the painting of your mother? I bet he doesn't. I bet Charlie Loxburg will forgive almost anything but not that. Not desecrating his precious art."

For the first time a flash of fear crossed her face. I pressed on.

"Let's concentrate on what happened that night in the Bank. You're a strong independent woman, Emily, but I'm fairly sure you couldn't have strung him up and tortured Frank alone. So, who was it?"

"Me."

For feck's sake! I really *should* have been paying more attention to the outer door. How the little weasel had managed to slip in was beyond me – unless it explained Emily's sudden stabby episode. He must have crept in while we were all riveted on the stricken Murrough. Now he blocked the doorway, a grin on his face and a .22 LR semi-automatic pistol in his hand.

"Nice of you to join us, David," I raised my glass to him. "Sure, it wouldn't be the same without yourself."

Ignoring me, he turned to Emily. "Are you insane, telling this nosey cow details?"

She shrugged. "It's not like she can tell anyone. Once we find out where that fool stored the goods, you can finish her."

"You said the same thing about Frank. That didn't work out so well either."

"That wasn't my fault," Her voice was rising again and the hand that held the knife shook slightly.

"You cut his throat in a fit of temper," David Howard snarled. "Before he told us anything."

"Your methods weren't working. It was a waste of time. She's not going to put up that kind of fight."

Beside me, Simon Prendergast trembled slightly but to my surprise, I felt him move slightly closer.

"Leave her alone!" His bravery was only slightly marred by the slight squeak of terror in his voice.

David took a half step forward, but I raised my hand and said firmly, "Stop. You make me absolutely *sick*, the lot of you. *Sick* to my stomach. Like, genuinely *ill*."

Absolutely nothing happened. No one burst through the door and an armed response unit of highly trained Gardaí failed to abseil in through the windows. I tried again.

"And I'm *sick* of this grandstanding." Nothing continued to happen.

David Howard looked at me, his eyes narrowing. "What are you playing at?"

Okay, then. The cavalry were stuck in traffic or something. Great.

"I'm just saying, all of this is pointless. I have a stash of evidence that will miraculously appear in the SCS office if anything happens to me. You each have incriminating knowledge about each other. Simon here now has that information, and" I took a chance, "that balances out whatever Charlie Loxburg has been holding over his head all these years."

Murrough glared at me.

"A youthful indiscretion, that he would like to forget. Now, can't we work all this out without guns and knives? It's so uncivilized."

Emily gave a derisive snort, but Howard silenced her. "What do you have in mind?"

"Well, my original thought was to quietly and politely come to a mutually beneficial arrangement with our Emily here. My bosses need some favours, politically, with these bank reforms coming in. Any leverage I can bring them does a lot for me. Plus, with the economy the way it is, I'm sure both Simon and I would appreciate a …flexible and friendly bank backing our businesses."

"A little cash injection, perhaps," David said smoothly.

"Indeed. I'll keep your deposit boxes safely out of the way of any investigations, and you just…carry on. As normal, but with a very friendly working relationship with Jordan PR."

His gun arm lowered slightly. "You could be saying all this just to get out of this room."

"Yes, but ask yourself, why did I bother sending for Emily tonight? And Murrough? I could have just blackmailed them anonymously, you do realize that? This is about the long game, David. And speaking of which if we don't want another murder investigation on our hands, someone should probably take Murrough there to a hospital, he's fading fast."

Instinctively both turned to look at Murrough, and I took the opportunity to hit David Howard across the head with my "Public Relations Campaign of the Year, 2011" Waterford Crystal plaque. It's a testimony to the fine workmanship of the glass artist that it didn't even fracture, let alone shatter. And it gave a most satisfying thud as it made contact. Howard went down like a sack of potatoes.

For a woman her age, Emily had excellent reflexes. Her knife flashed at me and would have made contact if Simon Prendergast hadn't intruded his arm between the blade and me; to my horror it went into his forearm and stayed there, the hilt sticking out at an angle. There was a moment of utter confusion, as Emily tried to wrestle back control of the knife, Murrough started screaming and Simon and I tried to avoid being sliced. In retrospect it probably wasn't helped by my frantic shouts of "I'm SICK! I'm NOT WELL!" until finally I gave up and roared "Help!"

According to the cops, they burst through the door within seconds of my hitting David. I can only assume they decided to hang back and watch the fun for a few minutes, because I definitely recall struggling with a literal knife wielding maniac a lot longer than that, but at last a strong pair of arms grasped Emily from behind and she was hauled off me. I found myself looking up into the honest, freckled face of Powers, his expression a picture of anxious inquiry.

"I'm fine," I pointed at Simon. "The blood is his, and that one, over there, has been stabbed. That one, has been hit over the head by a PR award."

"Jesus, Caroline," Doyle helped me to my feet. "Why didn't you give the signal?"

"I did! I was screaming the freaking signal."

"What? The signal was Oxymoron."

"What? No. I said that was stupid. I told you to come in when I said I was sick."

"She did," Powers had busied himself making a makeshift tourniquet for Simon from his own tie. He paused to add, "I told you it was "sick.""

Doyle shook his head. "But that's a daft safe word. I told you it was oxymoron; you don't get to just change it."

"It doesn't matter." I rubbed the bits of me that were battered and bruised, "I'm sorry, I should have just gone with the original one. Tell me you got that all on tape though."

"Ah. Sorry. We had some technical difficulties…" My face betrayed my utter horror because Doyle started laughing. "Joke. We got it all." It's no wonder people don't get his sense of humour.

Over his shoulder I could see Emily Cleethe struggling with two burly uniformed officers, holding her own despite being handcuffed. Simon Prendergast was being tended to by a solicitous female officer, who apparently was dead impressed by his bravery as told to her by the man himself. I couldn't begrudge him his hour of glory. I would have been lost without him. A fat lot of use Murrough had been, for all his tough talk about survival of the fittest; I looked forward to recounting his utter uselessness to Michael T and Derek.

Simon met my eyes and gave a faint nod, one survivor to another.

"Prendergast did well," Doyle muttered, apparently reading my mind.

"It'd be a pity if his past got dragged into this," I looked at him inquiringly. "I hope he said nothing incriminating…"

"Nothing that can't be carefully edited out," Powers chimed in with a grin. Then reddened, "Not that we'd do that, but…"

I laughed. "You do whatever it is you don't do, and we don't talk about, with my blessing."

"Ah," said Doyle. "Now you're getting the hang of the Special Crimes Unit."

Chapter Thirty-Six

Caroline Jordan

"You're okay!" Paula squealed, enveloping me in a huge hug. "Oh, thank God!"

"Gerroff," It would ruin my image to admit it but I was touched. "It all went off without a hitch. Oh, except Murrough Loxburg was stabbed and Simon Prendergast too. But turns out Simon is basically a decent person, and Murrough is a coward. But neither are murderers. Emily Cleethe is a psycho, by the way, and…" I was torn between feeling sorry for Paula and gloating that I had been right about him, "David Howard is a murderer."

All three of my audience, including Stephen and Marie, reacted with stunned horror. It was the quietest I've ever seen the lot of them.

"Give me a chocolate biccie, and I'll tell you all about it." I directed, perching myself on the comfiest chair in Paula and Stephen's apartment. Marie stood automatically, but Paula laughed and made her sit back down. "You're not in work now. I'll get the tea, and biccies and you sit there."

Marie looked quite pale, I noticed. And Paula was in full on mothering mode. There was something going on there, and I made a mental note to wrinkle it out of them once I had recounted the evening's events. It was very late, or rather early morning. I had arrived at Paula's as they were getting up, while I had yet to make it to bed. Processing a crime scene and taking statements takes time, or so Doyle informed me when I complained for the umpteenth time. Between waiting in the police station and endless calls to and from Derek Fields, I felt like a week had passed rather than a few hours.

By this time, I'd repeated the story so many times it had taken on a slightly unreal quality; but at least this time I could swear and give my unvarnished opinion on the characters involved. Apparently using what my mother would call "unladylike" language in a police statement tends to prejudice a jury; Claire MacPherson had to ask me several times to rephrase things.

When I reached the part where Simon threw himself in front of Emily's slashing knife, his character was fully redeemed in the eyes of Jordan PR.

"And DS Doyle said he would keep the poor man's past out of it?" Marie asked anxiously.

"Yes, he's not anticipating any problems there. Even if they do try to throw that at him in court, youthful past crimes tend to be outweighed by heroic actions in the here and now." I was repeating Derek's words; he had also promised to use all his influence to help Simon, but that was for my ears only.

As the city stirred into wakefulness beneath us, Stephen cooked a proper breakfast; the full Irish fry of sausage, rasher, egg, mushrooms, black and white pudding,onions, and toast - thankfully unsullied by baked beans. I was so tired I could barely eat but being handed a bite of food does wonders for morale. After that I crawled into their spare bed dressed in one of Paula's many themed night shirts – this one said "Sweet Dreams" over a picture of a huge wrapped sweet. Exhaustion dragged me under within seconds and it was getting dark by the time I opened my eyes again. The long twilights of an Irish summer had yielded to Autumn weeks before but it was still bright past six o'clock. I had slept twelve hours.

The other three were back around the kitchen table when I emerged from the shower, dressed and ready to face the world. Paula had taken my phone and recharged it, in the sitting room, well away from me so it wouldn't disturb me. I dreaded to think how many messages I had missed.

"It's fine," Paula read my thoughts, "I explained to everyone who needed to know, and I put off everyone else. Derek signed off on the urgent stuff. Oh, our beloved Taoiseach sent a huge bunch of flowers. Why do I get the impression they are delighted with the current turn of events?"

"Because it's highly embarrassing to our political rivals and reinforces the need for Bank reforms. Ooh," A huge dinner of steak, onions, chips and a fried egg appeared in front of me. "Thanks Stephen." It was decadent but I hadn't eaten all day, since the giant breakfast, so it evened out. The others let me eat in peace, chatting among themselves, until I pushed the plate away and sighed happily.

"Okay, then, my lovelies. What's been going on? Why do I get the feeling there's a whole other story I've missed?"

Stephen glanced at the women. "I'll let them fill you in."

"It's a bit of a tale. Long story short, remember those creepy gifts that arrived for me? Remember me telling you about Marie's rotten ex-husband? Guess the connection…"

My heart bled for Marie, whose embarrassed misery was obvious.

"I totally understand if this changes your mind about employing me," She said. I admired her quiet dignity.

"Don't be daft. I do however expect you to help us get the wee goat." My blood absolutely boiled. Paula grinned. "I told her you would never blame her. In a similar vein, we also have the JJ McDonnell issue."

"Give me a day." If I could take down that nest of vipers in the Bank of Leinster, I could put manners on the likes of JJ McDonnell. "I know what to do about JJ. Declan Healy is another matter." Marie's face fell. "No, I don't intend to let him get away with it, but I think I know the perfect person to deal with him. Trust me."

By Monday the crime scene that was our office was cleared for habitation; Marie spent a good half hour walking through it clanging some kind of cymbals and singing. "It drives out bad energy," She explained. "My mother used to do it, sort of a spring clean for negative energy. I'd normally use my Bodhran but it's at home in her house." I could only be grateful she hadn't managed to drag a bodhran, a large drum used in Irish music, into the mix.

I opened my mouth to scoff but Stephen frowned at me. "Don't mock the old ways. People knew a thing or two back then. It can't hurt." And in fairness it did make the place feel better. The cleaning company had done a good job, and I had replaced the carpeting in my office because a nasty big blood stain is distracting. The weekend had been largely spent catching up from my laptop at home, and Derek Fields had dragged me out to a dinner with Una Linehan. She was discreetly curious about the arrest of Emily Cleethe, but careful not to press for gory details. By the end of the evening, I had a new client and as Derek remarked, another name in my political network. "You'll need all the friends you can get in this job, Caroline. Una is an ally to be proud of."

It was with a clear conscience then, that I could devote a little time to our problems. A dozen phone calls, in my most persuasive manner, and I was ready.

"Paula, invite JJ to the Schoolhouse, will you?" The Schoolhouse was the restaurant attached to the hotel of the same name, a redbrick mid-Victorian building with a rich history. It was originally as the name suggested, a school, and the restaurant was housed in one of the original classrooms. The interior, with exposed wood and vaulted ceilings, was worth the visit alone. The menu was wonderful, if pricey – your Fresh Seafood Linguine and Summer Berries Pancetta would buy a lot of subway sandwiches. It also boasted a magical bar, with the same authentic mid-19th century charm, where we could retreat afterwards.

It was the ideal place for what I had planned.

From the alacrity with which he accepted the invitation to lunch, JJ was also a fan. When Paula purred down the phone at him, "Caroline and I are absolutely dying for a chat with you," one could almost hear his little brain working overtime. To be sure of everything going smoothly we arrived at the Schoolhouse twenty minutes early; the usually tardy JJ arrived in five minutes early, smoothing his hair back and practically rubbing his tummy in anticipation.

Much as I would have liked to box his nasty ears for bullying Paula, this was an occasion for a full-on charm offensive. Our greeting was so effusive I was sure he would see through it, but luckily his ego was in full flight; no flattery was too outrageous for John James.

A pleasant young man with lovely manners took our order, ignoring JJ's rudeness with aplomb. As the food arrived – my thyme breaded chicken fillet looked so perfect it could have been a magazine illustration – JJ continued to regale us with his opinion on everything from women who don't wear makeup to why the moon landings were fake. A woman seated at a nearby table approached us, interrupting his flow.

"Could I borrow your salt cellar? There's none on my table," Margo Kealy asked politely.

"Of course," Neither Paula nor I gave any indication that we knew her. She gave a brief nod to JJ, as she passed, and he looked away.

"Sorry, JJ, you were saying...?"

"Hmm. Well, never mind. Perhaps we should talk about this issue of the magazine," he began, but another woman detached herself from a table, where she was sitting with two others, and interrupted him.

"Hello, it's Caroline Jordan, isn't it?"

"Yes, and you're..."

"Annmarie Murphy. It's so nice to finally meet you in person! Just wanted to say hi." And she returned to her table, smirking broadly.

JJ had reddened slightly but recovered. "It's like Piccadilly Circus in here," He grouched. "I was trying to talk about the new promotions for the in-house magazine..."

"Is that you, Paula?" A tall girl, with a mop of frizzy brown hair and a pleasant, open face bounced up to our table. "Jennifer Lacey here. Good to finally meet you! And you Caroline." She stared directly at JJ, looking him up and down in contempt before turning on her heel.

His eyes followed her back to her table, lingered on her companions and then on the other tables in the restaurant. Every table. Every table filled with women, all of whom stared right back at him. Marie was among them, grinning encouragingly at us.

He went red, white and pink in rapid succession. Like a fish gasping for air, his mouth opened and closed silently.

"Yes," I said. "They're all here. Or most of them. Everyone in this room. All the women you picked on, sleazed over and bullied. Oh, and my colleague Paula, whose life you've made a misery over the last few weeks."

His face went to a deep purple, and he croaked "This is outrageous. You can't say these things to me! I'm leaving."

"Sit down!" Paula snapped. His limbs obeyed instinctively, the authority in her voice over-riding his conscious brain. "You can face this now, or you can face a sexual harassment lawsuit. I'm ready to file a formal complaint with your employers. And there's Marie Flynn over there – she is ready to tell anyone who's interested how she had to leave Best Budgets s because of your behaviour. I know you remember Margo Kealy. Margo is about to write a series of articles on workplace bullying, do you want to be the star of that?"

"This is defamation!" he blustered, "I have never- I'll sue anyone who writes a word about me."

"Don't be silly, JJ. She writes for the Evening News. They've run scandalous stories about politicians and cardinals and avoided court. They'll make mincemeat of you. Speaking of lawyers, Jennifer there has just qualified as a Barrister. I'd say a – what was it you called her, when she was a mere student working part time at that magazine? - a "feisty young filly" like her would love a high-profile harassment case to kick-start her reputation. Oh, I wonder now. See Clara Brown over there, that's Clara Brown of CB Designs. She's dying for a bit of publicity for her company. I'm sure I could get her a load of high-profile interviews, especially about being a woman of colour working with racist men."

"Remember what you did to her?" Paula produced her dossier and began to read, *"Clara was 22 when she started work in the publication "Fashion Today," where JJ McDonnell was an editor. He repeatedly made comments about her appearance, asked her for her passport to "prove she was Irish" and made both racist and sexist comments resulting in several complaints…*all catalogued meticulously by the HR department there, by the way."

"Oh, the things I could do with a story like that," I mused. "Of course, I would have to inform Best Budgets of a conflict in interest. I wonder what would be easier for them? Terminating you during your six-month probationary period or trying to break a contract with me? And have the headline "Best Budgets fire PR firm for representing victims of workplace harassment.""

JJ's face had returned to a sickly pale shade. He looked around him wildly and the women he had victimized all waved at him.

"You can't…" He said weakly.

"I can and I will. And I'll enjoy every moment of it. The thing you need to understand about me, John James, is that I am petty. I bear grudges. And I have endless patience."

He sank back in his seat, like a balloon deflating in front of our eyes. When he asked in a small, sullen voice, "What do you want?" I knew we had him.

"Well, number one is this. Paula is going to give you a list. You are going to write an apology to every single woman on that list and anyone else who comes forward. A proper apology. And you'll start with Paula. Also, if she so much as *feels* uncomfortable around you, I'll unleash merry hell. Is that clear?" He nodded. "Say it, JJ. Loud and clear."

"Yes! Fine. I understand." He muttered.

"Secondly, you are going to attend this." I pushed a leaflet across the table. The words "Dr Margery Fields, Workplace Counselling, Sensitivity Training, Anger Management and Professional Development" was emblazoned across it with details of group and individual courses in smaller print underneath. A grey-haired woman with glasses and an air of authority smiled at us – Dr Margery Fields, wife of a certain Derek Fields. I wondered how horrified JJ would be when he finally made that connection. "If you don't, I'll know" I warned him. "You attend for a minimum of 6 months, and you do everything that woman tells you. If you don't come out of it a better man, you will at least come out of it knowing how civilized people behave towards each other."

"Fine," His cheeks were scarlet now. He folded it up and tucked it into his shirt pocket with trembling hands. "Fine. Can I go now?"

"Sure. Oh, one final thing. Lunch is on you, JJ. Everyone's lunch." I gestured to include all the ladies, at all the tables in the restaurant. "Call it a goodwill gesture."

As if by magic, the nice young waiter materialized at JJ's side.

"Card or cash, sir?" He inquired politely. JJ's reply was far from polite, but he pulled out his card, nonetheless. The waiter took his time, while

JJ fidgeted from foot to foot, shrinking smaller by the moment under the relentless and eerily silent gaze of the women whose lives he had made miserable. Finally, he was able to retrieve his card; he made for the exit as fast as his legs could move, but not fast enough to outrun the spontaneous roar of cheers and jeers that followed him out onto the street.

Chapter Thirty-Seven

The moment the hospital rang I called Paula's mobile. When she answered the noise level coming down the phone was so bad, I winced. It sounded like they were at the notorious Copperface Jacks Night Club, on the night of a county final. I could hear a woman screeching "the face on him!" followed by an outburst of raucous cackling.

"I can't hear you, Alan!" Paula shouted, adding to my earache. I waited impatiently for her to reach somewhere a little quieter. "Sorry about that, Alan. Bit of a celebration here. We're in the Schoolhouse Bar if you'd like to join us…"

"Paula, Tomas Warskowski – the hospital rang." I drew a breath and ploughed on. "Is Marie with you? Milena needs her!"

"Oh no! Oh, the poor girl. Poor Tomas. Oh, hang on, I'll get Marie. I'm so sorry for that poor girl…"

"No!" I was shouting myself at this point. "Paula, listen. Tomas has woken up. He's going to be OK. Milena asked for Marie to come sit with him while she gets some rest. Did you hear me? He's pulled through."

There was another outbreak of noise at her end, followed by the unmistakable tones of Caroline Jordan roaring "SHUT UP!" A hush followed and I could hear Paula relaying the news. Then she was drowned out by another, even louder round of cheering and whistling. I was about to give up and resort to texting instead when the sound level abruptly died down, to be replaced by the background noises of traffic.

"Alan?" Marie's voice. "Alan is it true?"

There was a strange catch in my chest at the sound of her voice, and I almost forgot to answer.

"Yes," I managed. "The news came through a few minutes ago. Milena is looking for you, if you can go to her?"

"Of course!" I loved that she didn't even ask why she was needed, she was just willing to step up.

"I thought I would swing by and pick you up," I added. "Where are ye? It sounds like a riot." She gave me concise directions, another thing I liked about her. The list was growing longer every time I encountered her. As promised, she was waiting outside, coat in hand, as I pulled up. Paula and Caroline were flanking her. "Give Milena our regards," Paula said, bending to talk at eye level through the passenger window. "If there's anything we can do, let us know."

Caroline caught my eye over Paula's head and grinned. "Yeah, take good care of Marie, Doyle. Maybe you could make sure she has a lift back from the hospital later?"

Both women grinned broadly at that, and Marie's cheeks went red.

"You don't have to," She said quietly as we pulled away. "I mean, I know you're busy and all. Although it would be nice. I would like that."

All my life, I've been told I miss social cues and misread signals. Caroline Jordan once called me a troglodyte. Claire MacPherson said I couldn't take a hint if it hit me over the head. My ex, Karen, went further; she called me a cold fish with no social graces.

It wasn't that I didn't have feelings. My feelings were all there, raw and unprotected, and easily damaged. I insulated them because most of the time I was wrong about how other people felt about me; it was exhausting, trying to work out all the unspoken signals and false flags.

Marie seemed different. And what I felt for her seemed different too. Maybe I should trust what Paula and Caroline said.

"Marie, can I ask you a question? I'm not good at this. If I am wrong, just tell me and no hard feelings. I swear, I would never hold it against you. In fact, I am fairly sure this is one-sided but if I don't ask you, I'll regret it.

What I mean is, you and I get on well and if that's just friendship then that is absolutely fine except if it wasn't just friendship, that would be better." There. Rather well articulated, I felt.

Marie gave a lopsided smile, that made her lovely face even prettier. "Alan. Are you asking me out?"

"Yes."

"Oh good. But after we get Milena and Tomas sorted, okay?"

Okay.

The rest of the drive was spent in an easy, happy chat about Tomas' miraculous recovery, her first week as a member of Jordan PR, how lovely Paula was, what a nice couple she made with Stephen – I realized if all went well, I would be going to the wedding as a couple, which was a weird but pleasant thought – and finally, plans to attend that trad festival event on the weekend.

There was one small part of the story I hadn't told even Marie yet, but time enough for that. Caroline rang me the day before and explained about Declan "Dead Head" Healy. About nasty gifts and stalker behaviour, and how it was aimed at Paula but also Marie. Information I shared with Locke, MacPherson and Fellows over a pint in the Long Hall Pub, adding in my own details about his gambling, saddling his ex-wife with his debts and general weaselly behaviour.

If this was a Clint Eastwood movie, the cops would of course turn vigilante; we would meet him on his way home, late at night, to his one bed-roomed flat in an unsavoury part of town. MacPherson would explain to him in her inimitable style why his behaviour deserved a good battering, while Locke and Fellows, collars turned up and hats low on their brow, would menace him with detailed descriptions of what they planned to do to him if it happened again. I'd hang back, a shadowy sinister figure while the man admitted his "joke" and promised never to stalk his ex or her friends again. And the scene would end with a sobbing Declan, untouched, but broken by his own cowardly fears.

Of course, in real life that would be highly unprofessional, not something well behaved Gardaí would do at all; and the fact that Declan had transferred six thousand euro into Marie's account and paid off the outstanding debt on the car that had been repossessed was pure good timing. A sign that good things did indeed something happen to good people.

255

Chapter Thirty-Eight

C*aroline Jordan*

"Ms Jordan."

Murrough was back at a desk, looking like his old, sleek self. He greeted me civilly enough; I had been expecting a chilly welcome at best. His face was as unreadable as ever, and some of his old confidence had certainly returned but I could still hear his voice begging Emily to spare him and kill Simon and me instead. I doubted I would ever be impressed by him again.

"Murrough. Please call me Caroline. Ms. Jordan is so formal. After all, we've been through quite a lot."

"Indeed." There was a world of meaning crammed in those two syllables. He shuffled papers on his desk in a show of brisk professionalism. "We have a lot to discuss. The Bank has suffered quite a hit to its reputation, thanks in no small part to your extraordinary involvement with SCS. I am sure you can appreciate that it is untenable for the Leinster to continue in partnership with Jordan PR after that."

"Not at all, Murrough. I see no reason why the Bank should in any way object to honouring their contract with me. Incidentally, the Board agree with me, and we've already had quite a productive meeting. Yesterday. I understand you've resigned your seat? Probably for the best, in the circumstances. But it's nice to know we'll still be working together." I glanced pointedly at the title bar on his medium sized desk, in his small office. "Marketing Manager. I'm sure that will be such a good fit for you."

He didn't bother to reply, as I took my leave. The Board, free from the twin stars of Sean O'Dwyer and Murrough Loxburg, had been happy to continue with Jordan PR. Our chances of rehabilitating their image had improved immensely now the worst of the underhanded dealings were out in the open, like a lanced boil. Paula had charmed a financial journalist into doing a very fair piece, praising the Leinster for addressing the corruption and for dealing with circumstances that could not reasonably have been foreseen.

Frank Clarke had also come in for a fair share of praise, for which Doyle said his parents were grateful. Once the full story of his heroism in removing the evidence was revealed, he seemed to be fleshed out in the public imagination. Paula and I paid a visit to the Super-Ukers, partly out of curiosity but also from a sort of fellow feeling. They were his friends, the people he trusted with a deadly secret and thanks to Amy and her friends, he hadn't died in vain. We found them in a little hall attached to the local Church of Ireland, another of the red bricked Victorian buildings scattered across the city. A group of about forty people, every gender, every colour, every age group, singing cheerfully about rainbows and summer days, while strumming multi coloured ukuleles. I could see why Frank had found himself drawn to this.

"Is it weird," I asked Paula on the way home, "that I feel as if we knew Frank Clarke?"

"Nope. I feel it too. I suppose, we got invested in his life and death. We cared. So yes, in a way, we got to know him."

I thought back to the conversation with Doyle in the car-park. How it was caring that made the difference, even when things were grim.

"You were right about Doyle," I told her. "He's a good person. Irritating, but good."

"I was wrong about David Howard," She replied somberly. "I thought he was so nice, but it was him that attacked me in Howard Castle. And he attacked poor Tomas Warskowski. Emily is a psychopath, but David is as bad."

"I know. But in fairness, he was clever at hiding it. Even the SCS never fully considered him a suspect. I was sure it was Murrough."

"What will happen now? About Charlie and the break in at Bellingham House, I mean. And Murrough's forgery. Surely, they'll face charges?"

"I doubt it. Technically they could be, yes but believe it or not Emily is loyal to Charlie, to the bitter end. She swears blind he had nothing to do with the robbery. He insists he was nowhere near Bellingham. It's all too long ago. The lawyers are fighting it out, but Derek thinks he'll probably get away with it, as long as Emily sticks to her version. If we could open the boxes, maybe there's enough in there to prove it but…maybe not. And we may be old and grey before they get those boxes open. The orphaned boxes will be opened long before the law sorts out the Kinsella, Howard, Loxburg owned boxes mess."

"Well, at least the exhibition is going ahead. And Charlie doesn't seem to hold the slightest grudge against us."

"Why would he? I suspect he's been terrified of Emily for years. Emily, loyal and loving, behind bars is a lot safer than Emily loyal and murderous out here." I shuddered. "She was besotted. I blame Loxburg, I do. She was a troubled teenager, and he took advantage of her. He did the same in a different way to Simon. He's a leech."

Simon, freed from a decade of paranoia about his past mistakes, and thoroughly rehabilitated into the hero of the hour, had blossomed. He had also become friends with the Twins: Brendan and George were a good influence; he was quickly losing his air of jealous dissatisfaction. I suspected sales at his gallery would benefit.

I'd also had an interesting conversation with Leslie Howard. She had travelled up to Dublin the previous day and asked to meet. I half-thought she wanted to break ties with us, but it was the opposite. She filled me in on Peter's background, his relationship with his father and his pain at his murder. "But there's also relief too," she admitted, "he was a terribly difficult man. Peter loathes all that far right nonsense. It scares me too. It's growing every day, Caroline, and no one seems to notice or care."

"We notice," I promised. "And we care. We just need to wake up a bit. Anyway, you're happy to host the exhibition despite everything?"

She nodded, a steely look in her eyes. Her family had hung on to their conquests for generations, through worse than a mere family murder. "It'll be a roaring success, you know what people are like. They'll come precisely because of the scandal."

I smiled. "Grand, but promise me, go back to happy family getaways and wedding parties, OK? Make it a happy place. Don't let anyone – even your family – spoil it for you."

As I glanced at Paula, a thought occurred to me, and I hugged Paula impulsively. "It's six months to your wedding!"

She blushed happily. "I know. And thanks to new clients, we can properly afford to get married. All we have to pay for now is the honeymoon and that won't be too bad."

"What have you in mind?" I asked, thinking of the two tickets to Bali and the five star resort I'd booked for them, as a surprise. I'd finally cracked and told Stephen for fear he would book them a fortnight in Wales or something.

"I don't know, but it won't matter. We'll enjoy wherever we are."

I looked at my best friend and thought, how lucky I am. Frank Clarke found his tribe in the Super-Ukers. I've had mine around me for years. And despite everything we had been through, it was growing bigger. Marie and Doyle, and now even Simon. George and Brendan. Derek and dare I say it, Michael T O'Mahony in his lofty way. Graves, Locke, Fellows and my favourite cop, Claire MacPherson.

"Let's look forward," I hugged Paula again and she linked her arm through mine. "Onwards and Upwards. Next stop, your fabulous nuptials and a whole new chapter for Jordan PR. I'm half nervous. Where do we go from here?"

"No matter what, Caroline – there'll be you and me. You're my best friend. Nothing will change that." She fished in her pocket and pulled out a small velvet box. "I asked Marie to make something. One for each of us." She handed it to me shyly.

Opening it, tears sprang to my eyes. Sitting on a bed of silk was a silver bracelet, adorned with Celtic spirals, and ending in two circular knobs with an opening between them to slip it on the wrist. Tiny ogham markings, the ancient written alphabet of Old Ireland, ran the length of it.

"Oh my god, Paula." I spoke. "it's beautiful. What does it say?"

"That bit says *"friend."* And that bit there says...*Jordan PR.*"

I slipped it on and held up my wrist, admiring the silver flashing in the autumn sun.

Friendship, and Jordan PR. It sounded like a manifesto. It sounded like a plan.

About the Author

Did you enjoy The Body Count? please consider leaving a review wherever reviews are left. They make a huge difference to authors.

Geraldine is a writer and poet from Dublin, Ireland. She studied in UCD, worked in Advertising and Publishing and finally returned to her family roots to run a famous music shop in Dublin, retiring after almost 30 years in October 2021.

She lives with her husband, a long suffering and very brave man who often has to answer questions like "Where do you think it would hurt most to be stabbed?" and her two boys, who love that their Mam writes about murders. She also knits, crochets, makes jewellery, stitch markers and handmade cards; it's not so much that she is any good at any of this but it fills her life with creative, colourful people.

Her work draws on a variety of inspirational sources - Old Irish mythology,

Irish literary forms, modern politics mixed with the ancient tradition of Satire.

Her first mystery novel was published in February 2021; The Body Politic (A Caroline Jordan Mystery Book 1) is available in e-book on Kindle and in all bookstores in paperback. ISBN:9780956240361 ASIN:B08WR7DTPM

Poetry recent work:

She has several poems in the anthology Poetry From the Lockdown, Willowbrook Press, and her short story "A Stranger Among Friends" was a prizewinner in the Cunningham Short Story Comp and is included in the winners anthology 2020.

Her poetry has been published in Anthologies and Magazines (inc Asian Geographic -frontispiece)as well as E zines (inc Prairie Poetry; Poetry Life and Times.) Her recent work includes Gods and Radicals Anthology "A beautiful Resistance"; The 1916 Rising Commemorative Magazine "Sixteen" (several issues, featured poet.) In 2011 she was a prize winner, Listowel Writers Week John Creedon Inaugural Poetry Competition. Her work has been performed by theatre groups in the USA and UK - notably "Death of the Hero" and "Bealtaine"

You can connect with me on:
- http://www.celebratingwords.com
- https://www.twitter.com/gercelt
- https://www.facebook.com/geraldinemoorkensbyrne
- https://www.instagram.com/gercelt
- https://bio.link/germoorkensbyrne

Subscribe to my newsletter:
- https://dl.bookfunnel.com/fb0gvizpnf

Also by Geraldine Moorkens Byrne

263

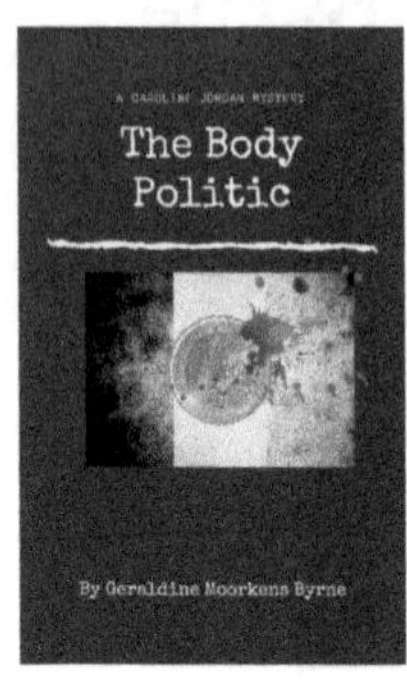

The Body Politic

A fun Modern Murder Mystery; ideal for fans of classic murder mystery, cozies with attitude.

Caroline has a dead minister of state, a new job to manage, a fledgling PR company to save - the last thing she needs are rumours of murder and a strange policeman dogging her steps. Can she outwit the murderer, save her company, impress her new VIP client and most importantly, survive? She's not sure but fueled by vodka, rage and steely determination, she's going to give it a good try!

When Minister Damien Fitzpatrick is found dead at his desk, everyone assumes it was natural causes. Caroline Jordan has spent 4 years keeping the Minister on track, hiding his volatile personality and building his public image as a good family man and serious politician. Now she's facing social Siberia and a serious setback for her new PR firm, not to mention her best friends and colleagues Paula and Stephen.

Meanwhile DS Doyle is faced with the unwelcome news that a Minister has been murdered and the prime suspects include the leader of the country, another Minister, several high ranking officials and Ireland's most brazen gangster turned property developer.

When Caroline finds herself dragged into the mess, one thing becomes clear. She is going to fight to the bitter end for Jordan PR, her employees and her new VIP client. And if she can manage a romance with the gorgeous but elusive Rory Fitzpatrick at the same time, why not!

Praise for The Body Politic

"You won't want to put it down, so clear your diary, get comfortable and settle in for a treat." Ita Ryan author of ***IT can be Dangerous***

""...a life-like and fast-paced world that really drew me in, and I ended up feeling like I knew each of the characters personally! Can't wait for the next one!" Reader Review